# ATHENA'S PIANO

## Allen Johnson

**Boroughs**
Publishing Group

www.BOROUGHSPUBLISHINGGROUP.com

PUBLISHER'S NOTE: This is a work of fiction. Names, characters, places and incidents either are the product of the author's imagination or are used fictitiously. Any resemblance to actual events, locales, business establishments or persons, living or dead, is coincidental. Boroughs Publishing Group does not have any control over and does not assume responsibility for author or third-party websites, blogs or critiques or their content.

ATHENA'S PIANO
Copyright © 2021 Allen Johnson

ISBN: 978-1-953810-81-6

*For Debi Eng in celebration of her gift for music and passion for young musicians*

# ACKNOWLEDGMENTS

I tapped many resources while researching this book. Alan Joseph helped me understand the art of self-defense. He even gave me a hands-on lesson at a local dojo. Jay Hendler was precise on the correct usage of architectural terms. Mike Rector was a wealth of knowledge when it came to firearms. Melinda Woodward was my go-to girl for questions about modern-day fashions and millennial speak. The National Weather Service of New York City was helpful in describing the city's weather patterns. Jan Jackson was an excellent resource for information on automobiles from the 1920s.

Special thanks to Claiborne Rice, associate professor of English at The University of Louisiana at Lafayette for her expertise in the linguistic intricacies of African American English. Special thanks also to Robert Berkman, former recording artist and chief operating officer for QRS Music for his extensive knowledge of player and reproducing pianos in the 1920s. I'm equally grateful to DeeAnna Galbraith for her sharp editing skills.

Early readers are always a treasured resource. My thanks to Pat King, Mike Navalinski, Gene Parulis, Allen Brecke, Ana Rahimlou, Jane Kirkendall, Paula von Lindern, Sharon Clement, Nancy Rosselli, Sue Peterson, Candy Curtis, Amber Dawn Miller, Terry Barber, Sue Benedetti, and Roberta Lewandowski.

Finally, special thanks to my extraordinary editor at Boroughs Publishing Group: John Trevillian, and to Jennifer Blackwell-Yale, copy editor.

# ATHENA'S PIANO

*The law of love knows no bounds of space or time*
—Mahatma Gandhi

# 1

*Harlem, New York City*
*January 1924*

Athena Cruz didn't hate Cal Craven. She didn't trust him. The Nest had closed, and she felt uneasy sitting alone with him at a table in the darkened nightclub.

"You were sensational tonight," Craven gushed. "And what a looker."

"Thank you," she said in a tone meant to be polite but restrained.

"Really, you drew an ace from the deck when you were born. You have your African mama's spirit and your Spanish papa's sex appeal: bourbon skin, yellow eyes, black wavy hair."

*I don't like where this is going.*

"And, damn, don't get me started on your body—so sleek and supple."

*God, he's undressing me.*

He studied his cigarette as he rolled it between fingers and thumb, a gesture that somehow appeared obscene. "With your looks, you should be arrested for indecent exposure."

She avoided his gaze and fidgeted. "It's all part of the show," she said, desperately trying to sound composed. "A singer has to look her best for the customers."

Craven cocked his head. "And for me, I hope."

Athena took her time by uncrossing her legs and primly tucking one ankle behind the other. She took in the man's raven-hued face—one that could easily get lost in the shadows—with sleek conk-styled hair, prominent cheekbones, and large piercing eyes set back in their sockets. "Of course. You're the boss."

"And a friend." He half-turned and side-eyed her. "A very good friend."

Athena was silent. She wanted to like Craven. She wanted to like everyone. But there was something too slick about the man. He dressed like a banker with starched collars and double-breasted suits. That was fine, but his smile put her off, a smile foreshadowing danger. "And a friend," she said with downturned eyes.

He straightened his back. "That's good. Because I have a surprise for you."

Athena looked up out of curiosity. "Tell me."

"I like to invest in quality, and you're prime quality, babe."

"Well, I don't know about—" She broke off.

"Which is why I bought you a new piano for your apartment."

Athena's mouth went slack. "A what?"

He was outright grinning. "I think you heard me."

She spoke slowly in a half-whisper. "I think you said 'a piano.' Did I hear right?"

The club owner leaned back and laced his fingers across his chest. "That's right, doll." He paused long enough to glide a forefinger across his lower lip, then pulled his hand back as if drawing a thread. "That is, if you want it."

Athena started to speak and thought better of it. Of course, she wanted it. Her piano was a mess with three dead keys and as many broken strings. She would treasure a new piano. *But at what cost?* "I— I can't. It's too much."

"Not that much. You don't know him, but Frank Milne came in to hear you last week. He's the recording engineer for a company called Aeolian. He loves your sound and wants to record you on a piano roll. That's when I got the idea." He moistened his lips. "Are you interested?"

Athena couldn't suppress her excitement. "You know I am."

"Then get this. Aeolian contracts with Steinway to make player pianos. I did a little high-rolling and told Milne he could record you if he sold me a piano below cost."

Athena's eyes widened. "And?"

"We cut a deal. Steinway mostly makes grands. But in your case, Milne said he'll deliver a special-order upright as soon as you record a few numbers." Again, he pasted on his catty smile. "Of course, I'll pay the difference," he winked, "but you're worth it. What do you say?"

She felt giddy as if overtaken by a perfect melody. *A new piano and a recording.* "I say— I don't know what to say."

"Thank you would be good."

Athena reached across the table and tapped Craven's hand only once. "Yes. I mean thank you." She shook her head in dismay. "I mean . . . yes."

# 2

*Greenwich Village, New York City*
*April 2019*

Tony was on the fourth day without a shave, but this Saturday morning he was anxious to get in his ride. He checked the air pressure on his road bike, slung the crossbar over his shoulder, and descended two flights of stairs. On the main floor Jessica Sweet was checking her mailbox. When she saw him, she swept a wayward strand of blonde hair over her ear. Lithe and long-legged, she wore a lemon-yellow spring dress with a hemline six inches above her knees. She was bright-eyed, quick-witted, and as flirty as they came when it suited her. Although college-educated in New York, she was born and raised in Savannah, Georgia, and had never lost her Southern drawl or country cheek. In fact, she was famous at MacDougal Ale House for rebuffing a shady player with her blistering stare and a Dixie threat. "You better back off, cowboy," she'd said, "unless you want to be shucked from a stallion to a gelding."

Tony forced a tight-lipped smile. A single bead of sweat bubbled and channeled down his forehead and the length of his nose. It was ludicrous. He cut into people's bodies, held no horror of thunder and lightning, and no dread of standing at the edge of a precipice. But Jessica rattled his nerves. Not because he disliked her, but because she chafed the open wound he called "Sophia's curse." *Sophia. beautiful and irrepressible...but gone.* The stony memory chilled his blood. Jessica could never understand, and he would never explain. The Southern belle would always remain the unwitting victim of his guilt.

"Hello there. I see you're fixin' to go for a ride," she said, her words as silky and fluid as quicksilver.

"Hey."

She fluttered long lashes over green eyes.

He looked away and lifted his bike off his shoulder and onto the lobby floor.

Jessica stepped between him and the exit. "It's right what women are saying about you."

"I'm sorry."

With a flirty smile, she edged in closer and lightly touched the center of his chin. "You're definitely the neighborhood hunk. You with your blue eyes, six-foot-two frame, and enough waves of black hair for a family of five."

He held his silence as he studied the handlebar's twist of tape. He pulled on a loose thread that unraveled until he finally snapped it off.

Jessica leaned back and dialed up her hot-brandy timbre. "Tony, I'm sorry about what happened just then."

He hummed in false bewilderment. "Nothing happened."

She giggled. "That's what I'm sorry about."

Tony took a half step toward the door, but Jessica stood unmoved.

"You know, I have a bike too, although I'm thinking the wheels may be cattywampus. For sure, the tires need to be air-upped." She eased in closer and moistened her lips. "Would you like to come to my place sometime and see if it's still useable? I'm not even sure I know how to work that silly ol' tire pump. It'd be great fun to ride with you. Maybe take a spin through Central Park." She had a hand on his handlebar. "You could teach me all about gear ratios, disc brakes, and such."

He signaled his direction toward the exit. "Well, got to get my miles in."

"Bless your heart," Jessica said, unclenching the handlebar. "You skedaddle now. But don't forget to knock on my door one night to check out my wheels."

"Okay. See you." Blasting through the front door, he drew his first deep breath. He didn't despise Jessica. In fact, he admired her banter and beauty.

His "issues" were not her fault.

# 3

*Harlem*
*1924*

Athena always loved her workouts with her brother, Zalo. She was tough, but Zalo—tall, lean, and sinewy—made her tougher.

This time he reviewed the power punch. "Remember, the blow comes from the floor, through the hip, to the fist. Got it?"

"Yes," she said, capering about and swiping her nose with her thumb.

"Then what else?"

"Punch six inches through the bad guy," she said with a straight-arm jab.

"How do you do that?"

"Shuffle the back foot forward an inch or two."

"Good, you've got this."

After the lesson, Athena made scrambled eggs and ham, seasoned with black pepper, cilantro, onion, and a pinch of salt. She mastered the kitchen, and Zalo always ate heartily, which delighted her. When they'd finished, they both sat back and sipped their coffees at the kitchen table.

"What are you doing these days?"

She beamed. "I'm enjoying Charles Dickens. What a talent. I've read all his masterpieces, and now I'm rereading my favorites."

"What a bookworm."

Her words softened. "That comes from Mama." Her theater of the mind envisioned the nights Zalo and she lay in bed and listened with dreamy eyes to their mother's narrations of *Heidi* and *Jungle Book* and, Zalo's all-time favorite, *Treasure Island*. The images still gamboled in her head.

"A child who *can* read and *doesn't* is no better than a child who *can't* read," they said in unison, quoting their mother.

Zalo stared at the kitchen table as if spying a squashed bug. "Man, I miss her. Tuberculosis is a rotten disease."

Athena examined the same phantom bug and reflected on her mom's death. How she hated the meanness of an unfinished life. "She taught us so much. Literature, music, all her Caribbean recipes." She passed her hand through her cropped hair. "But what was left unsaid? What...?" She fell silent and listened to the slow relentless drip from the kitchen faucet. "Sometimes I feel like half a person and only half awake at that."

Zalo reached across the table and squeezed his sister's hand. "You're wrong, Thena. She taught you everything you needed to know. Look at you, you're the perfect combination of wit, charm, and beauty."

Athena rubbed her arms as if to warm them. She was not perfect. She was too often scared, something that irked her to her bones. She despised retreating from trouble. That was cowardly, and not something her mother would have tolerated.

She parted her lips to speak but said nothing.

Zalo patted his sister's hand and cleared his throat. "I want to get back to your reading. Tell me, why Dickens?"

She pushed out from the table and boosted herself onto the kitchen counter. "I never thought I'd like him. I thought he'd be too depressing. Sure, he knew about poverty, but he also knew about grit and courage and perseverance. And, goodness, can the man write."

He swiveled sideways to face her. "Okay, give me a taste."

She rolled her eyes up, searching for the perfect passage. She could quote from any book she'd ever read. When her eyes lifted, she was seeing the page.

"All right. *Great Expectations.* 'Love her, love her, love her! If she favors you, love her. If she wounds you, love her. If she tears your heart to pieces—and as it gets older and stronger, it will tear deeper—love her, love her, love her!'" The thrill of quoting the passage shivered the length of her arms.

"Why do you like that so much?"

Athena puckered her lips. "Are you kidding? That's the kind of man I want. Someone who loves me no matter what." She hovered a beat. "Someone who will not run off like our deadbeat father."

Zalo's expression hardened. "Don't even talk about him."

"No argument there," she said under her breath.

Zalo kicked his chair onto two legs, folded his arms, and swished his tongue across the inside of his lower lip. "You should have a man who loves you no matter what. I don't know why you haven't found him already. It's not like no one in Harlem has his eye on you. You know what the boys on the backstreets call you?"

Athena rolled her eyes. "I don't think I want to know."

"'Caramel delight' for your flawless skin."

"That's just silly."

"Maybe so, but the point is they notice you." He canted his head. "And you are twenty-eight now."

"Yeah, Z, and you're thirty."

"It's different for a man."

She snapped him a wicked look. "Just like a man to say that. Your attitude is no more evolved than Master Bates in *Oliver Twist*." She waited for the double entendre to sink in. It didn't. "The fact is, I'm not interested. The boys on the block have windowpane hearts. I can see right through them. I know what they want. No thanks." She smiled at her brother. "Besides, I've got you. I'm fixed."

He pursed his mouth, either as an air kiss or a dismissal of the compliment. "Okay then. Maybe this is the right time." He drew a small box from his shirt pocket. "For you, sis," he said, presenting the gift on the palm of his hand.

Athena leapt from the counter. "Huh? It's not my birthday, and Christmas—"

"I want you to know I'm in your corner."

She felt her face flush like a schoolgirl as she opened the box. Under a slip of paper gleamed a gold chain with a heart-shaped pendant the size of a quarter. The two-sided engraving read FOR ATHENA and, on the reverse, FROM ZALO FOR ALL TIME.

"Oh, Z. I love you so much." She held his face in her hands and pecked him three times on the cheek. She gave him the necklace and said, "Please, put it on for me."

With the necklace latched, she returned to her chair, patted the charm, and said, "You'll always be right here for me."

"Okay," he said quickly. "This doesn't mean we're going steady. It's a reminder you have a big brother looking out for you." He squirmed. Although his love was pure, he was always more at home wading in shallower, less revealing waters.

After she stopped patting the pendant and the babbling eased, Zalo asked, "So what else is new?"

The question was a clock key that reset her timing. "I got a contract with Aeolian Music," she squealed.

Zalo shook his head. "Who?"

Athena told him about Frank Milne and her piano-roll recording session at Aeolian Company. "They've recorded George Gershwin." She posed with both palms out. "And now me."

"What did you play?"

Her words percolated as they always did when she was excited. "It's a new song. It's called 'It Had to Be You.' Would you like to hear it?"

"Of course, but you don't have a player piano."

"I do now," she said with a showtime grin. "I've had it for a week. Don't tell me you didn't notice."

They wandered into the living room, and Zalo stepped to the ebony upright piano, the glossy finish reflecting his face. "Yeah, this is definitely new." He hunched his shoulders. "What can I say? For me, all pianos look alike."

"My old piano was a clunker and mahogany. Don't you know the difference between mahogany and ebony?"

He hugged his elbows and buried his head into his shoulders. "So, all of a sudden I'm a piano expert?"

Athena spit-bubbled with excitement. "You want to hear me play? Do you? Huh?"

He chuckled. "Yes, Thena. Please play."

When she opened the fallboard, the ivories' pent-up moonglow gave her a shiver.

Zalo whistled his approval as he swept his hand over the keys, his discovery hesitating over the last two notes on the treble end of the keyboard. He traced two fingers across the scrolled scrimshaw etchings.

"What's this?"

"Don't you recognize the letters?" she chirped.

He bent at the waist, cocked his head, and grinned as he made out the calligraphy. "Oh my goodness. Athena Cruz."

"Made especially for me," she said with a little hop and a clap. "It'll always be mine. But it gets better."

Opening the spoolbox doors, she revealed the piano-roll's credits.

IT HAD TO BE YOU
WORDS BY GUS KAHN
MUSIC BY ISHAM JONES
PLAYED BY ATHENA CRUZ
1924

"Ta-da," she sang out, both hands framing the title. She pulled a small brass knob located on the upper right corner of the spoolbox, and the music played.

"That's you," Zalo said, his eyes shining. "I recognize your style. No one plays like you. Not like that."

"That's what I'm telling you. They recorded me. Little Athena Cruz."

When the song had rolled to the final resolve—a bell-tone octave on the upper register—Zalo brushed his fingers along the glistening edge of the upright's lid. "This is a beautiful piano, Thena. What is it exactly?"

"A Steinway Duo-Art Pianola," she said, her speech racing again. "Much better than an ordinary player piano, which can only play at one volume. My Steinway reproduces the *exact* performance. Phrasing, dynamics, tempo changes." She gulped for air. "It's incredible, right?"

He swiped his face. "Yeah, but how could you ever afford it?"

Averting her brother's eyes, she mumbled, "It was a gift."

"Huh?"

"It was a gift," she said with the flicker of a glance.

He tilted his head to capture her gaze. "A gift. From who?"

"From *whom*."

Zalo crossed his arms. "Thena?"

Although she wavered, she could never lie to her brother. "Cal Craven."

"Cal Craven." Zalo squinted. "Wait a minute. Are you talking about that cake-eater dandy from The Nest?"

"He's the owner."

His inflection evoked more sarcasm than anger. "Oh yeah, I know who he is. You see him strutting around 133rd Street with one tomato or another hanging on his arm like he was the neighborhood pimp."

Athena skimmed the white keys with her fingertips. "He's not a pimp."

"Are you sure about that?"

"I'm sure," she mumbled.

He caught her gaze. "Come on, Thena. You don't sound sure to me."

Athena dredged up a hint of conviction. "He's not a pimp."

"Then what is he?"

Her words softened the way they always did when she defended an underdog. "He's not so different. He grew up dirt poor and without a father, like you and me. Only *his* mother did anything she could to survive. I mean *anything*. You know what I mean?"

"Of course." His tone stiffened. "She was a whore."

Athena winced at the word. "He beat the odds. It wasn't always pretty. He scrambled and wangled but somehow made a life for himself. Now, he owns the best club on Swing Street. Doesn't that count for something?"

"Maybe," Zalo said after a long pause. He gripped his sister's shoulders. "Look at me, Thena."

She lifted her gaze.

"I'm going to say only one thing." He spoke softly. "A young buck doesn't give extravagant gifts to a beautiful woman for no reason. You know that, right?"

Athena bowed her head, not so much for being scolded, but for the veiled sexual connotations.

"Look at me," he said.

She faced her brother. "I can take care of myself." Her bottom lip trembled as she tried and failed to tame the urge to cry.

Zalo took her into his arms and stroked her hair. "I know you can. Please be careful. I don't trust Cal Craven."

Recapturing her breath, she kissed her brother on his cheek. "I will. I promise."

# 4

*Greenwich Village*
*2019*

Winters can be brutal in the boroughs, but when spring elbowed her way in, overcoats were ditched, shorts were donned, and the outdoor spirit of the city came alive.

When the weather allowed, Tony began his day cycling—his pace swift enough to give his heart a fierce workout. But on this morning, he had two goals in mind.

His first mission was to stop by the apartment of Roberto Rosselli, who lived just up the block on Minetta Lane. Rosselli was his kind of guy: a jovial Italian and, although now retired, the neighborhood's favorite baker for forty years. Tony's love for the man began as a schoolboy when his mother would send him to the shop for a loaf of bread. Rosselli always rewarded him with a chocolate-glazed donut for what the baker called "delivery services." His love for the man had only deepened over the years.

Tony never knocked on his friend's door; that was too formal. He tapped on Rosselli's first-floor window. As always, the baker drew the blind and opened his window. He was wearing a wifebeater undershirt. His whimsical eyes, full cheeks, and shock of white hair gave him a merry quality.

"Hey, Tony, I've been thinking about you. I have something to show you."

Rosselli escaped from sight and returned with a vintage .45.

"I bought this World War II automatic," Roberto said with pride. "Would you like to feel its heft?"

Tony flashed on his Green Beret days. Although trained, handguns violated his Hippocratic oath. As a field surgeon, he treated wounded GIs and civilians. He knew how a high-speed bullet could shatter a bone, yaw sideways, and create a massive exit wound. Although his blood was never shed, he was still a victim. In war, there were no impervious soldiers.

Even now, as a respected surgeon at Columbia Orthopedics, he had seen too many shattered bones from shootings. He would never carry a gun.

"I'm good," Tony said. "But it does suit you."

"Well, I do like to be where the action is."

"Good enough. I just hope you know how to use it."

Rosselli recoiled with a jerk. "Oh, *mio Dio*, you're not the only New Yorker who's done his time in boots and battledress."

"Oh yeah, I forgot. Hang on. It's coming back to me." His expression deadly somber, he paused for comic effect. "You served pork and beans to the Union troops at Gettysburg, right?"

"Get out of here before I load this peashooter," Rosselli said.

With a lazy salute, Tony threw his leg over his road bike. "Give my best to your sweet lady." As he slow-pedaled on Minetta Lane, he added, "Be good."

"No other way."

***

Tony's second mission was to cycle north on the Greenway. At West 110th Street, he turned east to drop into the north entrance of Central Park. He cruised through the entire park from top to bottom, then rolled to a stop at Alexander Piano on West Forty-Fourth Street.

The music store was a warm, unpretentious ground-floor shop with early-twentieth-century character. Inside were dark floors topped by Persian runners and a splendid trove of restored upright and baby grand pianos. He'd played a keyboard through medical school but gave it up when he joined the army, but not because he wanted to. There was something magical about a piano, especially the way its orchestral range filled his senses and calmed his mind. Today, he chased a soulful piano.

He'd known the shop owner, Andy Alexander, for years. They were so close Tony called him "Ragtime" or "Rags" after "Alexander's Ragtime Band," a nickname that suited the musical shopkeeper. A lanky, easy-going sort with a degree from Carnegie

Mellon School of Music, Ragtime fostered a passion for American jazz standards.

On occasion, Tony would drop in with his trumpet and play a Gershwin or Cole Porter melody over Ragtime's piano chords and fills. Each time they finished a song, they'd nod to each other in mutual admiration, the way musicians do when the music shivers their insides.

By Ragtime's invitation, he rolled his bike into the store and inhaled the intoxicating drafts of aged birch, maple, fir, oak, and mahogany. The potion filled his senses with nostalgia for all the music played on the instruments—every sentimental waltz, every blistering rag, every ungainly or gifted rendition of a Chopin etude or Beethoven sonata.

Ragtime pushed up from a piano bench when Tony entered. "Hey, my man. Got your horn?"

"Not today, Rags. I'm in the mood to buy an upright. Something special."

Ragtime's eyes flashed with boyish excitement as he dusted his hands. "Cool. Guess What? An instrument came in a few days ago that will spin your socks."

He chuckled. "You've got me hooked."

The two men threaded a path to the back of the shop to a glossy ebony upright pressed against the back wall under a ceiling fan and light.

Edging back to absorb the full impact of the instrument, Tony brightened, then stepped forward to tease the real ivory keys with his fingertips. "Steinway Duo-Art Pianola. Is that a player piano?"

"A *reproducing* piano to be exact." Ragtime explained the difference. "You've got to hear this." He opened the spoolbox doors to the music roll and, with a tug on the brass knob, started a performance of "It Had to Be You."

The flesh on Tony's arms pebbled. Player pianos were paramount during the height of ragtime. He expected a heartless slam-bang version of the venerable tune, but instead, this rendition cast a spell. Each crystalline passage told a story of first love, the rise and fall of passion, and the heartbreak of loneliness.

The room blurred and disappeared with music his only guiding light. As the notes rose and fell, he drifted into a night sky without fear or sorrow. His heart throbbed in iambic cadence. There was no disquiet, only peace—sweet peace. He embraced the music and the infinite cloak of space.

The last note faded.

"Doc?"

Tony heard his name called from a distance. He was neither worried nor hurried. Finally, in his mind's eye, the piano store became real again.

Someone touched his shoulder. "Talk to me."

Tony unsealed his eyes and released a yammering moan.

"There you are," Rags said. "I thought I lost you, buddy."

Tony took his time before speaking. He pressed his fingertips to his lips and shuttered his eyes. "I'm okay. I mean I think I'm okay. That was the strangest thing I've ever experienced. I'm not sure what happened, but I loved it." He swiped two fingertips across his eyebrow. "Who in the world was that?"

Ragtime said, "Her name was Athena Cruz." He passed a hand down his friend's arm. "Listen, are you sure you're all right? Would you like to sit?"

Tony turned, looked straight into Ragtime's eyes, and patted him on the chest. "No, Rags, I'm fine." He laughed at himself. "That performance shook me down to my shoes. Hey, maybe my socks *did* spin." Feeling more like himself, he smiled broadly. "Please go on."

"If you say so." He rested a knee on the piano bench. "The song was recorded in nineteen twenty-four. I did extensive research and discovered Athena Cruz recorded for Aeolian Music. They were the people who made the piano rolls. An old catalogue said she also recorded 'What'll I Do,' but I couldn't find it anywhere." He glanced at Tony. "Beyond that, I found a single sentence online that mentioned she played at a club on Swing Street in Harlem called The Nest back when Harlem was the place to go for moonshine and hot jazz. But that's it."

Tony was tantalized. He sat at the piano and skimmed his hands over the keys. "What's this?" he asked, fingering the engraving on the last two treble keys.

By lowering his pitch, Ragtime added drama to his response. "Her name. Athena Cruz. It was *her piano*."

Reaching to clutch Rag's arm, he missed and let his hand fall to the piano's keys lip. "Oh my god." Athena's music had shaken him to the core. To be so close to her now was like touching something ethereal. He played middle C and allowed the vibrations to linger in his chest. That single note was their bond for she had known the same tone and vibration. Although separated by a century, in this moment, they were as one.

He brushed his fingertips over the scrimshaw etching. After reliving Athena's rhapsody, he leaned over the keys and played the first eight measures of "What'll I Do," caressing one note at a time. He then added a simple counterpoint bass line for the next eight measures. On the break, he surged into full-body alternate chords, playing spirit-filled, though well short of the magic Athena Cruz had coaxed from the keys.

As he played, a rush of electricity purled through his entire body, culminating in his chest. The feeling mimicked the physical response to Beethoven's "Ode to Joy," the hair follicles at the base of his neck vibrating like tuning forks. He'd never been in love. Hell, he hardly spoke to women, let alone loved one, but he imagined love must feel like this.

When he'd finished, he bedded the fallboard and said, "Ragtime, this is the piano for me, but it must come with the Athena Cruz piano roll."

"Don't you want to know the price?"

"It doesn't matter. I'm in love, Rags."

Stuffing his hands into his pockets, Ragtime made a clicking noise at the corner of his mouth. "Doc, I'm so glad this piano is yours. I think it was meant for you."

Tony bit the inside of his mouth to resist choking up. "I know it was."

# 5

*Harlem*
*1924*

Athena leaned into her Steinway, playing and singing the new Irving Berlin song "What'll I Do." A whirlpool of lyrics, melody, and wistfulness created a yearning as soft and deep as the still of night. The music had its way with her and grabbed her by the throat.

> *What'll I do*
> *When you are far away*
> *And I am blue,*
> *What'll I do?*

Her brother's distinctive knock ended the recital. When she opened the door, she saw Zalo escorting Isabella Concepcion. In her mid-sixties, Isabella was a native Cuban. She stood tall and regal, her head turbaned in a yellow headdress with red pinstripes. The same material was used for her handmade dress, cut low enough to give her bust room to breathe and shade her rounded belly. Although not related by blood, Isabella was the family mystic, matriarch, and godmother.

Of all the people Athena knew, Isabella was the funniest, wisest, and certainly the most spiritual. Her aura manifested the power of a queen, a priestess, an enchantress. Perhaps she held court as all three in former lives. It made no difference. Athena became calm in her presence.

"Oh good. Don't stand out there in the hallway. Please, come in."

They gathered around the kitchen table and enjoyed Athena's tea and oatmeal cookies.

"Zalo told me about the new piano," Isabella said, her words spilling out in a Caribbean melody that made her dimples wink. "I should visit you, I thought."

"I'm so glad you did."

"After all, you are my favorite compatriot, even if you are as skinny as a rail." She laughed and slapped her well-padded hips. "Besides, I promised your mama, bless her soul, I would look after you. You are my godchildren, and I will always keep you safe."

Athena covered the mystic's hand. "Oh Isabella, I do love you. Thank you for thinking of us."

Isabella's smile deepened her dimples. "My sweet child, I would like to bless your piano. May I?"

"Yes, yes. I'd love that."

The three moved from the kitchen to the living room and surrounded the piano. Isabella fished out a fresh cigar and a box of matches from a large hip pocket. Opening the matchbox, she rolled her fingers across a matchstick, and said, "Give me fire." Whether by frictional sleight of hand or magic, the match head ignited. She lit the tip of the cigar, inhaled, and blew a stream of smoke that curled around her head. "Ooh," she droned.

"Are you summoning the gods?" Zalo asked.

"Are they here now?" Athena asked.

Isabella laughed as she passed the length of the cigar under her nose. "No, my children. Sometimes a cigar is only a cigar, and this one is the best. Cuban, you understand."

Again, she plunged her hand into her hip pocket and drew out a white feather.

"What kind of feather is that?" Zalo asked. "A great egret? Or maybe a snowy owl?"

Isabella examined the feather with curious eyes as if seeing it for the first time. "Harlem pigeon, I would say."

"Oh," Zalo mumbled.

Isabella inhaled another draw, leaned over the piano bench, and blew smoke across the full length of keys. Feathering the ivories, she chanted, "Oh-so-lama-komo-sayko. Oh-so-lama-komo-sayko," or something like that. Athena couldn't be sure.

Although Athena was a modern woman, she'd seen the otherworldly powers Isabella held. She would never dismiss her magic.

Isabella stood still, and Zalo broke the silence. "Did you want to blow more smoke?"

Their godmother shook her head and wagged her finger. "Magic is like any vice. A little is a good thing, but too much of a good thing invites danger." She turned and winked at Zalo.

"Good safety tip."

Isabella asked Athena to sit at the piano and rest her hands on the keyboard. Then she faced Zalo and said, "Stand beside your sister."

With feather in hand, Isabella haloed Athena's hair, closed her eyes, and hummed a celestial melody that Athena imagined could have calmed a raging sea. Isabella spoke as if in a trance. "Bless our child, Athena, and bless this piano. Let the artist and instrument become a source of peace and joy. Let this piano be a vessel for unconditional love, hallowed by hearts that are good and faithful and true." On an impish smile, Isabella glanced at Athena and added, "Let this instrument unite and fortify two lovers, whoever they might be, and from wherever they might appear." After Isabella pronounced her last words, she placed two fingers to her lips, kissed them, and pressed her fingers on the scrimshaw engraving of Athena's name.

Athena questioned her own eyes. Had the piano keys released a phosphorous glow? Her ears chiming, she passed her fingers over her eyelids, then stared again at the engraved keys whose luminance receded and extinguished, not in a flicker but with sunset stealth.

*What magic bewitches these piano keys?*

# 6

*Greenwich Village*
*2019*

Even though Tony scheduled the Steinway upright for a morning delivery, he decided to take the entire day off to ensure a seamless installation. His pulse quickened, telling him something extraordinary was about to happen. It was hard to explain what he felt. He had never been a man who believed in magic or otherworldliness. Still, he had seen the ravages of war and the miracle of soldiers who pulled through when the odds were stacked against them. He could not dismiss *something* unknown beyond hope and medical competency.

He anticipated a world of melody and harmony, certainly, but also an entry into a realm of mysticism, a world populated by dreams made real.

Hearing Athena's rendition of "It Had to Be You" was transformational. He'd always known music was more than a series of notes. It was about heart and soul and the mysterious relationship between musician and listener. After his experience in Ragtime's shop, Tony was convinced the piano was the embodiment of Athena Cruz, that it would allow him to connect with her, despite the barrier of space and time.

He guided the movers up the stairs and around each corner to his third-floor apartment. "Watch out for the handrail on the right. Two more steps to the first landing. Avoid the radiator at the left. It has razor-sharp edges."

Jessica opened her apartment door. She stood barefoot in a loosely tied black and gold kimono-inspired duster. "Oh my, you rascal. What devilment are you up to now?"

"Kind of busy," Tony said, his attention on the corners and edges of the magical instrument.

"Get serious," she said, her sultry delivery louder as he moved farther up the stairs. "Are you turning your apartment into a love nest with booze, candlelight, and music? I love it. You know, darling, I hanker to be the first one on the invitation list."

Although Tony didn't answer, he noticed when her voice softened. "Looks like a beautiful instrument. I'm looking forward to hearing your melodies cascade over the fire escape."

"Me too. Got to get back to work." He turned to the movers and said the only thing that came to mind. "One more flight, guys, and we're home free. Nice and easy does it."

\*\*\*

With the piano set, the fingerprints wiped clean, and the movers long gone, Tony considered the sway of the piano on his apartment from the outside-in. From the exterior, the MacDougal Street building was a split-level brownstone with a stoop that led to an arched French-door entry. It featured a Victorian Z-shaped fire escape, and beneath the stoop was the MacDougal Street Ale House. All these features animated the building with a quaint early-twentieth-century air. He'd fallen in love with the brownstone at first sight.

In contrast, the interior of his home was something of a city chalet—sophisticated but comfortable. The hunter-green walls, leather wing chairs, and gas fireplace radiated warmth and cozy luxury. The shower and countertops glowed in polished black granite with swirls of emerald green. His eclectic paintings pegged him as a devoted art buff, regardless of the period. He bought what he liked, not what would fetch him a good return on his investment.

The addition of the piano was a perfect extension of the ambiance he'd created, adding a sense of tradition within a modern setting.

He sat at the piano, his hands folded across his lap. Taking his time, he raised the fallboard, yet resisted playing a single note. Slowly, he leaned toward the last two ivories on the keyboard and skimmed his fingertips over the engravings. Athena's piano.

A song from the 1920s came to him as though whispered from the music shops of Tin Pan Alley. He could hear the haunting lyrics and full orchestration of strings. He positioned his fingers, teased an introduction, and graced Athena's piano with Gershwin.

*Somebody loves me, I wonder who.*
*I wonder who she can be.*
*Somebody needs me, I wish that I knew.*
*Who she can be worries me.*

# 7

*Harlem*
*1924*

Five nights a week from seven to eleven, Athena played at The Nest for the diner crowd. Her vocals were heard over the crowd now that the club had installed a brand-new Western Electric carbon microphone. She could whisper into the mic and still be heard at the far side of the bar. Every night, after Athena's last number, the showgirls came on, performing in scanty costumes to the raucous delight of the audience.

As usual, Buddy Jefferson greeted Athena at the curb with a glowing smile. Everything about Buddy was big. He was over six feet six and topped three hundred pounds. On top of his thick, unruly hair he crammed a straw skimmer with a hatband that read THE NEST: WHERE ALL THE BIRDIES GO TWEET, TWEET, TWEET.

He continually fussed with the hat, but he looked natty in his prized full-length doorman's overcoat with two vertical lines of brass buttons down the front. "Looking handsome as always," she told him.

Although she'd seen Buddy bounce patrons for no more than a dirty mouth, he was tender with her. He embraced her softly as if she were the most rare and fragile Caribbean orchid.

He cocked his head and flashed a toothy grin. "You go on in, Miss Athena," he said, his voice scuffed with rust.

"Thank you, Buddy. You're a sweetheart," she said, even though the endearing word made his feet shuffle. She enjoyed the exchange. It was their ritual. A way of being affectionate without sexual undertones.

When she entered the basement club, she paused as her eyes adjusted to the darkened room. At the bar, she pulled out a stool and ordered a cup of hot orange pekoe tea with lemon, her customary drink before each performance. As she sipped her drink, Cal Craven slipped in beside her. He had his back to the bar, both elbows resting on the padded edge. As always, he was impeccably dressed, tonight in a pinstriped smoke-gray double-breasted suit. A navy silk tie, matching pocket puff, and French cuffs completed his ensemble.

Zalo called him a "dandy." And he was right.

"Hello there, babe," he said. "I swear, you are one dolled-up Sheba."

She said nothing.

Craven fished out a gold monogrammed cigarette case from an inside pocket and passed it to Athena. "Butt me."

She expelled a long-suffering sigh, opened the case, and plucked what was probably a Lucky Strike. Snapping the case closed, she offered the cigarette to her boss. He ignored the offer and countered by presenting a gold-plated lighter—also monogrammed—with a flick of his wrist as a magician reveals the ace of spades. She exchanged the cigarette case for the lighter and, lifting the cigarette to her mouth, flicked on a flame, lit up, and handed the smoke to him.

Craven's performance made her belly sour, churning as if riled by blasphemy or larceny or…murder. His swagger, his arrogance all added up to an overbearing willfulness by a man adverse to accepting disappointment.

At first, she thought her reaction to him was swayed by Zalo's apprehensions. But for over a year, she had stifled a gag response to Craven, ignoring the warning signs for the love of music. Over the past couple of months, she saw him for what he was: depraved.

She could no longer dismiss her fears.

"Hello, Mr. Craven."

He smirked. An expression that conveyed not only irritation, but a shadow of peril. The look gave Athena a chill as if awakened in the middle of the night by footsteps at her bedroom door.

"Mr. Craven? What's with that? You know me well enough to call me Cal."

"Sure, Cal. Whatever you say."

He turned sideways, rested his forearm across the edge of the bar, and planted the toe of one shoe behind the other. "Listen, dollface, how 'bout you and me stepping out after your last set. We could get something to eat. Maybe see a show."

Athena decided to be civil but evasive. "Let me think about it, Cal." With that, she turned toward the bandstand and added over her shoulder, "Excuse me. I need to get started."

By the time she stepped on stage, she managed to shake off Craven's cloying lewdness and donned her show face.

She stood with her back to an unadorned upright piano, her figure stunning in a black silk floor-length spaghetti-strap dress. Isabella had stitched the festoon of silver sequins in place one loving bangle at a time. Her hair was swept behind her ears, which accented her high cheekbones and flawless complexion. At five feet eight, she was toned like a dancer but curvy like a starlet—both sexy and elegant.

"Good evening, ladies and gentlemen. Welcome to The Nest. The only place in New York City where you can laugh as you please, make whoopee as you please," a squall of whistles shrilled, "and drink as you please." That ushered a hoot of caterwauls and a sloshing of beer mugs and whiskey glasses. "But for now, since many of you are still eating our famous barbeque ribs, I'm here to provide a little ambiance. That's French for 'nice and easy.'" With splayed fingers, she grazed her thighs. "Oh là là."

She rode on the applause into her opening song, George Gershwin's "Somebody Loves Me," beginning with a piano solo and following with a smoky vocal. As she sang, the lyrics held new meaning. Did she teeter on the brink of romance? Would she soon discover the love of her life? If so, with whom? One thing was certain. It would *not* be with the parlor snake, Cal Craven.

The lyrics flowed from her heart like a prayer.

> *Somebody loves me, I wonder who.*
> *I wonder who he can be.*
> *Somebody needs me, I wish that I knew.*
> *Who can he be worries me.*

Athena's belly fluttered. Were the lyrics and melody overwhelming her? Or perhaps she was feeling the unctuous dross of Craven's words.

Whatever the reason, she freed her emotions, which revealed her hidden dreams of a certain but unknown love. She could feel the patrons go with her, their faces softening with every line, a communion between singer and audience.

***

Throughout the night, Athena noticed a willowy little girl sitting in the shadows. Gradually, the child inched her way closer to the stage. She seemed entranced by every note Athena played and every lyric she sang. Only a child with music in her soul would be so attentive from beginning to end, so Athena motioned her to approach.

The girl scampered to the dance floor below the piano.

"Come sit with me," Athena said from the stage.

"Really?"

"Yes, sweetie."

As Athena played, the girl followed the movement of every piano stroke.

All the while, they chatted. "What's your name?" Athena asked.

The youngster was a graceful girl with luminous brown eyes and two perky pigtails that sprang when she spoke. "Eleanora Fagan."

"Hello, Eleanora. Pleased to meet you. How old are you?"

"I'm nine," she answered with a puffed-out chest.

"Such a big girl. Where are you from?"

"Baltimore, ma'am."

Athena oohed her mouth. "So far away. Why are you in New York?"

"My mama is visiting my papa."

"Are they here?"

She pointed to a man and woman muffled within the shadows "They're over there. But they don't like each other very much."

Although the light was low, Athena was able to make out Eleanora's parents, who blew cold when she smiled at them.

"I see. But you like music, don't you?"

The girl's eyes lit up. "Oh yes."

"Do you sing?"

She shimmied on the piano bench. "Yes, ma'am. I surely does."

"Would you like to sing with me?"

Her face glowed under the stage lights. "Could I?"

Athena hitched her chin toward the audience. "Sure, they won't mind. They'll love you. Besides, it'll be the last number for the night. What song would you like to sing?"

The girl puzzled, then brightened. "I love Louie Armstrong. Could we do 'Saint Louis Blues'?"

"Of course. Why don't you stand right here," she said, tapping the side of the piano facing the audience.

Athena also stood, placed her arm on Eleanora's shoulder, and tucked her into her side. "Ladies and gentlemen, may I have your attention. I've met the sweetest young lady. She's visiting from Baltimore and her name is Eleanora Fagan. She's all of nine years old and would like to sing a grown-up song for you. Please welcome little Miss Eleanora."

The audience applauded politely while Athena played the introduction. Half watched with hopeful expressions while the others seemed to anticipate disaster. The hopeful guests were rewarded. When Eleanora sang, her melody was pitch-perfect and slyly improvised as if imitating the waggish lines of an Armstrong trumpet solo.

She received a warm ovation.

Athena motioned her to take a bow, which prompted an even greater round of applause. Drawing the girl into her arms, she said, "You're a singer, young lady. You'll always be a singer. Don't ever let anyone tell you differently."

Eleanora straightened her back and raised her chin. "I don't think I'm singing. I'm playing a horn. What comes out is what I feel."

Athena said softly, "What comes out is a bit of heaven." She wrapped her arms around Eleanora Fagan, the powerful little singer who would one day be known as Lady Day, Miss Billie Holiday.

# 8

*Greenwich Village*
*2019*

All medical events intrigued Tony but especially mysteries outside
his field of orthopedics. So, when he experienced hypnagogia—the
transitional state of consciousness between wakefulness and sleep—
his curiosity flamed.

It occurred the same day Athena's piano was delivered. He
composed at the keyboard for over three hours. Then, he played and
replayed the piano roll, "It Had to Be You." As Athena's rhythms,
voicings, and arpeggios infused his apartment, he held his hands
over the keys until he could anticipate every note. In the end, it was
as though the twentieth-century pianist and he played in unison, his
fingers overlying hers, feeling her every touch, her every shift in
mood. The closer he arrived at matching her cadences, the more his
body prickled, inspirited by the seductive music of Athena Cruz. He
found himself blinking back tears.

Retiring near midnight, he closed his eyes and waited for
slumber to slip in and overtake his consciousness. But sleep was a
stubborn child.

Although his eyes were closed, he was fully awake. The sounds
and images lurked like tree branches shapeshifting into monster
tendrils. From medical school he knew about hypnagogia—the
shadowy half-awake hallucinations that often appear as random
figures or geometrical patterns. But Tony's hallucinations were not
shadowy. They were vivid, dreamlike animations. To make sure he
was awake he opened his eyes and the imagery disappeared. When
he reclosed his eyes, the strange figures returned. The first was a
nickel-plated, pearl-handled revolver, the barrel glistening, then

fading. Next, the sight and sound of his feet bounded into a dark passage. Then he glimpsed a reddish geometric pattern of rectangles. Inspecting more closely, he discovered the figures were bricks, first wavering at a forty-five-degree angle, then horizontally, then angled again. His heart clamored against his ribs.

As Tony's interior screen darkened, a cold sweat misted his body. He shivered and flexed his back muscles against the dampened bedsheet.

The movie continued.

A murmur… No, humming that turned into the lyrics to "It Had to Be You." Then, a caramel-skinned singer faded in as she accompanied herself on piano. Although he had never seen her photograph, he knew the musician was Athena Cruz. He willed his internal movie to zoom in. The woman—tall, slender, and graceful— wore a crown of short black wavy hair brushed away from her face. As if on cue, she turned and faced him straight on. Her thick lashes accentuated her golden eyes with flecks of yellow. Her gaze was transparent and vulnerable, as if she trusted him…loved him.

How he longed to speak to her, at least to introduce himself, but however magical, hypnagogia was not interactive. It permitted the dreamer to only observe.

Tony projected himself closer to the spectral musician, but as he approached, the beauty fell back into a lightless void. He stretched out his arms, his fingers groping for her. "Come back."

She vanished.

He was a pitiful lummox around women and certainly would be around a woman as luminous as Athena Cruz. Yet, in his dreamscape, he sensed no uneasiness. He calmed in her presence. If he dared hold her hand, he would not shudder. If he braved a kiss, he would not swoon. He'd be himself.

But dreamscape visions laugh at reality. Anyone can feign courage in dreams. He doubted he'd feel so emboldened if she were close enough to touch her skin, to inhale the perfumed folds of her hair.

*I'm pathetic. Athena Cruz is long gone and all my dreams with her. The only woman who captures me lies in a forgotten grave. I've fallen in love with a ghost.*

*But what if…*

# 9

Athena stepped from the stage and weaved through the outcrop of small circular tables. She greeted the regular patrons by name and introduced herself to new guests with a soft touch. At every table, people praised her beauty, style, and musicianship. Typically, she deflected the compliments.

"You're too kind."

"It's a joy to play for such a fine audience."

"It's a desecration to bury our gifts, don't you think?"

A waitress with a tray of drinks touched Athena's arm and whispered into her ear. "Mr. Craven would like to talk to you before you leave."

She thanked the barmaid, wished the table of patrons a good evening, and sauntered to the bar where Cal Craven lolled with a drink in one hand and a cigarette in the other.

"Great show, as always."

"Thank you, Mr. Craven…Cal."

He stubbed out his cigarette. "Now, how about that dinner, babe?"

Athena set her feet—a firm foundation for the excuse she had to weave. "I'm sorry, Cal. I'm beat. Maybe another night."

His eyes flashed. "Maybe tonight."

The heat turned up and rose from her belly to her throat. "No, seriously—"

The boss man's expression changed as though his bone structure had morphed into a primeval wolf—the edges of his jawline, cheekbones, and eye sockets sharper and more angular. And yet, his words were stilted, without emphasis, without passion. Placing an order for a cup of coffee was more furious, which menaced his words all the more. "I don't want to hear no jive talk tonight. You work for me, remember?"

"Of course, I work for you," she said, her speech quavering. "And I'm grateful. But when I'm not working, my time is my own. I hope you appreciate that."

After setting his drink on the bar, Craven snatched Athena's hands. "I'll tell you what I appreciate. I just gave you a fucking piano. I'd appreciate a little something in return."

She toughened her words. "Do you want it back? You can pick it up anytime."

His right eye twitched, which fired a chill down her spine.

His grip tightened. "No, goddammit, I don't want it back. Nobody ever called me a damn welsher, and I ain't starting now."

Resisting the urge to turn her smile into a smirk, she said, "Honor's a good thing."

"Don't give me that crap. That's not what I want."

It came down to the same old story. A gift in exchange for sex. Zalo was right. The truth struck her with the force of a jackboot to the gut—a thinly disguised contract between a john and a moll, and she the willing harlot.

*The hell I am.*

She could feel the blood throb at her temples. "I know what you want, Mr. Craven. And, respectfully, you're not getting it."

His face hardened, becoming even more angular and blazing-eyed. He turned over her hands, pressed his thumbs into her open palms, and bowed her wrists as if intent on splitting a pair of twigs.

Falling to her knees, Athena screamed in pain. She could visualize her musical life ended in one cruel snap. "Stop, stop! You're hurting— You'll break my hands!"

The monster snarled, his chest rounded like a fighter before the bell, his eye twitching in double time. "Do you want to reconsider now, bitch?"

Patrons were standing and backing away from the scene.

It was hard to be sure in the smoke-filled room, but, yes, Craven levitated.

His glossy-toed shoes with gray spats lifted off the ground—higher and higher still. He released Athena as he eeled in midair, his mouth ajar, his eyes bulging.

Scrambling to her feet, Athena backed away, her heart drumming. She massaged her wrists and gaped at the scene that played out surreal and comical.

Craven dangled in the air like a marionette with Buddy Jefferson his puppeteer. The bouncer held the flailing boss man by the throat with both hands—not tight enough to kill him, but firm enough to gain his attention.

When he tried to speak, he only guggled.

Without breaking a sweat, Buddy said, "You needs to calm down, Mr. Craven, and leave Miss Athena alone."

Craven continued to thrash.

"Maybe you ain't hearing me good, boss. I don't want to hurt you, but I will if I gotta. Can I put you down now?"

Craven let his arms and legs go limp.

Grounding his boss, Buddy adjusted the man's lapels, which Craven shrugged off.

The club owner stroked his throat, loosened his tie, and popped open his collar. He still had nothing to say.

Buddy regarded his boss, his eyes soft but admonishing. "What you done to Miss Athena weren't right, and you knows it. I'm sorry I done that, but you gone crazy like."

As Athena watched, all compassion for Craven flagged and stilled. Despite his loveless upbringing, there were no hardships dire enough to forgive cruelty. Although shaken, she awaited his response.

With the heel of his palm, Craven swiped a polished thread of spittle from his chin and spoke in a shattered voice. "You're right, Buddy." Catching Athena's eye, he added, "I apologize, Miss Cruz."

Something in his eyes frightened her. The words suggested regret, but his spirit said something else, something outside her grasp. She could not define it, but she could feel it in her belly squirming like scavenger blood flukes.

Despite her dark premonition, Athena stood erect, her shoulders drawn back, her face somber. She pushed back against a wave of nausea. "Do I still have a job here?" she asked with more defiance than submission and loud enough for the crowd to hear.

In chorus, the crowd said, "Yes!" "Yeah!" "You bet, sister!"

Expelling an exaggerated huff, Craven turned to Athena. "I guess you do."

"What about Buddy? Does he have a job?"

He looked at the bouncer, who returned the regard with a broad, open-mouthed grin that revealed a gap between his two front teeth. "Yeah, Buddy still works here too."

The crowd applauded.

Athena hugged Buddy, her hands barely able to round his massive shoulders. "Thank you so much, you great big lovable bear."

The bouncer blushed.

When Athena turned to leave, Craven's eyes came to mind. His pride burned hot under the ash, waiting to reignite in uglier ways—the crux of the writhing blood flukes in her belly.

*** 

It was near midnight when Athena unlocked the door to her apartment. She should have gone straight to bed, but her mind swirled on the events of the night. Craven haunted her. He was a precarious game of jackstraws. *Draw the wrong stem and the game is over.*

Unsettled, she sat at the piano to calm her fears. Given the late hour, she pressed the soft pedal as she played one tune after the other. Time disappeared as her brain yielded and her fingers made all the decisions. But time scoffed at inspiration. It may have vanished for Athena but not for the universe. It was now three o'clock. As her eyes grew heavy, her fight dwindled and flamed out. She crossed her arms over the curved lip of the fallboard, pillowed her head on her forearms, and dreamed.

In her veiled dreamscape, she still sat at the piano. She played "It Had to Be You." Upon finishing the first chorus, she heard a trumpet enter, unlike any trumpet player she knew. Certainly not the flashy, rough-edged, and wide vibrato of Louis Armstrong. If anyone, it recalled the sweet ballad cornet of Bix Beiderbecke, each phrase sounding more composed than improvised. More like Claude Debussy than King Oliver.

The specter invented a fresh melody over the familiar chords—silky, wistful, mercurial, and introspective. The sound resembled a soft summer rain: at first gentle, then persuasive enough to stir the trees and seductive enough to awaken the songbirds. Athena searched the edges of her vision, but she could not find the trumpeter. He escaped into the misty gloaming of slumber, but she would never forget his beckoning call.

# 10

After a light day of surgery—one new hip—Tony wanted to unravel his visions and thought of his best friend at Columbia Medical, the psychiatrist Harlan Lowe. He made the call and set an appointment for five o'clock that evening. Walking to Harlan's office, he rehearsed his speech, which quickly collapsed into a chaotic riddle. He only hoped his friend could unravel the quandary.

Harlan Lowe was a trim and good-natured thirty-seven-year-old bachelor with smoke-gray eyes, abundant dark brown hair, and an unlined, boyish face. At home in his own skin, he usually wore suspenders and a hand-fashioned bow tie, both of which suited his playfulness and weakness for groan-worthy puns. Best of all, he always listened, seldom rattled, and never sniped. Tony gravitated to him when he hired on at Columbia Medical. Now, he was a trusted friend, as close as any Green Beret brother.

When he entered Harlan's office, the psychiatrist called out in Brooklynese, "Yo, ya big palooka. How ya doin'?"

Though reticent to play, Tony returned the accent. "Eh, I'm doin' good, but I gotta question to axeya."

"This sounds serious. Maybe we should switch to English."

He added gravity to his voice. "That's probably a good idea, doc."

The psychiatrist caught the dire quality of his tenor and boosted his professional demeanor. "Sorry. I can see you're not here for Doctor Lowe's Punch-and-Judy show. I'll shut the hell up."

Tony dismissed the concern with a flick of his hand. "Not to worry. Your sense of humor is one of the reasons I love ya, you crazy shrink. Though sometimes I can't believe what comes out of your mouth. I'm never sure if you're in the business of battling psychosis or halitosis."

Harlan wagged his finger in appreciation of the wordplay. He rounded his desk and moved to a leather lounger and matching sofa. Harlan took the lounger, Tony the sofa. When they had settled in, Harlan asked, "Is this about Sophia?"

Although he tried not to show it, a surge of heat stoked his chest, annoyed that Harlan would mention her name right off the bat. *Screw you* was on his lips, but fortunately, he only said, "No."

Although his tone was compassionate, the psychiatrist continued. "Are you sure? I notice you working that gold band on your pinky like you're trying to unscrew your finger." He waited for the gestalt metaphor to penetrate. "I can tell you're tortured. Right now, you look like you could kill me and eat me and not necessarily in that order."

Tony examined his hands, set them on his lap, and willed them to be still. Through his teeth, he said, "Not today."

The psychiatrist raised both hands in surrender. "Okay. Just remember, you have work to do. Don't let it fester too long."

"I won't."

"That's all I needed to hear."

Tony hesitated long enough to tamp down the noise in hearing Sophia's name. *This is not about Sophia. Damn, maybe it is. But for now, Athena's on my mind.*

His patchwork of thoughts played out more by emotion than reason—hardly grounded in the scientific method. He had to find some way to still the confusion.

He recounted the discovery of Athena's Piano—how, all at once, the sound of it filled him with passion and longing and malaise. His speech softened. "I feel like she entered my skin, that I know her and she knows me."

Harlan listened intently, only interrupting to clarify a timeline or definition of terms.

Kneading the vertebrae at his neck, Tony pushed against the pressure. A vertebra snicked. "Something incredible happened. You know about hypnagogia."

"Sure. Did you hallucinate?"

He swiped his hand across his mouth. "To put it mildly." He explained the full series of half-awakened dreams, all still vivid in his mind.

Harlan tugged on his lower lip in concentration. "Fascinating. What do you make of all that?"

"That's just it, I don't know. My life's been…intense. Maybe I'm snuffing out my candle."

Harlan stared for a second as if his friend had switched to a foreign language. "What do you mean?"

Tony looked away. "You know me. I like everything in its right place, which makes this screwy admission damn humiliating." He turned to face Harlan directly. "Am I losing it?"

"I suppose that's possible. We all have a finite reservoir of energy." The psychiatrist splayed and steepled his fingers. "How are you sleeping?"

"Not bad. I don't always get eight hours, especially when I'm gigging, but I can always count on six or seven."

"Try to make it seven." Harlan stroked his chin. "Tell me more about Athena Cruz."

Tony took his time as Athena's dream sequence flickered like a silent movie. "That's the most mystifying piece. She's well over a hundred years old. But…" He fidgeted, uncrossing one leg and crossing the other. "But I think I love her. Now that's *got* to be—"

"—delusional?"

"—wacko."

"Don't be so sure." On a long pause, Harlan asked, "You know what the mathematical equivalent is for emotions like loneliness and guilt?"

He shook his head.

"A negative number."

"And?"

"And sometimes a person can feel like minus infinity."

Tony pulled up short and aimed two fingers at the psychiatrist. "I think you just tiptoed from preaching to meddling, Brother Lowe."

"My point is negative emotions can feel crushing, like a huge minus number, but that doesn't make it crazy. Just hard to live with." He undid his bowtie and unhooked the collar button. "You don't mind."

Tony flagged his indifference with a wave.

"Look. Love is no critical discriminator. We love those who are dear to us, but it doesn't stop there. We can also love inanimate things. I know a guy who says he's in love with his Lexus. And millions of people swear they love God with every fiber of their being."

"But can you be *in* love with someone from the past?"

"Why not? I never met her, but I think I may be in love with Julie London, and she died about twenty years ago." He hunched his shoulders and shuddered. "I mean what she does with 'Cry Me a River' still curls my toes."

Knowing the rendition inside out, Tony cracked a smile, touched his friend would choose a musical example.

"Here's my point. Don't be afraid of who or what you love. If you're not harming yourself or others, you're on safe ground. Besides, any definition of normalcy requires a good deal of wiggle room." He patted a rhythm on his knees. "Would I like you to find a real-live girl one day? Sure. But that has more to say about my personal preferences than psychiatry."

Tony searched the far end of the room where the wall met the ceiling.

Lifting off the back of his chair, the psychiatrist snapped his fingers. "Hey, have you done any research on Athena Cruz? I'm wondering if reading an obituary or visiting a graveyard might bring some kind of closure to your fascination with this phantom lady."

Tony's head listed, his gaze lowered. *What a great friend. Loyal to the bone. But I'm the only person who can make sense of this.*

"As a matter of fact, I have. And so did Andy Alexander, the salesman who sold me the piano. We both came to the same conclusion. She vanishes after nineteen twenty-four." He chewed on his lower lip. "Look, brother, I'm like you. I'd like a real-live girl too." He stared at his hands. "But in the end, I'd like that girl to be Athena Cruz."

"I'm afraid I can't help you there. You entered *The Twilight Zone*, and I don't have a license to practice there."

He pretended to laugh. "Neither do I, but I'm not willing to give up the dream. At least not yet."

"Then don't. Play it out, and we'll see what happens." Harlan polished his hands. "I'll let you know when you're ready for a straitjacket."

On a sardonic smile, Tony embraced himself. "I take a forty-two long."

# 11

Athena still played at The Nest, and Craven kept his distance. However, when he *did* look her way, his eyes teemed with vengeance. His seething heart was impossible to disguise—as transparent as a child scheming to cover one deceit by inventing an even more outrageous lie.

With the mood so steeped in danger, she considered performing at another club on Swing Street. But The Nest dominated as the hottest place on the block and offered the greatest chance of being discovered. So, she stayed on.

After her last set, she slipped out of the club to avoid Craven's piercing stare.

"Good night, Miss Athena," Buddy said.

His graciousness gave her a tingle. "You're my favorite hero in all of Harlem."

Buddy flustered and ground the sole of his shoe. "And you my favorite chanteuse in all the world."

Setting her elbows akimbo, Athena asked, "Chanteuse?"

"That's what we call a beautiful singer back in New Orleans where I come from."

She patted his hand. "Chanteuse. I like that. It sounds so sophisticated and refined—just like you, Buddy Jefferson."

The bouncer flushed from the compliment. "May I walk you home, Miss Athena?"

"No thank you, Buddy. Don't you worry your sweet self. I live at the end of the block."

\*\*\*

While Athena strode home in the dark, her high-heel shoes clicking on the pavement, she heard footsteps behind her. But when she stood still, they fell silent. Stepping out on the balls of her feet, she again detected the sound of footfalls and glanced over her shoulder. No one. She quickened her pace and dashed down the steps of a split-level row house that led to a basement apartment. Under the stairwell's mantle of darkness, she stood in silence. In the shadows, she heard a whimper and glimpsed a spot of light on an otherwise all-black nose. A scruffy black and tan terrier mix.

She crouched. "Hey there, fella. Who are *you* hiding from?"

The pup trotted to Athena and nuzzled against her leg. A tag on his collar read BRAVEHEART.

She scratched the backside of the terrier's folded ears. "You like that, don't you?" The dog tilted his head and bellied in closer.

Athena hushed. Approaching footsteps like the slow dampened taps from a hi-hat. Closer and closer still. Her heart quickened. Perhaps the terrier sensed the danger. He whimpered again—louder this time.

Athena stood and surveyed the basement entryway, searching for some kind of weapon, some way of defending herself. Nothing. *No, wait, what's that?* She widened her eyes in the dark and spotted a two-foot strand of rope, the remnant of a schoolgirl's jump rope. She snatched the length of cord, wrapped the ends around both hands, and tested its strength. The strand shredded on the second yank. *No,* she said soundlessly.

Reeling for a solution of any kind, she remembered the belt that cinched her trench coat. *Of course.* She slipped the belt through the coat loops and wound it around both hands. If necessary, she could sling the belt around the assailant's neck and, with the edge of centrifugal force, slam him to the ground—if given the chance. She grew ghost-quiet as she grappled to master her breathing.

The rhythmic patter stopped at the crest of the basement stairs.

"Do you want to come out now, Athena?"

Cal Craven, his stony intonation unmistakable. She said nothing, stalling for time to plan her next move.

"You have nowhere to run."

Unwrapping her left hand, she stuffed her bound right hand into her pocket. She turned to the terrier. "Braveheart, stay," she whispered. The pup sat.

Athena ascended the five steps to street level.

"There you are. I'm glad I found you." He waved an envelope. "You forgot to pick up your jack for the week."

She feigned an uneasy laugh. "How stupid of me. You'd think I was born on Park Avenue."

When she reached for her salary with her left hand, he dropped the envelope and snagged her by the wrist. "Not so quick, sister," he said, sounding serpentine. "Why do you have to be so unfriendly? I'm not a goon, and I'm not a sap. I'm a regular guy trying to make a living. Is there something wrong with that?"

She squeezed the belt wound about her right hand. "I don't think there's anything regular about you, Mr. Craven," she said, making certain her meaning fell short of a compliment.

"Now there you go again calling me Mr. Craven. I told you my name is Cal."

"I think I feel safer with something more formal."

He stared at her as if waiting for a body of evidence. "Safer? What does that mean?"

She hesitated.

"Good evening, y'all," a deep voice said outside their circle of conversation.

Both turned to see Buddy's gap-toothed smile, appearing as sunny as a boy at a church picnic.

Craven released Athena's wrist.

"I hope y'all doing good this fine evening."

"Why ain't you at the club?" Craven asked in a snit.

Buddy's head wobbled. "Oh, I'm going back, sir, but I promised Miss Athena I'd walk her home. And, goodness, if I ain't forgot. I'm sorry 'bout that, Missy."

His words were fawning on the surface but defiant at heart.

Athena mirrored his double-talk. "That's all right, Buddy. Mr. Craven and I were having a nice friendly talk. Isn't that right?"

"That's right," Craven said a little too quickly.

Buddy looked down and spotted the envelope. "What's this here?" he asked, stooping to snag the envelope.

"Look at that," she said. "That's my pay for the week. Mr. Craven was kind enough to chase me down. It must have slipped out of my pocket. Isn't that silly?"

"Yeah, silly," Craven said, choking on the words.

"Well, that's funny. There ain't no money in this here envelope," Buddy said, opening and displaying an empty shell.

Craven and Athena regarded the barren envelope, then each other. When they made eye contact, Craven looked away.

"Now I'm the stupid one," Craven said in a breezy tone. "And I ain't even bent." He fished out his wallet from his inside suit pocket. "Here you go, Athena. Thirty clams and an extra five for doing great work this week."

She waved the bills at Craven. "Thank you. The landlord will be happy to see this. Now, if you'll excuse us, Buddy's going to escort me home. That is if you're still willing, Buddy."

He grinned and, with head bowed, offered his arm. "Oh, I'm willing just fine."

***

Craven watched from under his brows while the two turned and strolled along Swing Street, Athena clutching Buddy's arm, their shadows advancing and retreating as they passed under the narrow glow of one streetlamp to the next.

On a chill that pebbled the back of his neck, he snapped his suit collar, turned wearily, and trudged to the club—all the more stewing in a vengeant brew.

The burning quest for power rushed through his veins. He gloated when his human chattel winced and darted about in a frenzy. He ruled better than any damn white man and despised anyone who threw a shadow on his barony. That was the heart of it. Athena cast a long, contemptuous shadow.

***

When Athena and Buddy arrived at her apartment, she invited her escort to sit on the stoop. Buddy fished out his handkerchief and brushed the step. She rested, entranced by the moon-splashed street as if it were a frolicking campfire in a darkened wood.

Buddy cleared his throat and spoke haltingly. "Miss Athena. I don't know nothing from nothing, but I wonder if you scared-like of Mr. Craven."

She bobbed her head. "A little."

Fidgeting, he said, "Uh-huh. Well, I wants to say something that probably sounds cracked and broke up."

"I'm listening."

He spoke as if to an apparition manifested in the space between them and the streetlight. "You know, there's a lotta bad men coming to the club. Some from Chicago, some of them killers. They know how to take care of bad men like Mr. Craven, and—"

Athena lengthened her spine and turned to face him straight on. She was evenly tender and stern. "Look at me, Buddy. Don't say another word. Craven's not a good man, and he does scare me, but I would never hire a man to…" She stopped to settle her flutters. "I will defend myself if I have to, but I will not… Well, you know what I mean." She lowered her head to catch his downcast eyes. "Buddy?"

He glared at his shoes as if they might catch fire. "Yes'um, I know."

"That's good. We won't talk about this again."

"No, Miss Athena." He halted and restarted. "I hope you still likes me, even though I said something stupid."

Wrapping her hands around his brawny arm, she quoted her mother's favorite bedtime promise. "Oh Buddy, I love you as much as the flowers love the rain." She pulled his arm into her breast. "You never need to worry yourself about that. Not one tiny bit. We're friends forever, you and I. Do you understand?"

He hunched his shoulders over his chest.

She placed her fingertips under his chin and raised his head until he looked into her eyes. "Remember this, Buddy Jefferson. You're my sweet prince. Nothing can change that."

Rolling his lips over his teeth, Buddy moaned, which Athena took as regret.

She gave his arm a squeeze. "Good. Now say good night, Buddy."

Although tears thickened his throat, he said, "Good night, Buddy."

She laughed at the joke while he blushed with the warm grace of being forgiven.

# 12

Tony was called in late to set a child's fractured fibula. Although his hands and eyes were on the job, his mind flitted to Athena Cruz. It was near eleven o'clock when he arrived home. To unwind, he played his trumpet with a cup mute to avoid a knock on his door, especially from the steamy Jessica Sweet. When he finished, he set his trumpet on top of Athena's piano and sat before the keyboard.

He couldn't deny falling in love with Athena, and music was the source. It was as though melody completed them just as a chord progression resolves to its home key. There was no escaping her attraction. He whispered her name as if it were a sacred incantation. "Athena... Athena." He played her piano roll, "It Had to Be You." For the first time, he fingered every note as *she* played them—note by note, rest by rest.

Tony was thrilled by the duet. On an impulse of devotion for his muse, he placed two fingertips to his lips, kissed them, and pressed his fingers into the scrimshaw engravings of her name. *Was it another hypnagogic episode that glimmered the inscribed keys?*

A tingle radiated beneath his sternum, crept like minute runnels across his chest, over his hips, and down his legs. The tingle became a quiver, then a thousand serried pricks. *I'm having a heart attack.* But the symptoms were all wrong.

He stared at his hands and commanded them to move, even to twitch, but they no longer belonged to him. Nothing did. He was a prisoner in his own body.

The details of the room faded. Now his hands appeared frosted behind a diaphanous veil. Behind the shroud, a new image appeared. It was a twentieth-century apartment with a bare radiator, an armoire, and an upright piano. As the shroud lifted, he saw a woman at the piano. When he approached, she turned her head and smiled. Her eyes were bright and...beckoning.

"Please, Athena, I know you."

She said nothing. Her image yellowed, fissured, and fragmented like a time-lapse film of a rotting leaf. She was gone.

And now, *god help me,* his hands atomized. Pieces of fingernails, knuckles, and skin splintered and crumbled and drifted upward like snowflakes returning to the cumulus clouds that had shaken them loose. Bit by bit, his body faded into oblivion. But not death. He was still aware.

A keening wind chased overhead, underfoot, and through the field that once bundled his body. He churned in a rush of spinning space—so dark it seemed to vibrate. Nothing grounded him in the swirling void. Nothing earthly, nothing celestial. He could not be sure of anything, including his own reality. Tormented, he opened his mouth to scream, but if he wailed, he had no larynx to shout, no ears to hear, no mind to unscramble the sound.

The past and future dissolved. Only the present existed—suspended and parched of meaning—a psychotic fugue belonging to another entity.

Somewhere in the shredded moments, what was pestled and pulverized incrementally resurrected. Although he was still blind, powerless, and wallowing in murk, he sensed a kernel of himself remained. He clung to that promise of life.

It was then he heard something—no, *someone.* At first, he imagined the sound was a phantom creation of his mind. No. Although the sounds gibbered faintly, the emotions were clear. Anger and fear.

*Stop. Listen. Think.*

The words—spoken in English, thank god—echoed louder and more distinct. Although the voice was feminine, the meaning was fierce. "Who are you? What are you doing here? Answer me, or I swear, I'll kill you."

Like a slow dawn stingy with twilight, the world reappeared. He struggled to rise from the piano bench.

"Who are you?" the specter asked.

Tony turned a half circle toward the hollow words, peered, and detected a figure, all but an afterimage as if seen from within a bowl of egg whites.

"Start talking, mister."

*Talk about what? Who's asking? How did you break into my apartment?*

As he batted his eyelids, the figure became marginally focused. He opened his mouth to speak, but nothing vocalized. Then her face became clear. *My god, Athena Cruz.* He knew her instantly. She was everything he imagined, everything he dreamed: tall and graceful with short hair, Tahitian skin, and startling yellow eyes.

On a hard swallow to clear his throat, he took one bungling step around the piano bench and a second step toward her.

She didn't step back. She shuffled forward and, out of nowhere, threw a punch that caught his jaw. The sound, a crackling *splat*, and the taste of blood raveled his mind.

He staggered back into the piano bench—shaken, woozy, bewildered.

The world washed out and extinguished as his knees buckled, his back scalloped, and his body crumbled.

# 13

*Harlem*
*1924*

Athena stepped into the hallway and shouted with enough force and frenzy to awaken her brother.

In less than two minutes, he scampered down the two flights of stairs and bounded into Athena's apartment. "Who the hell is he?" Zalo asked, half out of breath. "And what's a white man doing in your apartment?"

Athena was not herself. Her jaw trembled, and her eyes darted. "I don't know… And… I don't know."

Zalo softened his tone. "Thena, what are you saying?"

She paced from one end of the room to the other. How could she explain a man who seemed not to *arrive* but *effervesce* out of the piano's ivory and wood? "Exactly that. I don't know who he is. One moment, I was alone. The next moment he was at the piano. I don't know how he got here. I don't even know how he got *in*. The front door and all the windows were locked. It's like he appeared out of thin air. I was alone, and then he was here." She snapped her fingers. "Like striking a match with your fingernail."

"Huh?"

She let her head loll. "If I could explain it any better, I would." She dazed for a beat. "It was the way he looked at me after I slugged him."

"Yeah?"

"It shook me."

"How?"

She froze as she played back the scene. "He batted his eyes. No anger, no fear, not even payback. Just bewilderment as if to say, 'Why would you do that?'"

"What?"

"That's all I've got."

Zalo hooked his thumbs over his belt, bent over at the waist, and gawked at the mysterious stranger. "Is he alive?"

"Of course, he's alive. I'm strong, but not *that* strong."

"Are you sure? Did you check?"

"I checked. See for yourself."

Zalo knelt beside the intruder. Placing two fingers on the man's throat, he canted his head as if listening to his fingertips. "He's alive, all right. Thank god for that. Otherwise, we'd be in one hell of a mess with a dead white guy in your living room." He stripped off the stranger's curious bracelet. "What's this thing?" He stood and gawked at a black rectangular screen. His head angled, he turned over the band and flipped it again to the smooth black surface. When large digital numbers flashed, he immediately dropped it. Bending at the waist, he poked it with his forefinger. "I'm an idiot. It's not like it's hot." With the watch in hand, he stood erect, rotated the instrument, and stared goggle-eyed as the device lit up. "What time is it?"

Athena looked at the windup alarm clock through the door that led to her bedroom. "Just after midnight."

"That's what this thing says. What day is today?"

"April nineteenth."

"Same date." Zalo bobbled his head. "I don't get it. Have you ever seen a watch that tells you the date?"

"Never."

Zalo clicked the small silver button on the side of the watch. A line drawing of a heart filled the screen. Under the heart were the letters BPM. He passed his hand over his short-cropped hair. "What's BPM?"

"You got me." Then she blurted out, "Beats per minute? But that doesn't make sense. Anybody knows there're sixty beats to the minute."

"Not according to this. This says seventy-two."

"That's weird." She pondered. "Let's look for a wallet."

She knelt beside the visitor. That was curious. "Visitor" was the word that came to mind. Not a thief or intruder or stranger. He was a visitor, as if he were an old friend, newly returned from foreign lands. Why would she think that?

Athena looked at him really for the first time. Tall, muscular, and definitely handsome with his full lips and waves of black hair. *For goodness' sake, he could have been the model for Michelangelo's* David.

The visitor wore a solid tan gabardine suit over a black, silky long-sleeve T-shirt. More strangely, his footwear, a gaudy pair of sneakers held together by a fine mesh, glowed in purple, turquoise, and lime green. "He sure dresses funny," she said as she peeled back the tongue on one sneaker. A label read MADE IN CHINA. "Since when does China export anything other than tea?"

On an impulse, she checked the stranger's pockets, beginning with his inside jacket compartments. "Nothing here." She patted his front right pants pocket.

"Hey, watch what you're grabbing," Zalo said.

"You watch what you're thinking," Athena snapped with a glare that could have fried nose hair. Still kneeling at his side, she drew out a black leather wallet, which sized slightly greater than a folded dollar bill. She extracted a black card, a little over three inches long and two inches wide. It read CITY NATIONAL BANK VISA. The card was as thin as tin but more rigid. She turned it over. "There's a long number here and a name."

"What's the name?"

"Anthony Marco."

"What's the number?"

"Just a long string of random numbers. It doesn't make any sense." She looked closer at the card. "Wait a minute. It says good through seven – O – one. Whatever this thing is, it was only valid until July nineteen twenty-one. This thing is worthless now."

She fished out a driver's license. "This is strange."

"How's that?"

"For one thing, it's in color." Her head snapped. "Man alive." She clambered to her feet and leaped backward from the unconscious body. "Damn!"

"What!"

"Guess when this guy was born?"

"I don't know…eighteen ninety?"

"Not even close," she said with a gasp. "Guess again."

"Eighteen-eighty?"

She tunneled her fingers into her hair and clenched. "Get this. Nineteen eighty-four."

"You mean *eighteen eighty-four*."

"Nope. Look for yourself."

Zalo stared at the card. "It says DOB."

"Date of birth."

As if learning to read, Zalo slowly pronounced the words, "Date of birth, January twenty-sixth nineteen eighty-four. Issued in twenty-sixteen. Expires twenty-twenty-four."

Athena returned to the body and retrieved the wallet at the visitor's side. She drew out a single one-dollar bill. "Do you have a dollar?"

"I think so." Zalo dug into his pocket, found a bill, and passed it to his sister.

She stared at the two bills, the visitor, the bills again. "You won't believe this. Your bill is a Silver Certificate, series nineteen twenty-three. *His* bill is a Federal Reserve Note, series two thousand nine." She pulled out three more bills from the visitor's wallet, two tens and a twenty, and speed-read the dates. "Series two thousand nine, two thousand nine again, and series *twenty-blessed-thirteen*."

Shaking her head, she rounded her lips and dragged on a long sigh. "You can slap me silly if you want, but…"

"You want to finish your sentence?"

"Our visitor is from the future."

However strange, the gentle whirlpooling of her blood told her she was safe, that the mystifying visitor could be trusted. Embracing the man with her eyes, she glided the back of her hand along the stubbled curve of his jawline and moistened her lips. "He's real."

Zalo paced a tight three-sixty. "Thena, cut that out. Listen to yourself." He wagged his head and snorted. "A man from the future. That's just goofy."

No matter. She *wanted* the man to be from the future. The visitor was the manifestation of every dream ever dreamt: every fantasy ever read. "Not according to H. G. Wells."

"H. G. Wells?" he howled. "You're talking nonsense. *The Time Machine* is a fantastic children's tale."

"Maybe not." Standing to face her brother, she recited the evidence with authority. "When was the last time you saw a man dressed like this with sneakers from China? When was the last time you saw a watch like his? A dollar bill like his? A driver's license like his? And what about this VISA card thingy? Explain all that, and I'll listen to you. But for right now, I'm telling you, this man— Anthony Marco, born in nineteen eighty-four—is from the future."

She regarded her brother, then the visitor. Arms folded, she narrowed her eyes and crimped one corner of her mouth. Ten seconds later, she snapped her head. "Let's get him to my bed."

# 14

Fifteen minutes later, Athena sat on the side of the bed, massaging her right hand, restless for Anthony Marco to awaken. She liked the look of him—his straight nose with a slight crease at the bridge, the way his hair curled around his ears, his chiseled jaw, only flawed by the bruised imprint of her knuckles.

The first words he mumbled were in his sleep. "Please, Athena, I know you."

*He's calling my name. How does he know my name?* "He's coming to."

"Careful, Thena. You don't know anything about him. He could be a madman."

"I don't think so."

"But you don't know."

"And you don't know either, Miss Mollycoddle. So hush up."

With a bleat of disapproval, Zalo moved from the bedroom door to the side of the bed opposite his sister.

Tapping her patient's cheek, she said, "Wake up, Anthony. It's time to get up now."

The visitor opened his eyes, not all at once but in a flutter. It was impossible not to smile. *Those eyes. Bold. Deep. Blue.*

"Athena," he said with such tenderness it gave her a shiver.

On a jitter, a flame ignited in her chest. "Good evening, Anthony, or rather good morning."

He tried to ease onto his elbows, wavered, and lay down again.

"Not so fast. You've got time."

His slow blink would have appeared theatrical in any normal circumstance. He cleared his throat. "Where am I?"

"You're in my apartment."

"Where? What city?"

"Harlem. New York City."

He seemed troubled, disjointed. "I don't know how to ask this, but—"

"What year is it?" she said, completing the sentence out of mercy.

The tension in his face fell away. "Yes. Please."

Athena touched his arm. "Nineteen twenty-four." She repeated with more meaning. "It's nineteen twenty-four."

He was already shaking his head. "I knew it. It had to be."

Zalo stepped in, his intonation not entirely friendly. "What do you mean by that?"

He looked at Zalo for the first time. "Who're you?"

"I'm the escort," he deadpanned.

"I'm sorry?"

His eyebrows came together in a half-scowl. "You do anything wrong to my sister—you even *think* about it—and I'll escort you to another life."

Athena pruned her face. "Back off, Z."

Although clearly steeping with pent-up angst, he obeyed.

Turning to the visitor, Athena referenced Zalo with a smirk and a head jerk. "He's my brother and sometimes overprotective, but I love him. His name's Zalo, although I sometimes call him Z."

"It's always good to have someone in your corner." He held out his hand. "Nice to meet you."

Zalo hesitated until his sister gave him a don't-make-me-kick-your-ass glare.

"Shake," she ordered.

Although Zalo's eyes wandered, he accepted the intruder's hand.

The visitor cradled his chin and wobbled his jaw. "Are you the one who slugged me?"

Fisting his hands below his belt buckle, Zalo flexed his shoulders. "If it was me, you'd still be asleep."

Fashioning a ragged smile, Athena offered a single word of contrition. "Guilty."

He whistled. "Man, you pack a wallop."

She dipped her head and peered at him from under her brows. She looked cute, and she knew it. "You didn't leave me any choice—the way you showed up."

"How was that?"

"Like this," she said, making a fist and flaring her fingers. "I turned and you were there, sitting on the piano bench." She searched his eyes. "Now, it's your turn to answer a question, Anthony Marco. How did you know you had to be in Harlem in nineteen twenty-four? And how do you know my name?"

He opened his mouth to speak, closed it, then blurted, "Wait a minute, how do you know *my* name?"

"We found your wallet," Zalo said.

He patted his empty pocket. "Of course. I would have done the same thing." Pressing his hands into the mattress, he managed to set himself upright. "First, I only use Anthony for official documents. Please call me Tony."

She tried out the name and liked the sound of it. "Tony."

"Why Harlem, nineteen twenty-four? And how do I know Athena Cruz? That's a long story. I don't understand it all myself, but I'll tell you everything I know."

Zalo pulled up a straight-backed chair, his face unsmiling. "I'm ready, fella."

Athena snapped a scowl at her brother and returned to her guest. On Tony's gaze—stained-glass studies in blue—she looked down to resist jumping him.

"It all began when I saw your piano for the first time."

Athena twitched. "I don't understand. It's always been here."

Tony dragged his fingers through his hair. "I know this'll sound crazy to you. I didn't see it in nineteen twenty-four I saw it in…two thousand nineteen."

Zalo wriggled.

Athena settled in with interest.

# 15

With questions and speculations swirling like a New York blizzard, Tony's story took most of the night to unfold. When he described his experiences before and during time travel, Zalo leaped from his chair and returned ten minutes later with Isabella Concepcion.

Tony was spellbound by Isabella. Despite being rousted from bed, she entered the room with an air of royalty, not cloaked in smugness or arrogance but with the bearing of internal peace. She seemed incapable of harboring lies or regrets.

Captivated by her kindness and presence, he leaned in to the sage. They exchanged a warm smile. Whether it was intuition or the enchantment of the witching side of dawn, he trusted her. And he sensed she trusted him.

Together the three of them told a more concise version of Tony's story, often all speaking at once.

Zalo faced Isabella. "Do you think a man can travel in time to find the love of his life?"

Athena flushed and spoke in a whispery snit. "That's enough, Z."

Zalo raised both hands, signifying *stop*. "It's my turn to tell you to hush." He pivoted to Isabella. "Is it possible?"

The sage studied Tony in the buttery lamplight, her lips curling up ever so slightly. She spoke to him as though he were the only person in the room. "Love knows no boundaries. It can cross all lines. Color, time, space. All of that is unimportant."

She listed her head to catch Zalo's eyes. "You are really asking if I think this man's story is true. No, I do not *think* it is true. I *know* it is true." She tugged on both sides of her dress. "I know your heart, Zalo Cruz. You have nothing to fear. Athena is safe."

Isabella returned to Tony and patted his hand. "You are safe too. You are home."

Tony was touched by a warm sense of togetherness. It was an unfamiliar feeling. As a boy, he was left to fend for himself. His father seemed blind to the needs of others, and his mother, trapped in a loveless marriage, bled out the days by propping herself in bed and escaping into one romance novel after the other, interrupted only by sleep and a steady dosage of Prozac. The Cruz clan was different. Each regard was transparent, a look that said, *I know you, you scalawag, and I love you.* They were a family.

Isabella met Athena's eyes. "My sweet child, you are such an independent soul. But never forget, happiness is a gift. Accept it whenever offered."

Although he felt safe, Tony clung to his shyness. When Athena looked into his eyes, he held her gaze for only a few seconds before turning aside.

Athena said, "'Happiness is a gift and the trick is not to expect it—'"

"'—but to delight in it when it comes,'" Tony said, finishing the quotation.

Looking at each other, they said in unison, "Charles Dickens."

"You know Dickens?" Tony asked.

"About every word."

Thrilled to discover a thread of connection, his face stretched at the seams. "Well, I certainly don't know every word. But he is my favorite author."

"Mine too."

Invading each other's eyes, both mirrored the other's sense of wonderment.

Isabella and Zalo exchanged a look and giggled.

"What?" Athena asked.

Isabella and Zalo shrugged in childlike innocence, their faces saying, *Huh? I couldn't possibly know what you mean.*

***

The minutes lengthened into hours. Tony happily accepted an invitation to spend what remained of the night in Zalo's apartment.

He didn't want his presence or, more accurately, his concealed love to frighten her.

Athena accompanied her guests to the front door.

After an exchange of kisses, Isabella and Zalo slipped into the hallway.

Lingering, Tony took Athena's hand and looked into her yellow cat-eyes. *Man, I could swim in those eyes for a month and come out a Jesuit monk.* "Thank you for your kindness but mostly for believing in me. At least, I hope you believe in me."

She trailed a finger down her neck, a gesture so unpretentious yet so sensual it nearly unraveled Tony's last fragment of self-confidence.

"I'm working on it," she said. "Don't run off yet."

He liked the sound of that. "No chance."

They were quiet for three long beats, Tony rejoicing for holding her gaze the entire time.

"Hey, are you coming or what?" Zalo chided.

"Coming," Tony said, his gaze still on Athena.

Zalo scuffed his shoes.

"My host is getting restless." But his feet refused to move as if he were shipping out at daybreak, never to see her again. "Until tomorrow, if that's all right with you."

Her smile was sweet but ambiguous. Was it shyness or flirtation? He guessed the former but hoped for the latter.

"I'm looking forward to it," she said.

In a flourish of ridiculous flamboyance, he thumped his hand over his heart and tipped his head lower than was necessary. As he backed into the hallway, his heel caught the threshold edge, and he bungled into Zalo's arms.

"Eh, sorry, man," Tony said.

"Cripes."

Concocting a crooked half-smile, Tony turned to catch one last glimpse of Athena as she closed the door and pressed her hand over her mouth to muffle a chuckle.

The visitor from another time followed Zalo to his fourth-floor apartment. *Who pats his heart and bows? A doofus, that's who.*

\*\*\*

Zalo made a bed for his guest on the living room couch.

Although his feet would easily surpass the end of the divan, it made no difference to Tony.

Before escaping into his bedroom, Zalo sat in a slat-backed rocker, haloed by a meager floor lamp. "You know, our mama used to lull Athena and me to sleep in this rocker when we were kids."

"I can picture that."

"But we're not kids anymore."

"No, you're not."

"We had to grow up fast to take care of each other."

"I can imagine."

"And if one is hurt or injured, we come running."

Tony thumbed his stubbled beard. "I know that already. It's one of the things I love about you."

Zalo cocked his head. "Now that's what I'm talking about. How can you love us? You've known us for only a few hours."

Tony shifted his weight, which carried him forward to the edge of the couch. The move foreshadowed the gravity of his words. "This is not easy to explain, but I feel I've known you much longer. And, as strange as it sounds, I'm sure I've known your sister, or the *longing* for her, my entire life."

Zalo stared at his guest in silence as if waiting for him to dissolve back into the future. "Maybe so, but listen up. Like I said before, if you hurt my sister in any way, if you even think about it, I will…"

"Go ahead."

"You get me."

"Yeah, I get you."

He didn't doubt Zalo's sincerity. His devotion to his sister so stirred his heart he squeezed his eyes to keep menacing tears at bay.

"Damn you," Zalo said. "You've got that doglike loyalty in your eyes." He pounded his fist into his hand, not as intimidation but as contrition. "I'm sorry. What I said a minute ago was unfriendly, wasn't it?"

Unable to squelch a chuckle, Tony said, "Well, not compared to Attila the Hun." After gathering his thoughts, he leaned in. "Please don't worry. I'm not a player."

"What's a player?"

"Someone who uses women."

His face went hard, his eyes cold. "That better be the truth."

"I'm no good around women. Frankly, they scare me. But not Athena. I knew from the first time I saw her in my dreams she was special." He trailed his hands to his knees. "Now that I've met her in person, I'm even more certain. She's strong, loving, and compassionate. Absolutely perfect."

Zalo looked at the ceiling and swept his hand from his temple to the nape of his neck. His rocking picked up pace. "So, what do you want from her?"

He knew Zalo was thinking about sex. Of course, Athena was desirable—he'd have to be lifeless not to see it—but his ache was more profound, more exquisite. "I want to know everything about her, especially what makes her spirit so—"

"—soulful?"

"Yes, so beautifully soulful."

"What else?" Zalo asked with less intimidation.

There it was. He edged up to the precipice of a new belief, teetered for only an instant, and then embraced it. He wanted to build a family. It was time to say it out loud. "If it brings her joy, I want to share our lives together."

Zalo's rocking stopped on the beat. "Even though you're from a different time?"

He thought of Harlan Lowe's wish for him to find a real-live girl one day. Well, he'd found her all right. He had to backpedal ninety-five years, but there she lay, two floors below, so close he could enter her dreams. She was no longer a beguiling phantom. She was real. "Even though we're from different times. I agree with Isabella. Love knows no boundaries."

Zalo raised his chin and stared at his guest, appearing calculating and judicious. "What are you going to do now?"

Tony was stymied. "I'm not sure. I think I'm going to let destiny take its course—and enjoy the ride."

# 16

Tony awakened refreshed and ready to ride his road bike to work until he remembered he wouldn't have his bike or his position at Columbia Orthopedics for ninety-five years. He glanced at his watch—a timepiece that would be useless in a few days without a USB port. It was nine fifteen.

He found a note on the small table that skirted the couch where he'd slept.

*Tony,*

*I normally work as a laborer, but today is Sunday, so I'm going to the gym. There's some oatmeal and coffee in the kitchen if you're hungry.*

*See you after my workout.*

*Zalo*

Military habits being hard to break, Tony made his bed, carefully folding, smoothing, and squaring away his blanket at the end of the couch. Then, famished after his leap in time, he made his way to the kitchen, poured a cup of coffee, and reheated the oatmeal. He enjoyed both, even though the coffee was anemic.

As he ate, he thumbed through the morning newspaper, taking a special interest in the ads. You could see Clara Bow in *Wine* for ten cents. "AN ULTRA-MODERN THRILL FOR THE FAMILY. SHE WAS PRETTY AND INNOCENT UNTIL HER PARENTS ERRED AND SHE WENT PLEASURE MAD."

On the next page, an ad read, "MAKE YOUR RIDE A FORD TUDOR SEDAN: COMPACT, ROOMY BODY." *Which was it?*

68

*Compact or roomy? Must depend on the customer's needs. You want compact, you get compact. You want roomy, you get roomy. Advertising. Some things never change.*

After reading the sports page (it looked like the Washington Senators would have a promising season with Walter Johnson on the mound), he found the bathroom and scrubbed his hands and face with a new bar of Ivory Soap. BE SURE THEY SAY NICE THINGS ABOUT YOU—ALWAYS.

He appraised himself in the bathroom mirror. He needed a shave. He found Zalo's safety razor (thank goodness, he wasn't using a straight razor), a brush, and a puck of soap in a ceramic bowl. It wasn't the closest shave, but it would do. Although using Zalo's shaving kit without permission pricked his notion of good form, he was sure he wouldn't mind.

When finished, he scanned the entire apartment. *Yep, everything's shipshape.*

His mind reeled back to Athena. The fact that he loved her without reservation was thrilling but also mystifying. *Why her? Why a woman from 1924?* He shook his head. *Why not her? I love who I love, and that's it.*

He pumped his fist and headed downstairs to her apartment. He was mid-flight when he pulled up with a jolt and leaned against the banister—his belly bilious, his thinking muddled. *My god, what if she doesn't love me? What then? Maybe she already has a lover. What am I thinking? With her beauty, she could have a dozen men in her life. Why didn't I think of that?*

*Nah, not Athena. Surely not. But it's possible. You're damn right, it's possible. Or what if... what if she thinks I'm too strange—a crazy lunatic from the future? Crazy lunatic is redundant. Yeah, maybe so, but no one could blame her for having the thought. Right?*

*Hey, maybe—*

*Knucklehead! Stop it. You're killing yourself. Be yourself. Let love happen—or not.* He heaved a prayerful sigh. *Just don't let it be "not."*

Tony stood at her door. On the first knock, soft enough to be courtly but loud enough to be heard, he detected the sound of shuffling feet. Fearful he may have called too early, he didn't knock a second time. Several minutes later, Athena came to the door, looking like she'd stepped out of a beauty salon. She wore a belted celadon green dress with a matching ribbon on one shoulder and a cascade of folds that draped from her hip pockets. *Cue moonlight and the string orchestra.*

"Good morning. Please come in."

With her gentle smile, his confidence quickened, which prompted a self-scolding. *You see, you nutjob? You've nothing to worry about.*

"Thank you. I wasn't going to step in until invited." He raised both hands in defense. "I didn't want to get poked in the kisser again."

"Stop that." Roughening her tone, she added, "But you better not step out of line." She mimed a one-two punch. "I might have to sock you from here to Yankee Stadium."

He loved her playfulness, at once flirty and spunky. "I'll be good," he promised. "I wanted to come with flowers, then realized the few dollars I have came from twenty-nineteen. How would I explain that?"

"That's a sweet thought, about the flowers I mean. Please, have a seat."

She directed him to the couch where they sat at opposite ends, both pitched at an angle to better see the other.

"How do you make a living in your time?" she asked.

"I'm a doctor."

Normally, women brightened when the conversation turned to his occupation, images of mansions and luxury sedans scrolling behind their eyes. But Athena's eyes didn't flare with greed—only curiosity.

"Orthopedics, though I'm afraid I'd be lost in today's medical world without penicillin or—"

"What's penicillin?"

"It's an antibiotic used to treat bacterial infections. But it didn't come into full use until World War Two."

The color dropped out of her face. "World War Two! What?"

He winced when he saw her expression. "I'm so sorry. It just slipped out. World War Two started in Europe in nineteen thirty-nine. We entered in nineteen forty-one."

"Who were we fighting?"

The burden of recounting war news knotted his gut. "There were two fronts. The Japanese in the Pacific and the Germans in Europe and North Africa."

She blanched. "In the Great War, I cheered when our boys boarded transport ships for England. So many died. I was ashamed for cheering their departure." Her eyes teared, her words quivered. "The Germans again. How's that possible?"

"It's complicated. An evil dictator came into power in Germany."

"Was it as bad as our war?"

"Worse."

She cringed. "How much worse?"

"The death count—"

"No, wait. I don't think I want to know."

"Maybe it's best you don't."

Athena seemed transfixed on the unknowable *Beyond*. When she did speak, it was with a note of quiet introspection. "It's so meaningless. Why are we intent on killing each other? It makes no sense."

"That's why I chose medicine…and music. I want to be an instrument for healing."

With that, her eyes came into focus. She looked at Tony endearingly, the way loving parents watch their children when they're asleep. "Music?"

"I play trumpet and some piano, though well short of your artistry."

She beamed, stood, and clutched Tony's hand. "Come over here."

Her hand was a velvet glove. It was thrilling the way she took his hand so freely, so naturally. His heart picked up a beat.

She led him to the piano and skimmed the lid's edge, her fingers leading to a muted trumpet. "Is this yours?"

It took a moment for his eyes to see and his brain compute. "Oh, my goodness. It came with me. I remember now. I played my horn, placed it right there on the lid, and sat to play your piano. It traveled with me." He picked up the horn and tested the valves. "It seems to have made the journey all right."

She quieted his fingers with her hand, a touch that jittered his heart.

"Well, don't just tinker. Play."

He removed the cup mute, raised the trumpet to his lips, blew warm air into the horn, then snapped the instrument under his arm. "Aw, maybe some other time."

On cue, she howled. "Oh, no you don't, Tony Marco. You play or I'll *really* sock you this time."

He winked. The tease was a theatrical bit—viable only because he had the chops. He brought the horn to his lips and played a silvery concert F cadenza that led into the opening strains of "It Had to Be You." He closed his eyes and could hear Athena's piano roll rendition playing in his ear, and so he accompanied her. Midway through the first chorus, he opened his eyes and saw Athena playing live at the piano. He sat beside her with his back to the keyboard, their music in a slow dance of swoons.

When the last note had drifted into memories, they were both silent. Tony leaned back against the piano to see Athena's face, her eyes awakened and credulous.

She half turned on the piano bench. "It was you. It was you in my dreams. I would know your sound anywhere, from any time."

They shared a look as intimate as a kiss.

He held her gaze until, betrayed by Sophia's curse, he regarded his horn and fingered the trumpet valves. He'd given himself entirely to Sophia. Now Athena required the same devotion.

Whispering her hands across his cheeks, she turned his face toward her and closed her eyes.

Like a dolt, he petrified. If he didn't kiss her, would he be sucked back into the future, a broken, loveless man? He yearned to caress her beckoning lips. But he was seized by the friction between his heart—a chalice convexed beyond the brim—and his neurotic, jumbled mind.

"Come here," Athena said.

She was so close he could taste the sweet moisture of her breath.

She held his face, captured his lips, withdrew, and kissed him again.

His chest heaving, he fell back and hunched over his knees, his hands barely able to grip his trumpet, and stared at the floor planks.

A gale of questions blew through him. *Am I ready? Is this happening too fast? Will I break her heart?*

*Will I kill again?*

# 17

When Tony uncoiled and searched Athena's eyes, he witnessed a cascade of emotions. Dismay, disappointment, remorse, and, worst of all, shame. Her gaze tortured him. "I'm sorry."

"What is it?"

Explosions pounded his sternum. He ached to rip the torment from his brain. *How to explain?*

A new assault whiplashed his mind—irrational, superstitious but unrelenting. *What if I say nothing? What if I shut her out? Will it send me spinning back to the future and Athena to her grave?* The thought was crushing.

"I..."

She took his hand. "Say it."

When he slipped his hand out from under hers, he saw the sorrow in her eyes. "Don't touch me. You may never want to touch me again." He dragged his hands down his face. "I have to tell you something." He searched his mind, an imbroglio of guilt and loneliness, and seized his darkest secret. "I'm a killer."

Athena lunged to her feet and retreated toward the front door. She slapped her chest as if to jump-start her heart. "What're you saying?"

Hardly present and seemingly immune to her reaction, he sat transfixed on the piano bench. "She's a woman like you. Beautiful, intelligent, brimming with life."

Her question sounded distant and grievous. "You're married?"

"No."

"Engaged?"

"No."

The sound of morning traffic shrouded the terrible space that separated them.

"What's her name?"

He raked back his hair. "Sophia. She was an army lieutenant. We were both stationed in Mosul, Iraq. I was a surgeon at a field hospital. She protected the grounds." He swallowed hard against a thickening throat. "I love her with every beat of my heart. Always will."

Pressing her lips together, Athena looked aside and mumbled a word.

He lifted his left hand. "This is her ring."

After sighting the gold band, she set a straight-back chair across the room and sat. "Go on."

He placed his trumpet on the floor. Unable to frame a coherent sentence without breaking down, he spoke in fragments. "Mid-July. Hot as hell. I worked through most of the night. Dead tired. She arrived on a stretcher. Unconscious. Blood everywhere. A shot to the chest. Her heart sputtered." His jaw trembled without mercy. "I had to open her chest."

In sympathy, Athena covered her sternum with both hands.

He made a sad moaning sound as tears welled his eyes. "I massaged her heart. Found a catastrophic wound to the blood vessels that fed her lungs."

She stood and approached him with slow, measured steps.

As he swiped at tears, his speech pleaded. "I couldn't save her." Suspended in taut silence, he kneaded his temples. "She died on the operating table. Before my eyes. Her heart in my hands. Too slow. Too incompetent." He dropped his head over his racking chest. "I killed her."

Athena rushed to the piano bench, sat, and cupped Tony's face. "You did all you could."

"You don't understand."

"I do. I—"

"*You don't.*" He collapsed into himself. "She was my kid sister."

Athena gasped.

"She idolized me. Followed me into the army… I failed her." He raised his head and looked into her silken eyes. "What if"—he took a hard gulp of air—"I fail you? I can't live with that…not again."

Athena took his arm and shepherded it around her waist. She pressed her body against his and kissed his face. "Wherever you are is where I want to be."

She pierced his heart. Of all the words left to say, only hers purged his guilt. He awakened.

At that instant, the nexus of his life, the neural pathways in his brain disconnected, reshuffled, and realigned themselves to a new reality. A vibrant, beautiful woman gave herself to him. Freely. His heart thumped in his ears, and his blood churned as if coming to a boil.

In a storm of understanding, passion, and release, he drew Athena into his body and crushed her mouth to his with such desperation his head staggered. He could feel her pitching in his arms, her entire body quaking. When her tongue boldly trespassed his lips, his gut curled with desire.

"Touch me," she said. "Touch me all over."

Ravenous for each other, they were aflame, their hearts pounding, their lips searching, their hands roaming as if they had the perfect right.

*** 

Athena took flight. Plundering her most secreted cravings, she never felt so naked, yet so unashamed.

Her nerve endings sizzled like fuses burning to the core—ready to explode.

How strange. She hadn't planned to fall in love. Her music lent sufficient passion, or so she said. But the undertow overwhelmed— tumbling heart, mind, body, and soul—controlling, releasing, controlling in pounding waves of dominance and submission.

They shared equal rights—hunter and huntress, master and servant—both having their own way with their lover.

Each time she arched and reared and shuddered, it was like a little death as if she would never take another breath. When his lips raced down her body in a furious flame, she was revived—only to be shattered again in the next wave.

She burned for it all. To be enfolded *by* him and emboldened *for* him.

And the covenant was divine.

# 18

Zalo loved the feel of the Harlem boxing gym: the heat, the coppery stench of blood and sweat, the rhythmic swish of jumping rope, and the snap of whirling strikes into a speed bag. But the greatest draw was the neighborhood hero, Samuel Battle, the first black police officer in New York City. He was the real reason Zalo trained.

At six feet three and two hundred and eighty pounds, Battle was a bruiser—assuring for good folks and intimidating for thugs. His good looks and gentle way of speaking endeared him to the entire community.

Zalo and Samuel sparred in the ring. Even though Battle was forty-one years old, he could still outmaneuver the younger, high-spirited boxer.

"Good solid punch," Battle said after Zalo launched a hard straight right. He beckoned him on with both gloves.

Zalo threw two quick jabs and a right cross, which Samuel easily sidestepped.

The policeman stepped back and dug his mitts into his hips. "I know you have a strong punch—you've proven that—but your opponent ain't likely to stand still and wait for it. You have to be able to move. Strike misery and slip trouble."

"Yeah, I know my footwork stinks."

Battle looked over his shoulder and shouted at the club manager. "Hey, Mac, is whining allowed here?"

"Hell no."

"I didn't think so."

Zalo rolled his eyes. "Okay, I get it. Just tell me what you want."

Battle led the young fighter through a series of footwork and punching exercises, advancing and circling the ring. Left-step jab, right-step cross. By the end of their workout, they were both drenched in sweat.

The two men sat on a bench and unlaced their gloves.

Battle toweled his head. "You know, Zalo, I like training with you. You're a good man."

Zalo smiled with indulgence, then, not wanting to appear cocky, slackened his grin. "Thank you, Samuel. That means a lot coming from you."

Battle placed a big hand on Zalo's shoulder. "I only speak the truth."

"I know that. I mean, I know you're a truthful man. And I *do* want to be a good man myself."

The policeman threw one leg over the bench. "I'd like to propose something to you." He let his words sink in. "Are you listening?"

The question startled Zalo. He always listened to Battle, so the question seemed unnecessary and, consequently, ominous. He scanned the policeman's eyes. "Yes, sir."

"Good. I want you to think about becoming a police officer."

Zalo wiped his eyes with the back of his hand—partly to clear the sweat, partly to erase the idea. "Oh, I don't know about that. No offense, but I don't have much respect for bulls."

"Do you respect me?"

"You know I do."

"Why?"

That question was easy. "Because you're on the level. I know I can trust you."

"Yeah? Why's that?"

Zalo thumb-massaged his palm. "I've seen you in the neighborhood. Nobody's afraid of you because you're never on the take." He looked away. "You don't club down folks for getting in the way of police corruption. You do the right thing."

Battle straightened his back. "It ain't been easy."

"What do you mean?"

"Like it or not, we live in a white man's world."

The young man sneered. "Imagine that."

The policeman whorled the towel, laid it across his neck, and tugged on the ends. "But if you set your mind on something—I mean all out—there's no telling what you can do."

Zalo dug deeper into his palm. "I'm not so sure about that."

Battle curled over his knees, maybe to stretch out his lower back, maybe to give himself time to think. When he uncoiled, he asked, "Would it be all right if I told you a bit about my life?"

"Are you kidding? Of course."

"Good." His eyes became distant. "My ma and pa were slaves in North Carolina. They were treated like dogs. And I swore that would never happen to me. So, I came north. I got me a job as a redcap porter at the Grand Central depot. I didn't make hardly nothing. But I wasn't no damn slave."

Emotion stirred in Zalo's belly, impressed Battle escaped the tyranny of the South, and proud he entrusted him with his story.

"I'm telling you this because it might help you make a decision." He stood, planted one foot on the bench, and leaned over his knee. "You see, I got it in my head to be a cop. I passed the civil service exam, but the police doc said I had a bad heart. That was a lie. They just didn't want a colored man in the department."

"What'd you do?"

Battle lifted a hand and let it fall. "I bucked the system. I found me a high-stepping white doctor to examine me. He wrote a letter giving me a clean bill of health. That letter went all the way to the mayor's office. Eventually, with backing from the colored press, I was in."

"Damn right," Zalo said, punching his fist into his palm. "You *made* it work. Good for you, Samuel."

Battle raised a hand and straddled the bench again. "I'm not done. For the first two years in the department, nobody talked to me—I mean nobody, no time. I wasn't allowed to eat in the cafeteria. I wasn't allowed to sleep in the dormitory with the other cops. No, sir, they moved my bed to the loft. I felt like the master's dog."

The young man could feel his belly knot. *Why did it have to be like that? Didn't anyone stand up for him? Or was it always a black man against the world?* "What about people outside the department? How'd they treat you?"

Battle huffed a single laugh. "I was a carnival sideshow." He expanded his massive chest and held it big. "They used to have tour buses come by to point out where the nigger cop worked."

"That ain't right."

The officer grabbed Zalo by both shoulders and gave him a single shake. "That's my point. Sometimes you have to do the right thing, even when it's hard. It took years, one street beat after the other, but I finally earned their respect." He tapped Zalo's cheek, a friendly touch confirmed by a wink.

"How?"

On a long sigh, Battle said, "I showed them I was a better cop than any white man on the force."

Zalo weighed the quality and heft of his grit. Could he be tough enough and good enough to make Battle proud...to make himself proud?

A new awareness took hold of him. *What if I do nothing? What if I coast, accepting whatever comes along, sometimes good but mostly ugly? What if I piss my life away? What then?*

The two fell silent.

Battle unlaced his shoes, bowed them into a knot, and tossed them over his shoulder. "Think about it. The department could use a good man like you. So could our people."

"I'll think hard about it," Zalo said—a promise he made to Battle *and* himself.

# 19

For the next three days, Tony sequestered in Athena's apartment. It was curious how immediately they felt as one—devoted and at ease with each other as if fated. Time, space, and the color of their skins existed but only in the background, like the nearly silent, soon forgotten rush of air.

"I'm not sure what to expect," Athena said.

"Are you afraid?" Tony asked.

She slanted a teal beret over one eye, brushed her hair over both ears. "Yes…no. Not afraid really. I've always been able to take care of myself." She turned to him. "Honestly, I want you to be okay."

"What do you mean?"

"I want you to be at home with me."

His body drooped. "I'll always be at home with you." He opened his left hand, swiped its palm, and looked into her golden eyes. "You are a part of me now, as real and trustworthy as my own hands. Nothing can change that—not in my time, not in yours."

Athena's eyes brightened. "Is it really like that?"

He opened his arms. "Come here."

She stepped into his embrace.

Holding her fast, as if surrendering her would let her drown, he kissed her mouth and cheek and the curve of her neck.

"Oh, you're a bad man. You're making me hot all over again." She kissed him softly, warmly on the mouth.

He stepped back and held her shoulders at arm's length. "Hold on. Remember we promised we'd get some sunshine today."

"But I like it here with you."

"So do I, but we promised."

She let a breath stutter out. Looking pouty and cuter than any woman should be allowed, she said, "All right. I just hope our world won't shock you."

"Something more shocking than a century leap in time?" He cockled his face. "Come on, we can do this. It can't be tougher than gangster rap."

"What's that?"

"All right, demonstration time." He closed the two middle fingers on both hands, swayed from one foot to the other, cleared his throat, and half-sung, half-spoke in a strange rhythm. "Pooka-chaka-la chaka-la, pooka-chaka-la chaka-la. Don't be talkin' trash. You're givin' me a rash. I never dig your hash. Just gimme all my cash...bitch." Performance completed, he curled his upper lip, crossed his arms, glared sideways at Athena, and froze for his close-up.

She slapped him across the arm. "You stop that right now."

He hugged himself as if wounded. "All things change with time. You know that, and music is always first in line." He gave her a peck on the cheek. "Now, let's see your world."

When they descended and opened the door to the outside world, they were greeted by a blast of sunshine. The neighborhood on West 133rd—what was affectionately called "Swing Street" in 1924 for all the jazz clubs and speakeasies—was alive with black Model Ts, friends in conversation, and vendors who sold apples, bananas, grapefruit, and roasted yams.

To Tony's delight, the men—evenly black and white—paraded in elegant dark suits, white shirts, vividly striped and madras ties, and flashy fedoras and bowlers. In contrast, Tony stood out like a horsefly on vanilla ice cream with his tan suit and psychedelic running shoes. In fact, his strange outfit incited the first insult.

A black schoolboy in a V-neck sweater, knickers, and high-top sneakers turned to what looked to be his older brother and said, "Hey, Booker, it looks like the circus came to town."

The older boy snickered but jerked his brother by his arm to stay clear of the peculiar white man.

"Sorry about that." Athena said.

Tony waggled his head. "He's right. I do look funny. But, trust me, I'd go unnoticed in twenty-nineteen."

She teased him with a wicked smile. "Are you sure about that?"

"Oh yeah." They rounded a game of hopscotch played by two giggling black girls in pigtails. "When it comes to fashion, anything goes in my time. Some girls have even taken to wearing bare-butt jeans."

Athena flinched. "What?"

"Their pants are ripped and frayed to expose their bare bottoms."

She stared at him with dubious eyes.

Raising his hands in a gesture of innocence, he said, "I'm sorry. It's been done."

She shook her head. "And I thought the twenties were risqué."

"You ain't seen nothing yet, kiddo."

As the couple strolled arm in arm, every man and woman—regardless of color—ogled the couple. Tony unhooked his arm from Athena, thinking it would be less embarrassing for her. She caught his eye, shook her head, and reclaimed his arm.

"You have to expect this," she said. "They're not mean, just ignorant. If they knew you as I know you, they'd love you."

He caressed her hand. "I just don't want you to be hurt. I am white, you know."

Athena pulled up and flinched. "Oh my goodness, you're right." She giggled. "And I just thought you needed more sun."

Their bantering ended when a young, light-skinned black man approached. "Athena, is that you?" he asked, shucking his black fedora and revealing a high sloping forehead.

Athena stopped and greeted the man with a warm embrace. "My goodness, how are you? I've missed you at the club."

"It's not for lack of trying. I've been so busy writing these days."

She turned to Tony. "Forgive my manners. Tony, I want you to meet my dear friend Langston. We've known each other since he was this high," she said, measuring three feet off the ground.

"Which was about the time I fell in love with Athena," Langston said, shaking Tony's hand.

"What are you working on these days?" Athena asked.

"Mostly poetry," he said in a soft, melodic voice.

"Anything I should know about?"

"Only everything." He laughed and surveyed the city skyline. "But a while back, I wrote a piece for the NAACP I like." He turned to Tony. "The National—"

"Association for the Advancement of Colored People," Tony finished.

On a step back, Langston gawked. "I'm surprised you know the name."

"Of course. I'm a New Yorker, which makes me the son of an international community. Listen, I adopted all the street kids as my family."

"Regardless of color?" Langston asked.

"*Every* kid. I played stickball or street hockey in the alleys with boys who cursed in foreign languages. Many had the exotic aroma of garlic or cabbage or curry infused into their T-shirts."

Langston chuckled. "I know that scent."

"My best friend was Ezra Cohen, an orthodox Jew who always wore a black kippah and never played ball on Saturday. I never considered the color or religion of the boys on the block. They were just a good hitter or fast runner or funny storyteller—and now, a great poet."

Silence overtook them as Langston peered at Tony and boggled his head.

"So what's the poem?" Athena asked.

Langston offered the slightest bow. "Kind of you to ask. It's called 'The Negro Speaks of Rivers.'" His speech became deeper and more resonant.

"My soul has grown deep like the rivers.

I bathed in the Euphrates when dawns were young.

I built my hut near the Congo, and it lulled me to sleep.

I looked upon the Nile and raised the pyramids above it—"

Tony finished the poem. "'I've known rivers: Ancient, dusky rivers. My soul has grown deep like the rivers.'"

The poet looked as though he'd found a gem in the sand. "Okay, who is this fella?"

Tony extended his hand a second time. "I'm Tony Marco. And I love your poetry."

Langston pumped his hand. "I don't know where you found this man, but you need to down him like a jaguar."

"Ooh, I love that image," she said with bright eyes.

He chuckled. "Well, a poet must always have a decent phrase in his pocket."

As they said their goodbyes, Tony faced Langston. "Never doubt the power of your words. You will make a difference. You're a powerful model for all people, black and white."

With puzzled eyes, Langston said, "You seem to know a lot about me."

"Who doesn't know about Langston Hughes?"

*** 

As the couple continued their walk, Athena said, "I love you so much," which stopped Tony like a stand-up slide into third base.

He turned and took her hands. "I knew you loved me. At least, I hoped you did. But this is the first time you've said the words. Is it true?"

When she spoke, he shifted his gaze from her eyes to her lips, wanting to engrave every word she said into his memory.

"You silly man. Of course, it's true. Does that seem so impossible?"

He led her to a bare brick wall, allowing the foot traffic to pass. "Well, yes...no. But what are the chances? Traveling so far to find someone with your beauty and wit?"

She circled her index finger in the air. "And?"

He jerked his head. "And what?"

With a knitted brow, she folded her arms and pointed a shoulder at him. "Really? Are you waiting for a telegram?"

"Huh?" His mind finally unscrambled her meaning. "Yes, of course, I love you." Again, with more meaning, "I love you, Athena Cruz. More than the Euphrates, more than the Congo, more than the Nile."

She looked askance at him. "So, you not only steal a girl's heart but her friend's poetry as well."

He shrugged. "What can I say? I'm an equal-opportunity thief."

Athena shook her head, turned him toward home, and swatted the seat of his pants on a giggle. "Too bad you're not wearing bare-butt jeans."

# 20

The following day, Tony could see Athena was brewing mischief. She had that telling look in her eyes, a secret tinged with self-satisfaction and delight. In a word, trouble.

"You and I are going to make music together," she said.

Tony raised one eyebrow—a flirty, on-the-prowl expression.

She wagged her finger at him. "Not *that* kind of music. We're going to shake the world at The Nest tonight. I want you there at eleven o'clock."

"Isn't that when you close your show?"

She grinned impishly. "Yes, but tonight, everything'll start cooking at eleven. So be there. And bring your horn." She teased his lips with a gentle kiss. "At eleven," she repeated with greater emphasis. "And don't be late."

"Where're you going?"

"I have to run a little errand," she said with a hint of wouldn't-you-like-to-know sass.

As soon as she left, the apartment fell silent.

From the couch, he studied the water-stained fleur-de-lis wallpaper above a painted paneled wainscot. Although worn by time, it struck Tony as a vestige of pride and nobility—still present, even in hard times.

Outside of wallpaper, there was nothing to distract him—not a computer nor a cell phone nor even a radio—so he escaped into his thoughts, which iced his bones out of nowhere. A queasy foreboding. Whether by superstition or an omen from Sophia's ghost, he worried Athena was in danger. He had seen how people gaped at them on the street. Could she become the target of a hate crime?

"Uh-uh," he murmured. *I'm thinking crazy again. I'm a scientist. I refuse to be gutted by fear.*

Still, despite his upbraiding, he could not shake off the dread.

He left the apartment, scuttled down the stairs, and into the sunlight. With no purpose in mind, he turned west, which took him to Saint Nicholas Park. Once in the park, he followed a winding northerly path into the woods. Soon, his body pulsated with malaise as though a massive meteorite had dropped from the sky and rippled the atmosphere. He spun around but only glimpsed a tall outcrop of jagged boulders edged with layers of pale-green lichen. He continued walking, but after a few steps, the pulsating waves jiggered the nape of his neck. He tramped to a stop and tried to wipe the feeling off with the palm of his hand as if it were so much sweat to be blotted.

The premonition lingered.

He turned to face the threat. As he backtracked, his temperature rose. He spotted shoulders surpassing both sides of an American elm. The tree, as thick as a cathedral column, did little to conceal the wide body pressed against its trunk.

Rounding the tree from a distance, he faced a massive black man, a prize for any professional football team. He sported a navy suit. *Tailored by a sailmaker?*

"Who are you and what do you want?" Tony asked.

The behemoth retreated a half step from the elm and passed his mitt over the tree's jigsaw-puzzle surface. "I doesn't mean you no harm, mister," he said in a deep lumbering cadence, the phrase sounding like coal tumbling down a steel chute.

"Then why are you following me?"

"I'm Buddy Jefferson. I seen you with Miss Athena the other day." He dipped his head in either respect for Athena's name or shame for spying. "You a good man?"

The mention of Athena gave Tony pause. Was he facing the object of the dread that had chilled him earlier? He ignored the man's question. "How do you know her?"

He spoke more to the tree than to Tony. "I workin' at Th-The Nest," he sputtered. "It be my job to take care of Miss Athena. She's awfully pretty, and some men is downright mean. That's why I wanna know if you a good man."

As his lips morphed from a knife slit to a gracious grin, he offered his hand. "My name is Tony Marco. I'm happy to meet you."

Buddy looked up for the first time and swallowed Tony's hand in his bear-paw grip.

"Can you keep a secret, Buddy?"

He tugged on his lapels. "Yes'um, sir."

"I believe you," he said honestly. "Here it is. Athena and I love each other." He searched the big man's eyes for a tell. Not to disappoint, Buddy responded with a broad pumpkin smile—a grin so effervescent Tony couldn't help but chuckle. "I think you love her too. Am I right?"

His skin emitted a warm tint of maroon. "Yes'um, I do," then added, "but not like you."

"I think we understand each other. Please do keep an eye on her." He patted the man's Herculean shoulder and added, "Buddy, this looks like the beginning of a beautiful friendship." Living in the past had its benefits. He could steal a *Casablanca* quotation and not be accused of plagiarism.

The two men ambled side by side through Saint Nicholas Park.

Without making eye contact, Buddy said, "You be a different kind of man."

"Oh?"

"I don't mean no disrespect."

"None taken."

Buddy searched the inside of his mouth with his tongue before speaking. "I feel like a field mouse being cozy with an alley cat."

Tony directed Buddy to a bench. When they sat, Tony extended his legs, crossing them at the ankles. In contrast, Buddy sat on the edge of the bench, back straight as if ready to lunge forward at full speed.

"And I'm the cat?" Tony asked.

"That's just it. You ain't no alley cat. You talk to me like I be visible."

Tony pulled off the bench backrest and turned toward Buddy. "Meaning?"

The big man's face soured. "Oh, I feel visible all right when something heavy need lifting and hauled away, but after that I'm nobody again."

A tightness rose in Tony's throat. "I see."

After dragging his big hand down his face, Buddy spoke slowly. "White folks don't know"—his lower lip trembled—"I have a heart made for loving and a soul fit for singing. Is that so strange like?"

"Did you always feel that way?"

"See, that's what I mean. No white man ever asked me how I feel."

"They should. Your story is important."

"But why do you care?"

Tony picked up a pebble and tossed it sidearm across the path. "Every storyteller needs an audience, every audience a storyteller. It's how we all connect. You understand me?"

"I think so."

"Then tell me. Have you always felt invisible?"

Canted over his knees, Buddy spoke to the ground. "Not always. My mama could see me real good." Affecting an airy tone, he straightened his back, placed his hands on the bench lip, and surely mimicked his mother. "'Buddy, every man, black or white, shits between two shoes.'" From under his eyebrows, he glanced at Tony. "I know that ain't polite talk."

"Doesn't have to be when it's true," he said over a laugh.

"She was my teacher—no schoolhouse for me. Just Mama and the Louisiana cotton fields."

"Tell me more about your parents."

Lowering his head as if in mourning, he said, "My mama died from influenza…and they hung Papa from a live oak tree for looking sideways at a white woman."

Tony laid a warm hand on the big man's back. "I'm so sorry."

"Nobody come to Mama's funeral," he said, bitterness stinging his words. "No reason to. She hired help, lent out for fifty cents a day."

"And your papa?"

A teardrop pearled and fell between Buddy's legs. "He hung from that moss-covered cross for three days until I couldn't take it no more. I creeps into the moonless night, steals a ladder, and cuts him down."

They were silent. Tony levered off the bench, crossed the path, and pushed his weight against an immovable tree. Sympathetic and heartsick, he turned to face Buddy again. Without returning to the bench, he asked, "Is that when you left Louisiana?"

He nodded. "At the next blossom time. I hoboed from New Orleans to Harlem—picking cotton, stacking hay, and shucking corn on my way north."

"Are things better here?"

"Some. Talk of lynching tapered off—leastwise the hanging type. Still, my soul dies a little every time whitey be slamming and bolting the door when I pass."

"Let's walk some more."

Buddy shoved off the bench and trudged alongside his new friend. "I knows who you remind me of."

"I'm listening."

"You like a good construction boss, checking off a punch list of work needing to be done. Thing is your checklist is all about understanding."

"What does that feel like?"

The big man expanded his chest as if indulging a swelling heart. "It feels like"—he conjured a smile under evasive eyes—"like you ain't talking to no damn fence post. It feels like...I'm a man."

**21**

At Zalo's apartment, Tony stood before the bathroom sink, scraping the lather from his face and neck.

"Athena has something special planned for tonight," Tony said.

Zalo leaned against the doorframe, his arms folded, his legs crossed. "Is that why you're preening yourself like a flaming peacock?"

Tony lifted his chin to shave the obstinate patch of stubble above his Adam's apple. "This is all new territory for me. Love does strange things. It's like I want to be the best version of myself, whoever that is."

"Don't you have that figured out by now?"

Rinsing and toweling his face, he asked, "What part?"

"Blazes," Zalo said, with heavy surliness. "Are all the people from your age ninnies, or is it just you? What do you think I'm talking about? The best version of yourself."

Escaping his reverie, he faced Zalo. "I always thought so, but for some reason, I feel like I'm walking a tightrope." He rinsed out the sink. "Any false move and I'm a goner."

"You've got my sister all wrong. You're not on trial here. Not with *her* anyway," he added with a cocky smile. "She's not waiting for you to make a false move. She's crazy about you, even with those dopey shoes."

Tony stared at his running shoes. "They are a bit over-the-top"—he wiggled his toes—"but these kicks are hot stuff in twenty-nineteen."

Shaking off a shiver, Zalo said, "Not so hot in our world. What's your size?"

"Twelve."

Zalo escaped into the bedroom and returned with a rag, a can of polish, and a visibly worn pair of black shoes. "These are twelves. They're a bit run down, but with a little polish and elbow grease…"

"Hey, no apologies, please." On a broad grin, Tony snared the hand-me-downs. He immediately started polishing the cap-toe shoes, adding a little spit to raise the shine. As he worked, he asked, "How's work going, Z?"

He made a face. "Could be better. Welcome to the world of a construction laborer. All brawn. I'm not allowed to have a brain."

"That's got to be frustrating."

"I'm thinking about a new career."

"Oh?"

Zalo told him about Samuel Battle, including his plug to join the police force.

"You'd make a good officer."

He shoved a hand into his pocket and jangled some change. "Maybe. For damn sure, I'd like a fatter paycheck. Have to, if a family's in the cards."

Tony put his hands on his hips and gave him a do-tell look. "A family? You must be holding out on me. You have a girl?"

With a shade of resignation, Zalo said, "Afraid not."

"Why's that?"

"I guess because I can't find a girl as good as Thena. Someone a little tough"—he flattened his hands to render a balanced scale— "and a little kind."

"Brave and tender."

"With a good right cross." He thumbed the contour of his jawline. "She may be out there. But I haven't found her yet."

Tony threw a slow-motion jab to Zalo's shoulder. "I'll tell you what. I'll be on the lookout."

"Appreciate that," he said without conviction.

*** 

At ten forty-five, Tony left Zalo's apartment for the short walk to The Nest, his trumpet tucked under his arm. At the entrance, Buddy Jefferson greeted him with a tug on his skimmer. "We waiting for you."

"Good to see you, Buddy," he said as he shook the bouncer's hand and pounded his cannon-chase shoulder. When Tony stepped through the basement door, Athena's slow, heartbreaking piano blues constricted his throat. A mixed crowd of black and white faces jammed the place while waitresses in short skirts and high heels worked the tables.

He spied a small table with two black bentwood chairs near the stage. He weaved his way to the table, snatched a chair, and set it on the wall-side of the table to have a straight view of Athena at the upright. When they made eye contact, her gaze was rife with carnal implications. *You naughty girl,* he mouthed.

"May I join you?" someone asked over Tony's shoulder.

Tony turned to a dark-skinned woman who posed with hands on her hips, her eyebrows sculpted, her hair layered and stacked on her crown with only a hint of a frizzy halo. Her eyelids hung heavy and low, a sleepy look that Tony's mother used to call "bedroom eyes." She looked strong and solid as if she'd been no stranger to hard work. He figured she could take a swift medicine ball to the gut without a flinch.

He half-stood and turned the second chair in her direction. "Of course."

"You must be Tony Marco," the woman said with a good deal of smoke in her voice. She settled in and sat upright, giving her a quality of authority.

His curiosity was piqued. "Yes, I am. Have we met?"

"Not yet, but I've heard talk. How could I not know you?"

The woman had his attention. Her style was confident and saucy—the kind of woman who had nothing to hide, even if some of it was scandalous.

"I'm sorry."

"I saw the way you and Athena looked at each other. You might as well mail out wedding invitations."

Tony laughed heartily, blaring louder than he expected. "Is it that obvious?"

"I'm afraid so, darling."

He glanced at Athena, who gave him a knowing smile, although what she knew was a complete mystery.

"May I ask your name?" he asked.

"I'm Joanna Mangum. But everyone calls me Johnny."

"Johnny," he said, sounding her name with approval. "I like that. I've always thought a man's name on a woman lends her a kind of strength and intelligence."

Johnny elbowed the table and rested her chin on the back of her hand. The pose limelighted the import of her words. "You mean to say a woman can't be strong and intelligent by her own means? It requires a man's name to make it work?"

He raised both hands in submission. "Whoa. You've got me. Let me dig myself out of this hole. What I meant is powerful human beings—men *or* women—have a good balance of feminine and masculine traits."

Her stare stayed fixed on him. "Keep digging," she said, her mouth cocked to one side.

Though jelly-kneed, he answered the bell. "They can be aggressive and diplomatic, demanding and merciful." Then, remembering Zalo's description of Athena, he added, "Tough and kind." He pulled up, sapped of dichotomies. "How'd I do?"

She tipped her chin and let out a free-spirited laugh. "I like you, Tony Marco. I can see how Athena fell in love with you."

He must have passed the test because Johnny's entire demeanor shifted. She skated from mysterious and forbidding to friendly and playful.

"You know her then."

"Since high school days. I always wanted to be like her."

"It's not easy for a woman to admit that kind of thing."

"I give praise where praise is due," she said as she pitched Athena a wink.

"You have me curious about something. Are you married?"

Some of the light drained from her eyes. "Not yet. It's hard for a woman like me to find a good man. Most men want a slave. My slaving days are done."

"You know something about slavery?"

Johnny fired him a scorched look. "Well, I was born after the Emancipation Proclamation, if that's what you mean."

*Uh-oh, here we go again.* "You know it wasn't."

Although Johnny's regard was gracious, her meaning was serious. "The point is slavery didn't end after the Civil War. My people are still picking cotton in Mississippi. They're being paid, but the pay is slave wages."

Their conversation ended with Athena taking center stage.

## 22

Tony was struck by Athena's stage presence. She blazed so brightly the audience immediately hushed when she rose and took a step downstage.

Holding the microphone close to her mouth, she created a warm sense of intimacy. "Ladies and gentlemen, welcome to The Nest. This is a night you will not soon forget. I know I won't. You're about to hear the music of world-class musicians. Get set to be enchanted. First on the list is a new trumpet player with a sound as sweet as maple syrup…laced with a splash of Kentucky bourbon." That line brought a laugh. Tony smiled as Athena worked a crowd more interested in having a night of freedom over the recriminations of the evangelist Billy Sunday. "Please welcome Tony Marco."

The applause pealed, but when the mixed audience saw a tall white man take the stand and blow a kiss to Athena, the clapping quickly faded to a funeral drumbeat. They had crossed the line.

Tony was smart enough to see the warning signs. Although he knew color barriers were challenged in Harlem's Roaring Twenties, the sight of mixed races on stage grated like slates ripped off a chicken coup during Sunday worship. He had kindled a flame of prejudices. Being the target of bigotry was new to him, and he didn't like the feeling. His first response was rebellious as he leaned in and kissed Athena on both cheeks. Even as the room huffed with displeasure, he knew his impulse was naïve and stupid, but there was no taking it back.

He turned to Athena. "Let me kick it off. 'Somebody Loves Me' in G."

Tony was familiar with the old recordings of the song. In 1924, Paul Whiteman and his all-white band introduced the George Gershwin song. An early photograph of the conductor flashed in Tony's head. With his porcelain cheeks, orbital midsection, slick-backed hair, and a mustache so refined it popped like a fresh tattoo, Whiteman looked more like a sumo wrestler in formal wear than a jazz orchestra leader. The chubby conductor played the Gershwin tune at a ragtime tempo with a heavy-handed banjo twanging out the rhythm. That was not Tony's style.

Without introduction, Tony brought his trumpet to his lips and played the melody at half-tempo. In the first four measures, he could make out the sour-grape faces in the darkened club. The audience expected a two-beat barnburner, and he gave them a dirge.

Tony was on fire. He could feel the music rise from his diaphragm and burn in his chest. He sang the blues from his mind to his horn—his trumpet anguishing with stolen time, languid vibrato, and half-valve slides.

When Athena entered at the eight-measure chorus, she swooned in the same mood. For the first seven measures, she played a descending A minor chord with A natural droning in the bass. Then, on the eighth measure, she chose an alternate chord. Paul Whiteman's version had played a soulless D7. Athena chose an Ab9+11 that sighed with layers of fullness and suspension into the final eight-measure verse.

On the second time through—when Athena broke into a slow swing tempo—Tony heard drums and bass kick in. At first, he imagined the side musicians sprang from his own closeted orchestra. No, the house-band bassist and drummer had sat in while he was internally composing.

The quartet swung with raw power.

When they came to the last note, the last sizzling cymbal tap, the last piano riff, the last trumpet wail, a suffocating hush fell on the room as though the patrons were quick-frozen.

One pair of hands clapped in quickening rhythm—hands belonging to Zalo Cruz. A second brave soul applauded, followed by a third. On a slow wave, the house scrabbled to their feet, having heard for the first time in their lives the sound of an inspired twenty-first-century jazz trumpeter.

Tony guided Athena downstage center where, hand-in-hand, they both took a bow.

A man shouted over the ovation. "You ain't got the right," he exploded, his anger brutal as if stomping on the face of an innocent man.

Shading his eyes, Tony detected a beefy white man in the middle of the room in a crumpled suit and an off-centered tie. A mousy woman with grizzly hair wrenched on his right sleeve with both hands. Shaking off the woman's grasp, the hothead faked a backhanded slap to her face, which sent her withering beyond his reach.

The man held a half-drained tankard of beer in his hand, a mug thick and heavy enough to floor a critical bystander. How many beers he had swilled that night was anyone's guess, but as he rounded his table to move toward the stage, he stutter-stepped to catch his balance. "You ain't got the right to be smooching or hand-holding with no nig—"

Something serpentine coiled in Tony's gut. He expanded his chest, ready to bludgeon the man in scornful terms. But before blasting the threat, he glimpsed a shadow pass along the length of the room. It was Johnny, moving with cat-grace and a feverish stare as taut as ratcheted wire. Tony stepped from the stage to intercede— as did Zalo from the back of the room.

They were both too late. Johnny squared off on the drunkard and snarled in a whisperous but chilling voice. "Sit down or be busted down," she said, her eyes so still they could have been fossilized.

The drunk was visibly rocked, but the hushed crowd was leaning into the scene, which seemed to spur his bravado. He chuffed as if purging the scent of old blood sausage or fresh Roquefort cheese. "*You* sit down, you piece of sh—"

To crush the obscenity, Johnny gripped him by the shoulders, kneed him in the crotch, and again in the face. The man fell to his knees like an overstuffed bag of dirty laundry.

She wedged her boot into his neck and toppled him to his side. "Buddy. Throw this muttonhead in the gutter."

The bouncer smiled when he hauled the drunk to his feet. "She ain't no woman to be trifling with," he said, more to himself than to the drunk.

The audience applauded as Buddy lugged the whimpering man to the street.

With gawp-smacked eyes and a mournful shake of her head, the mousy wife gazed at Tony. "I'm sorry," she murmured.

He patted the woman's hand and tendered his sympathy with a single word. "Hush."

Before returning to the stage, Tony stepped to Zalo, who stood with both hands stacked on his crown. "Some kind of woman, huh?"

Gawking at Johnny, Zalo shook his head and whimpered. "Mama."

Athena took command from the stage. "That was exciting. Folks, please give a round of applause to my dear friend Johnny Mangum, the toughest gal in Harlem."

In ironic contrast to her fierce, unladylike exhibition, Johnny curtsied and blew a kiss to the crowd.

"Now, I don't want you to even think about leaving," Athena said. "'Cause you ain't heard nothing yet."

## 23

The mean drunk was not the only person who had his eye on the duet. Athena spotted Cal Craven lurking at the entry of the club, his barrel chair balanced on two hind legs, his face flickering in the flame of a jazz cigarette—what he liked to call "tea"—the smoke wafting around his white-banded black fedora.

Athena recognized the madness, the fury. His eyes burning, his mouth turned down at the corners, he was a vat of nitroglycerin waiting to be jostled. But Athena didn't care to think about her boss now. This was Tony's night, and her surprise made her smile with anticipation.

*** 

Tony counted off a medium swing tempo for the next song, "Rock-a-Bye Your Baby with a Dixie Melody." At the end of the first chorus, Athena modulated a half-step higher. Playing with eyes closed to embrace the language of a new key, he heard the entrance of the now-familiar house drummer and bassist. But there was something else. The pianist comped in time but without Athena's grace.

A tenor saxophone and trumpet played fills at the end of every four measures. My god, the husky texture of that saxophone, the full-throated vibrato of the trumpet were as familiar as his own musical musings. They sounded from the archives of his cherished recordings, first heard as a boy with his bare feet on the couch, his arms enfolding his knees, spellbound by every passing note, every fresh and whimsical idea.

The crowd erupted. Tony opened his eyes. On his right was his favorite tenor saxophonist of all time, Coleman Hawkins. Wearing a narrow-brimmed porkpie hat, Hawkins blew a dreamy, breathy arpeggio of notes in the lower register that quieted all ills.

At the piano sat Fletcher Henderson, one of the most influential arrangers in jazz history, a bandleader who led the drive from Dixieland to swing. He was young, boyish really, with a wisp of hair so fine under his nose it took chutzpah to call it a mustache. On a celestial smile, he nodded with delight over each musician's creative riff.

On his left stood a short, roundish man with flashing wraparound teeth, a buzz haircut, and a white handkerchief draped like a victory pennant from his left hand. Only twenty-three years old, his sound was already legendary: his hand-triggered vibrato, his descending passing notes, his crystalline high C at the end of a verse. How he crazed an audience. Tony's musical hero, the man whose voice and trumpet heralded five decades of jazz from Dixie to swing to pop, the unforgettable Louis "Pops" Armstrong.

Tony reveled in the company of the greatest stars from the Cotton Club. This was Athena's surprise. She had enticed the trio of jazz legends to visit The Nest.

While Hawkins soloed, Tony searched the stage for Athena. Nowhere to be found. He scoured the room and spotted her to his left at the front table with Johnny at her side. He looked into her dazzling eyes, splashed iridescent from the stage lighting overspill. On a wave of emotion, he thumped his chest, a gesture brimmed with gratitude and wonderment.

His heart beating in tempo with the drummer's bass kick, he could not let this miraculous ruck in time slip away unfinished. At the end of Armstrong's solo, Tony stepped to the microphone and sang the first eight measures of the tune. Armstrong followed with an eight-measure mix of lyrics and scat. "Zot-dah-doo-be-bah." Standing side by side, arm in arm, they brought "Rock-a-Bye Your Baby" home in a raucous duet.

Armstrong had one final trick up his sleeve for the tag. On the first beat of the last measure, Louis pointed at the drummer, who played a four-measure cadenza followed—naturally, obviously—by one last ridiculous vocal: "Ooh yeah."

Always the performer and consummate lover of music, Louis doubled over and stamped both feet. He offered an open palm to Tony, who slapped and swiped it as if he'd won a million-dollar lottery, although no lottery could match the joy that quivered his insides.

"You know your onions," Armstrong said to Tony.

In one final expression of generosity, Louis dusted Tony's broad shoulders with his handkerchief as if he were the ascending king of jazz. He was not, of course—no one would ever dethrone Pops—but still, the gesture was something Tony was sure he'd never forget.

***

In the wee small hours of the morning, long after reasonable people had gone to bed, the five musicians formed a circle and swapped stories.

"How did Athena beguile you to take a night off from the Cotton Club?" Tony asked.

Fletcher leaned in. "Athena is beguiling, no question, but the Cotton Club was dark tonight. I think there were rumors about a raid."

"Not everyone is on the take," Coleman offered. "You never know when bulls might bust in with shotguns pumped, ready to blow holes in the ceiling."

"Whatever the reason, I was thrilled."

Flashing dazzling teeth, Pops patted Tony's shoulder. "I was thrilled too," he said in his gravelly voice. "I ain't never heard a player like you. You got chops. All of us dig what you do with your ax."

"That be true," Coleman said.

"Absolutely," Fletcher added. He glanced at Coleman and Armstrong, both of whom signaled agreement. "The band has a little extra scratch these days. How would you like to sit in with us at the Cotton Club?"

Joggling his head, Tony looked at Athena, who grinned coolly, knowingly. "Wait a minute. Would that even work? You're an all-black band, right? I think you saw what happened here tonight. I don't want to start a race riot."

"Listen here," Armstrong said. "I've got a story for you. My life ain't been easy. I grew up cabbage poor. Most times, I sang on the street for spare change. Sometimes Mama had to be with men to feed me and my sister." He stared vacantly for a long beat.

"But it wasn't all misery. There was a family called Karnofsky. They was Jewish. They treated me like I was family. They bought me my first cornet. Looky here." Armstrong loosened his tie, popped the top two buttons of his shirt, and drew out a chain with a Star of David pendant. "You see this? I wear this for the Karnofskys."

Armstrong dropped the pendant under his shirt. "Love ain't got no color. Any decent cat knows that. And music ain't got no color neither." He turned to Athena. "You're in love, ain't you?" he asked with a nod toward Tony.

Athena glowed. "Yes, Louie, we are," she said, sharing an intimate smile with her man.

"How can that be?" Louis asked.

"I don't know. It just is."

Armstrong patted his hands. "Yes'um. That's the way I thinks about music. *It just is.* It don't matter what color you is. If a cat can play"—he pointed a finger at Tony—"that's all that counts." He drummed the table. "Now, giving polite society a nudge can shake them up the first time around and maybe the second time, but sometimes the world needs to be shook up."

Tony pressed his hands into a prayer. "Louis, you're making me think about a song that was made for you. If you ever come across a tune called 'What a Wonderful World,' be sure to record it. It captures your spirit."

Louie crinkled his brow. "Can't say I know it."

"You will."

There was a moment of silence.

"What do you say, Tony?" Fletcher asked. "Are you in?"

Unable to stop from grinning, Tony opened his hands as if receiving a sacred blessing. "I'm definitely in."

The group called it a night. The five musicians patted and hugged each other and filed toward the exit.

Because Tony led the procession, he was the first to see Craven lying in wait for the Cotton Club musicians to pass. When Tony approached, he offered his hand, which Craven ignored. The club owner brushed by to corner Hawkins, Henderson, and Armstrong, pumping all three with two-handed handshakes.

Tony lagged to overhear the conversation.

"Thank you so much, gentlemen, for dropping by," Craven said, his tenor at once fawning and smug. His eyes rimmed red, and his breath hovered with the skunk scent of marijuana, something even Tony picked up from a distance. "Please come again—anytime. Drinks on me. Or if there's anything else you want, I'm sure I've got it or can get it quick enough, if you know what I mean."

The three musicians responded offhandedly.

"Uh-huh."

"Sure."

"Okay."

They formed an awkward tableau until Fletcher turned for the exit. When the five had stepped onto the street, and the door latch clicked home, Louis said, "That's one strange monkey suit."

Athena passed her hands over her hips as if to cleanse herself from the stench of Cal Craven. "You have no idea. And the depth of his meanness is too dark to know."

# 24

Craven plotted in the back office where he kept the good booze and a three-foot-high floor safe with a combination number drawn from his mother's birthday. The number pleased him, not that he had any reverence for his mother.

*Good cover. No one here thinks I have a mother. They think I was dumped in a garbage bin and raised by a pack of street dogs. But never breastfed by a mother who rocked me when I fussed. Never that. And that suits me fine. Let them think I'm wild. Beastly.*

There were only two things in the safe. Bundles of cash and his favorite Colt .32 with nickel plating and pearl grips. When anticipating danger, Craven packed the revolver in a horizontal shoulder holster under his left arm. This was one of those times.

A heavy thud shook the door, a sound that only Buddy could make with a hand as wide as a dinner plate.

"Yeah."

Nothing happened. The delay reminded Craven he'd ripped into Buddy the last time the bouncer opened the door before being acknowledged. "Come in, *please*," he said, his invitation varnished in sarcasm.

Cracking the door open, Buddy poked his head into the gap. "He's here."

"Send him in."

Buddy lowered his pitch, which, coming from the massive bouncer, sounded more like a distant foghorn than a whisper. "He do talk funny, Mr. Craven."

Craven turned up the volume. "Just send him the hell in."

"Yes'um."

\*\*\*

Buddy returned to the club entrance where the visitor waited at a table steeped in shadows. On his approach, the bouncer noticed a twist of shine as if emanating from under the closed door of a lighted room. As he drew closer, the glimmer reflected off a long hunting knife the man stropped on the palm of his hand. The blade mystified Buddy, its double-crescent guard arching downward.

"Mr. Craven's ready."

Without humor or courtesy, the man opened his coat and slipped the blade into a sewn-in sheath. Although not as tall or wide as Buddy, the visitor stood big and bullish.

"Follow me," Buddy said.

The two men moved like grand steers plodding through a single-file raceway toward the slaughterhouse.

Buddy knocked, turned the knob, and let the door swing open. Once the Russian tramped into the office, Buddy closed the door but not all the way.

"Shut the damn door," Craven barked from his desk. "And make sure nobody comes into the club 'til I tell you. Now beat it."

On a pained wince, Buddy eased the door closed and shook his head. "That be trouble."

\*\*\*

The Russian stood three feet from Craven's desk, his body mass snuffing the light behind him.

Craven considered the calloused hulk. He didn't appear bright—in fact, he looked Jurassic—but an Italian tough guy with Chicago connections vouched for him. Still, a bed of worms wriggled his brain with doubts.

Wearing a newsboy cap raked over one eye, the man resembled a butcher from the old country, accustomed to cleaving ham hocks with a single whack. His black peacoat was mottled with russet and ocher stains of what? Vodka? Vomit? Dried blood?

The Russian's black half-moon eyes hung close to a bulbous nose stippled with a stein of broken capillaries—disturbing features that suited the S-shaped lightning bolt tattoo on the side of his neck.

His pocked complexion sheened like swarthy snakeskin. Craven envisioned the butcher ripping his nose against a stone and slithering out of his skin. On a wave of the creeps, he pressed his left elbow against his holstered Colt.

"What's your name?" the boss man asked.

"Nikita," he said in a groggy grumble as if for want of sleep.

"Is that your real name?"

He hiked his shoulders, letting the gesture speak for him.

"How about your last name?"

The Russian's deadpan expression molted into irritation. "Is not important," he said, every syllable gargling from the back of his throat.

Craven was not going to argue with the Russian juggernaut. "You understand what has to be done?"

"Understant," Nikita said, substituting a "t" for the final "d."

Throughout the stilted conversation, the Russian's face remained impassive, his teeth hidden behind thick, blistered lips, his blank ebony eyes peeping through slits of granite. He stood rod-up-the-ass rigid.

Craven got down to business by matching the Russian's spiritless expression. "Half now, half when the job's done. Agreed?"

"Agreet."

He squinted. "What?"

"Agreet. I agree."

"Oh. I got you."

Drawing a silver money clip from his pants pocket, Craven peeled off a ten, two twenties, and folded the bills lengthwise. Without standing, he extended his arm, the cash scissored between two fingertips.

The Russian eyeballed the bills and moved for the first time to snatch the cash in his palm as if squeezing the life out of a mouse.

"Address," the butcher said with his uncanny knack of paring any sentence to a single word.

Speaking slowly so the Russian would get it right, he gave him the street address and apartment number. "You need to write it down?"

"*Nyet.*"

Rattled, Craven pressed his hands into the arms of his banker's chair and lifted himself enough to reset his hips. "You mean 'no'?"

The butcher nodded but only once.

Grumbling something vulgar, the club owner opened a desk drawer and fished out an eight-by-ten glossy. He jiggled the black-and-white photograph like tinkling a bell. "You've seen this photograph?"

"*Da.*"

Craven emptied a lung-full of air. "Christ almighty, does that mean 'yes'?"

Not one for idle chitchat, the butcher grunted, which passed for confirmation.

"You don't need to carry this?" he asked, rocking the photograph.

"*Nyet.*"

"*Nyet.* Okay, I've got it." Under his breath, he added, "Look at me. I'm fluent in Russian."

"Ven?"

His face crumpled, which uncovered his teeth. "What's that?"

"Ven?" Nikita repeated. "Ven you vant done?"

"Got it." Craven lowered his chin and stared at the butcher—a look intending to carry gravity. "Tomorrow. Tuesday at 2:00 pm. No sooner, no later."

The Russian composed the longest sentence of the day, maybe the longest sentence of his life. "You vant it fast or you vant it should jurt."

"Huh?" he grunted.

The butcher repeated the sentence on a scowl.

When Craven broke the code, he summoned a wolfish smile. "Yeah, I want it to hurt."

"Goot," the stone-faced butcher said. "I like ven it jurts."

**25**

On Tuesday morning, Athena filled a glass of water at her kitchen sink when a birdlike tap sounded at the door.

"Would you get that, Tony?"

"You bet."

Tony opened the door, looked out, then down into the eyes of a scruffy schoolboy gulping for air.

"Are you Mr. Marco?" the boy gasped.

"Hold on, son," he said, resting his hand on the boy's shoulder. "Take a good long breath."

"No time for breathing. This is for you, mister. Got to get back quick to tell him I found you."

The boy handed him a folded note and dashed dizzy-fast for the stairs. When he ricocheted off the banister at the first landing, he grunted and quickened his pace.

*That's one ambitious letter carrier.*

Tony's smile turned into a grin as he read the handwritten note:

*Mr. Marco,*

*It was a great pleasure to meet you and hear you play at The Nest. I'm looking forward to working with you.*

*I'd like to meet and talk about how we can best use your talent. Would you please meet me at the Cotton Club on Tuesday, 2:00 pm sharp?*

*Respectfully,*

*Fletch Henderson*

He danced into the kitchen and read the note to Athena. "Can you believe this? I'm going to play with Fletcher Henderson at the Cotton Club."

"I'm so excited for you."

His face brightened. "Hey, why don't you go with me?"

"Not this time. I don't want to jinx this for you. Besides, you have everything you need to make it on your own."

He tugged on her waist and leaned back to see her eyes. "Are you sure?"

"Just knock him dead," she said, boosting onto her toes and giving him a quick kiss.

Releasing her, he set a foot on a kitchen chair, leaned over his knee, and reread the note. "Fletcher Henderson. You know he was the composer and arranger for Benny Goodman."

Athena narrowed her eyes. "I know most of the great jazzmen on the East Coast but not a single Benny. Who's Benny Goodman?"

Tony rolled some numbers in his head. "That's right. What am I talking about? Goodman is only fifteen years old. But trust me, you're going to hear from him—a lot." He thumped his chest. "Pinch me and tell me I'm dreaming."

She folded a dishtowel and tossed it over her shoulder. "I don't want to pinch you," she said, moving toward him with a lot of hip action.

"The towel missed the counter," he said, making his voice crack.

"Who cares?" she said as she swept her hair over her ears. Playacting now, she gave him the stalking yellow-eyed tigress stare.

"Some say sex is not the answer."

"You're right," she said. "Sex is not the answer. It's the question. The answer is 'yes.'"

As his gut sparked and flared, he backed into the living room, embracing his role. "Oh, I never knew you were such a bad girl."

She moistened her fingertip and trailed it across his bottom lip. "You don't know how good a bad girl can feel."

That she was the aggressor and he the fool—roles that could reverse in a blink—only sweetened the game. "Oh please, Miss Athena. Please don't have your way with me again. It's too horrible to think about."

She kicked off her shoes and unbuttoned her blouse with impure meaning. "You stop right where you are, my devil sheik. I have something special I want to show you."

He chugged to a stop. "Oh no... Oh no."

With taunting eyes, she stripped off her blouse so hurricane-fast it could have been air. Hunkering low, she dragged her hand between his legs as she rose to full height.

On a whimper of pleasure, he pretended to be unfazed. "You know what they say. 'No shoes, no shirt, no service.'"

Her mouth was at his ear. "What does that mean?" she purred.

He corkscrewed his neck and let his diction quake. "Oh, nothing. A twenty-first-century thing people say. Beach kids started popping into cafes without shoes and shirts. Shop owners didn't like it. There's no law against it, but—"

"Tony darling?"

"Yes, dear."

"Shut up." Step-by-step, she shoved her prize into her lair. The window shade was closed—convenient for the huntress and the end for her prey.

The last thing he said was, "Oh, nice cat-woman. Please be gentle."

# 26

At one forty-five, Tony set out for his meeting with Fletcher Henderson at the Cotton Club. The nine-block walk from Athena's apartment on 133rd Street to the Cotton Club on 142nd Street would take no more than fifteen minutes if he headed north on Lenox Avenue.

He played out a dream within a dream. He and Fletcher would talk about the future of jazz. They would pore over his charts, including a look at his solos or duets with Louie or Coleman. Maybe afterward, they would all sit at a booth and nurse a drink while jabbering about chord changes or tonal inflections or the art of thrilling an audience—all this through the eyes of a man from the future who knew their music before they conceived it.

The exterior of the Cotton Club featured a neon art-deco design with clean elegant lines. A sidewalk billboard included eight-by-ten black-and-white photographs of Fletcher, Louis, Coleman, and the entire orchestra. He tested the double doors. They were open. When he eased into the lobby, he confronted a doorman with a flattened nose and a black Pershing cap with a gold strap.

"You can't be here," the doorman said without contrition.

"I'm Tony Marco. I have an appointment with Fletcher Henderson."

"How do I know that?" the doorman asked, looking like he'd either missed lunch or a stiff drink.

"I'm sure he'll welcome me if you announce I'm here."

The doorman mulled that over. "Hmm. You wait here."

Tony didn't wait. He followed the doorman into a hall filled with white columns, a floral fresco ceiling, a long bar, and an even longer dance floor that led to a raised stage with a grand piano alongside a tangle of music stands. Fletcher sat at the piano, a pencil balanced on his ear, noodling a melody with his right hand.

The doorman was midway to the bandstand when Tony called out from the back of the room. "Sorry if I caught you by surprise."

"Tony, come in, come in," Fletcher said. "It's good to see you." He turned to the doorman. "It's okay. Tony's one of us now."

Henderson's expression of brotherhood rippled Tony's heart.

The bandleader stepped from the stage to shake hands. "I've been thinking about you," he said, patting the edge of the stage where they both perched. "I have a hunch you like a good ballad. Something nice and easy. Am I right?"

"You've got my number," Tony said with a hint of chagrin in being found out. "I do like a slow tune. It gives me time to play with melodic surprises—from inspiration to breath, from soul to horn."

Because Fletcher was so boyish and soft-spoken, a fool might dismiss him as a lightweight. Not Tony. He valued musical intelligence, so when Fletcher spoke, he listened intently, measuring not only the meaning of his words but the tonal nuances.

Fletcher crossed his arms in a relaxed manner. "Here's what I'm thinking. I'd like you to compose a thirty-two-measure melody. Something that grabs your heart. Maybe a tune that makes you think of Athena," he added with a wink. "When you've got it, give it to me, and I'll score an arrangement. Unless you prefer arranging your own tune."

With a hand on Fletcher's shoulder, he said, "No, you're the master arranger. I trust you completely."

Fletcher acknowledged the compliment with an easy smile.

There was a lag in the conversation. "I'm thrilled to have this chance to play with you," Tony said. "Thanks for inviting me to chat with you today."

An inquisitive look played on Fletcher's face. "How's that?"

"I said, 'Thanks for inviting me today.'"

"I'm sorry, I'm glad you dropped by, but I didn't invite you."

Tony knotted his brow. "That's strange. There was a boy, about nine or ten years old, who came to my door with your invitation." He remembered he still had the scrap of paper. He fished out the note from his pants pocket. "Here it is."

As Fletcher scanned the message, his expression grew troubled. "I'm afraid you've been duped. This is not mine. That's not my handwriting, and I never sign my name Fletch—always Fletcher."

His mind spinning, Tony pictured how fast the boy wanted to deliver the note and scoot. Then he recalled Craven's ratchetted face, the look of a man who could easily savage the essence of beauty and sensibility.

On a tide of nausea, Tony sprang to his feet. "Athena's in trouble. My god, I've got to go right now."

Fletcher's face turned grim. "What is it?"

With no time to explain, Tony dashed toward the lobby. Midway across the dance floor, he shouted, "What time is it?"

"Eh…" Fletcher faltered. "Two thirty." Then louder. "It's two thirty."

A half hour. Athena had been with that monster for a half hour. He crashed through the club's double doors and onto the street. He was in a full sprint now. He figured he could make it to the apartment in five minutes. Maybe faster.

The awful truth of five minutes swished through his mind. *Strangulation takes five minutes. A slash across the carotid artery drains a soul in a heartbeat.*

He muscled his heart to the limit.

He was on Lenox Avenue heading south. Crossing 141st Street, a Lincoln's bumper skimmed his right leg. *Be careful. Being dead won't help Athena.*

On 139th he broke his pace when a woman coaxing a wicker baby carriage made a sudden left. Jumping sideways, he stumbled over the curb and into seething traffic. A convertible Piedmont barreled down on him. He had no choice but to dive headfirst over the hood. The radiator cap ornament mauled his gut under his ribs. The car braked, and he crashed over and onto the opposite side of the Piedmont. Staggering to his feet, he cupped his head with both hands.

At the head of teeming traffic, another car from the opposite direction loomed toward him. Although the car braked and fishtailed to a screeching stop, it was too late. The front bumper clipped the side of his leg and hurled him to the ground like an imploded building.

As the traffic shrieked to a stop, the driver in the Piedmont got out of his car, scurried to Tony, hooked his hands under his armpits, and dragged him to the sidewalk.

"What the hell's wrong with you?" the man snarled.

Although woozy, he wanted to say something but had no words.

Wearing a homburg hat slanted over one eye, the man stood over him with his hands on his knees. "I said, what the hell's wrong with you? Look what you did to my car."

Tony squinted at the man, now overpowered by the sun. His vision blurred. *Don't pass out.* The edges of darkness became wider and thicker, seeping in like black blood, oozing into every fissure of his will, and overtook him.

# 27

At two o'clock, a monster pummeled Athena's door. There was nothing gentle about it. It was an ultimatum. *You better open this door now, or I'll kick it in.*

Strangely, the fierce hammering spirited curiosity. Athena wanted to see the beast on the other side—not to make friends but to see the face of evil. She sought to cage the savage in her brain and, one day, tell the story to her grandchildren at midnight. She would say, "I was brave. I faced the monster, and I survived."

That was a half-truth. The other half was teeming with fear.

She tiptoed to the door and watched her hand approach and finger the knob.

The monster pounded on the thin barrier separating him from Athena's throat. The vibration pricked her hand. Even more, her chest tremored with visions of the beast.

She froze. Mute. Hardly breathed.

Turning from the door, she scanned the room and spotted the slatted straight-backed oak chair. She minced on cat feet to the chair, gripped it by the seat, and eased back to the doorway. The monster battered the door again.

*Boom, boom, boom.*

She wedged the chair's top rail under the doorknob.

Her eyes glared at the crease between the door and the jamb, linked together by one pathetic dead bolt. The latch had as much chance of holding as a spider's web against a broom. She cowered—one, two, three steps, and into the bathroom. Hunching over the claw-footed cast-iron bathtub, she cranked the faucet. If she could only melt into that pool of water.

***

In the hallway, the butcher clutched the door handle and wrenched this way and that. He heard the creak of a neighbor's door crack open. Whipping around, he eyed a gray prune-faced woman with white hair so fine it could be strained through a silk scarf. He growled, which by her reaction quaked the timbers under her feet. She snapped her head back and slammed the door shut with a decided thud.

He had enough.

The task was easy. Gripping his right wrist, he lowered his shoulder and battered the door. The first whack tore the dead bolt through the doorframe. The second blow splintered the bracing oak chair into kindling. Anticipating a gunshot, he whipped to the side. There was nothing. He kicked the door open. As it swung on frazzled hinges, he peered with one eye through the opening.

Tomb silent.

He unbuttoned his peacoat and drew out a stag-handled, twelve-inch-blade hunting knife. The knife was long enough to savage a retreating victim with a handle butt heavy enough to shatter a skull. Although the blade glistened, it wasn't perfect. Corrosion from unscoured blood pocked its surface.

The butcher advanced his head around the doorframe. Scanning the living room, he spied the tall mahogany armoire with louvered doors, tall enough to hang dresses or conceal a cringing target. He raked the tip of the knife along the fleur-de-lis wallpaper and, at the armoire, ran the blade in a slow chatter down the louvers.

"Der is no place to run," he droned, the trilled "r" of "run" so deep in his throat it sounded as if he were trying to cough up a wad of phlegm. Pressing his ear against the seam where the doors met, he listened for shallow breathing or a muted gasp. He popped the doors and gored his blade across the width of the closet, hoping to eviscerate the soft belly of his victim.

No one.

The killer stood in the middle of the room and listened. Running water from the bathroom. The door was closed but unlocked. He stepped into the room with a war yelp, his knife swiping left and right. Still no one. As he turned off the water, he listened and detected a twist of metal whispering from outside the apartment. The fire escape.

*****

Sixty seconds earlier, Athena turned on the tub faucet, hoping water pouring on porcelain would shroud her escape. After she opened the tap, she scampered spider-quiet across the living room and into the bedroom. She raised the window and climbed, leg and head first, onto the fire escape. So far, luck was on her side. The first apartment above hers belonged to Isabella. Zalo's flat was one floor above that, but he was at work for at least four more hours.

She stole up the fire escape and rapped on Isabella's window.

Glimpsing Athena's eyes, Isabella shuddered. She unlocked and ripped open the window.

Athena exploded through the open window and into Isabella's arms, panting as if she were hunted, the baying hounds at her heels.

Frenzied, Isabella said, "What is it, child?"

"Someone is trying to kill me."

"I heard strange sounds. I should have acted. I should have—"

Athena grabbed Isabella by the shoulders, her fingers hollowing into her skin. "You *can*. Let me leave your apartment and slip by him and into the street. From there I'll get help."

"Yes, of course," Isabella whispered.

With no greater plan, Athena dashed to Isabella's front door. "Lock it as soon as I'm out." Easing the door open, she peeked into the hall. It was clear, but as she scrambled downstairs, the man hurled into the hallway and spotted her. She jerked to a stop. He was a terrifying hulk, his eyes emblazed with satanic fury, his mouth turned into a greedy smirk as if content. The light pouring into the hallway from Athena's apartment cast a sliver of ice down the killer's long blade.

Recoiling, she turned, pelted up the stairs, and called Isabella's name.

The instant Isabella flung the door open, Athena plunged in.

Isabella slammed the door shut and latched it.

"He's in the hallway."

"Don't worry. I can do this, child. You take this," she said, handing Athena a heavy sharp-edged electric iron with an integrated six-foot electrical cord. Athena knew it could be a lethal weapon—equally lethal if turned against her.

The butcher's heavy boots thudded up the stairwell.

"What do you want me to do?" Athena asked.

The assassin bashed his weight against the door. It held. Maybe it could take one or two more blasts, but no more.

"Go out the fire escape and onto the roof. I know how to take care of this kind of man."

Athena clutched Isabella's face. "No, I can't leave you."

Her eyes piercing, words chilling, Isabella stripped away Athena's hands. "Do as I tell you. Go now."

Uneasy but yielding, Athena climbed back through the window, scrambled to the rooftop, crouched, and awaited the attack.

# 28

Tony awakened to city clamor—the skidding tires, the bleating horns, the jabbering New Yorkers. When he opened his eyes, a concaved ring of faces glowered at him like a murder of crows.

His head throbbing to every heartbeat, he struggled to make sense of his place. "Where am I?"

"On Lenox," someone says.

"Lenox and what?"

"Hundred and thirty-ninth."

He clambered to his hands and knees. Although buildings teetered and sidewalks wavered like funhouse mirrors, he forced himself to stand, despite the wringing pangs that wrenched his gut. "I gotta get to 133rd Street."

"Easy," a man said with a hand under Tony's elbow. "Maybe you should sit a minute."

"No, 133rd Street," Tony repeated as he squirmed through the crowd, his legs trembling, nearly buckling under him.

"You're going the wrong way," the same voice said as the faceless man reversed Tony's course.

"Thank you," he said under a pile of rubble weighing on his head. Vacant-eyed and sheathed in cold sweat, he lurched forward. Despite his battered body, his pace quickened with every step. *I've got to get to Athena. She has to be safe. She is safe.*

His mind reeled, a mishmash of horrific nightmares.

*It's on me. If she dies, it's all on me. I should have never left her alone.* He clenched his teeth against Sophia's curse.

His heart pounding, he plunged on, his legs churning pell-mell, the pedestrians scattering like cats when they glimpsed the desperation in his eyes.

# 29

Eyes steely, mouth grim, Isabella rushed into the kitchen, clutched something, and shoved it into her housedress pocket. When she returned to the front door, she stood soldier-tall. She crossed her palms over her chest, held her breath, then lowered her hands on exhalation.

When the butcher slammed into the door for the second time, the doorframe moaned. Isabella held steady. With chest expanded and chin set high, she unlatched the door and swung it open.

She bored into the killer's eyes as if trephining into his brain by the power of her mind. The regard riveted so intensely the butcher suspended in taut bewilderment. Although the long knife was in his hand, he let his arms fall limp.

"*Ya... Ya...*" he stammered.

"I see you are troubled," Isabella said in a soothing tone. "Please come in. Let us talk."

Stepping aside to give the man free passage into her apartment, she watched him blink at her walls—vibrant purple, red, yellow, and green. He tranced on the trove of African and Caribbean masks, some humorous, but most terrifying.

Although approaching timidly, he touched a wooden death mask: a pale face flecked with blood with darkened shadows down the center of the forehead and below the cheekbones. Encircling the mask from ear to ear were long leonine strands of straw. The teeth were bared, the eyes chevroned, affecting a murderous scowl.

"I see you like the African death mask," Isabella said. "It is not surprising. It holds a furious spirit and requires a powerful man to own it. Perhaps you are such a man."

Turning to face her, he quaked when Isabella touched his neck. "Do not fear," she murmured.

Seemingly becalmed, the butcher allowed Isabella to finger the jagged S-shaped lightning bolt that rippled across his thick, striated neck.

"You wear the sign of Satan."

His expression was stiff and noncommittal.

"So be it," she said. "You must be who you are."

"*Da.*"

"And I must be who I am. We both must be true to our spirits."

Isabella controlled his eyes.

Unhooking the death mask from the wall, she placed it over her face. She now glared at the butcher through the spirit of death and felt his terror fan and course through her own body. The butcher's face and shoulders began to shrink as if made of wax and kiln-fired. He flicked his eyelids to sheer the sweat that had trickled down his forehead, over his brows, and into his eyes. In freakish slow motion, his face turned into a Greek mask of tragedy.

"I now possess the spirit of death," Isabella said as she drew a bone from her hip pocket. She pointed the bone at the butcher. "This bone is the sacred dagger of the most powerful, the most evil sorcerer of all time, Chief Pórcachoópus." Edging closer to the shriveling man, she slipped her hand under his peacoat and twisted the ossein dagger over his heart.

Her speech belched from an unearthly region—if not hell, then purgatory. "If you hurt my godchild, the curse of Pórcachoópus will melt the skin off your face, puncture your ears, and draw snakes from your eye sockets. Your misery will not end with death. It will be eternal."

His snakeskin complexion molted fog-gray. As his arms dangled at his sides, the Russian unfolded his fingers. The hunting knife slipped and sliced through the jute mat and pierced the oak flooring, its long blade and crescent guard casting a tall quivering shadow. Even to Isabella, the shadow resembled a broken upside-down cross, the sign of Satan.

The butcher followed Isabella's gaze to the demonic shadow and escaped his trance. Reaching down, he clasped the knife and pulled it from its sticking point. As his body expanded, he ripped off the death mask that covered her face and flung it aside. Clenching

Isabella's hair, he set the tip of the blade under her chin even as she turned the voodoo bone deeper into his chest.

*** 

*Whack.* The crack exploded from the living-room window.

It was Athena. She could not stay long on the rooftop, not with Isabella in danger. Having stowed the iron, she returned as live bait to lure the monster away from her godmother.

Kneeling on the fire escape, her face and hands pressed against the window. She again pummeled the windowpane with open palms and bared her teeth. Her rant was bestial. "Here I am!"

The butcher turned and scowled at Athena. Withdrawing his knife from the underside of Isabella's jaw, he charged for her, his eyes glinting vermilion.

# 30

Below the apartment building, Tony spotted Athena scuttling across Isabella's fire escape and up the ladder toward Zalo's flat. Behind her, a brawny man with a long knife strained to pass through Isabella's window and onto the escapeway.

Favoring stealth, Tony repressed the urge to signal Athena. He thundered into the apartment house, stumbled up the stairs, and glimpsed Athena's shattered front door. Bent on taking the next flight two steps at a time, his legs gave out. He fell to his knees, the smack provoking a silent curse. He pushed on, his head reeling like a dust devil.

Rushing into Isabella's apartment, he jammed his hands onto his hips, doubled over, and chuffed for air.

The death mask in hand, Isabella's speech was a torrent of words. "He is a crazy man. He believes in evil spirits. Take this and wear it. Tell him you are the ghost of Pórcachoópus and you have come to kill him."

"I'm not—"

Clawing his shirt with both hands, she gave him a hard yank. "Do as I say. The ghost of Pórcachoópus."

She set the mask on Tony's face and cinched the leather strap.

"Jesus, I hope you're right," he said through the mask.

"Make your voice lower. And take this," she added, pressing a T-shaped bone in his hand. "He'll be terrified. For him, it's the all-powerful scepter of Satan. It will scare the hell out of him."

On failing legs, Tony wriggled through the window.

Two flights above, Athena hoisted herself onto the fifth-floor fire escape. All that remained was the bare ladder to the rooftop. The Russian gawked at her from one landing below.

Tony scrambled up the iron steps, but the soles of Zalo's borrowed shoes were leather and worn smooth. In a heartbeat, he slipped on one of the treads and bashed his right shin, already bruised and aching from the car accident. He stifled a yelp as three seconds of valuable time ticked into oblivion.

Athena clutched the highest rung of the uncaged ladder to the roof. Below, the Russian, who had sheathed the long knife to facilitate scaling with both hands, stood on the second rung. He reached to snag Athena's ankle but brushed air.

Soft-handing the sides of the iron ladder, Athena pressed her feet together and free-fell with all her weight into the Russians skyward-craning face. She heard the brittle snap of bone from under her bootheels.

The butcher groaned and waggled his head while Athena bounded up the ladder and onto the roof. Rooted over the ladder, she broadened her stance—ready to take on the killer.

At that instant, Tony stormed the assassin.

His glare aflame, Tony impaled the butcher's ankle with the supernatural bone—a flensing knife that ruptured the Russian's Achilles tendon.

The assassin wailed a mourning ululant cry, looked downward, and quaked.

Behind the death mask, Tony loomed like a spectral man-killer. "I am the ghost of Pórcachoópus," he bellowed so low and frightening he gave *himself* a chill. "I have come to kill you." He jerked the bone overhead and spiked it into the killer's right calf.

The butcher's eyes turned into pools of terror—the kind of eyes that stare into the face of doom with a guilty conscience. Although his right leg was nearly useless, he managed to hoist himself to the final rung of the uncaged ladder. He was within arm's length of the roof cornice.

Incarnated as Chief Pórcachoópus, Tony scaled two more treads, reached overhead, and plunged the bone into the butcher's hamstring. Simultaneously, Athena gripped the iron's electrical cord, whipped the weapon overhead, and with full fury hammered the Russian's temple.

The butcher lay out in space. Arms flailing, fingers combing the sky, he landed on his back across Zalo's fire-escape railing, which snapped his spine and flipped him one-eighty on descent. When his skull struck the pavement, echoes of shattered bone ricocheted along Swing Street. With sightless eyes fixed in horror, his blood pooled around his head.

Still masked, Tony hooked one arm around a ladder rung, stared at the broken body below, then up at Athena, who stood trembling, her gaze blank, the iron's cord still in hand. Tony scaled to the rooftop and tore off the death mask.

In each other's arms, they embraced long and hard, their lips and hands searching.

After a flurry of kisses, he said, "You're trembling. Are you hurt?"

"I'm all right. Scared out of my wits but okay."

"I'm so sorry"—his eyes misted over—"so sorry I wasn't here."

Athena's expression gentled so suddenly it surprised Tony.

"What is it?" he asked.

"I just realized you're my man, strong and devoted and tender," she said with a smile.

"But..."

She touched his lips. "It's not your fault," she said, kissing him again and again. "Really, it's not." On a deep breath, she brushed a tuft of hair from his eyes. "I think I know who's behind this."

"So do I."

"What're we going to do?" Athena asked.

"We're going to protect each other, but we'll have to be smart about it."

Pivoting, they surveyed the street, the city crowns, and the cumulous clouds that puffed the sky. "This is our life, Athena. And no one's going to take it from us." He turned to caress her face with both hands. "I love you so much."

She found his mouth. "I love you too."

The neighbors and random onlookers who had gathered across the street lowered their hands from their faces. As their relief settled, they applauded—haltingly at first, then with spirit.

Still shaken, the couple acknowledged the neighbors with timid waves.

Tony knotted the iron cord, slung it over his shoulder, and slipped the death mask strap over his arm. He edged down the ladder first, then asked Athena to descend under him, allowing his arms to act as guardrails. At the third-floor fire escape, Isabella greeted them with lavish embraces.

Having passed through the window into Isabella's apartment, they sat in a circle, the couple side by side on the davenport, Isabella on a black leather ottoman. Although the wound was not severe, Tony massaged his stomach where the Piedmont radiator ornament had left a globular green and purple contusion.

After the three versions of the story had spun out, Tony turned to Isabella. "I'm curious. Do you believe that curses can work?"

"Yes, I do."

"How's that?"

Leaning forward, Isabella placed her hands on her knees and flared her elbows—holding their gazes with mysterious eyes. "I believe that if an evil person believes in voodoo, the shock alone can scare him to death."

"There's physical evidence to support your claim," Tony said. "A radical fall in blood pressure can be fatal." He fetched the bone from his pocket. "But can a bone possess a curse? Does *this* bone, Pórcachoópus, carry a curse?"

Isabella bit her bottom lip, which belied her mischief. "The only thing that bone carries is a little gristle. There is no curse of Pórcachoópus. There is only a good *pork chop*, dear. And with a little salt and pepper"—she laughed despite herself—"that one made a heavenly lunch today."

In the distance there was the sound of sirens. The police were coming. They would be interrogated—soon.

# 31

The next morning, Tony repaired Athena's door and lock. He liked working with his hands. Whether replacing a worn knee or repairing a splintered entryway, he was at home with any mechanical challenge.

Once the work was completed, they sat at the kitchen table, shared a cup of coffee, and read the morning paper. There was one short paragraph on the case. UNIDENTIFIED MAN FALLS TO HIS DEATH. Athena read the entire notice aloud. "Tuesday at approximately 3:00 pm, an unidentified man fell to his death from the roof of a brownstone apartment on West 133rd Street in Harlem. The cause of death was provisionally attributed to a botched robbery or attempted murder. The case is still under investigation."

They were discussing the notice when someone hammered on the front door. Athena winced. Tony reached across the kitchen table and squeezed her hand. "I'm here, sweetheart. We're safe."

He approached the entry. "Who's there?"

A booming command echoed in the hallway and down the stairwell. "It's the police. Open up."

When he turned to Athena, her eyes were big and troubled. He smiled gamely and pumped his hands to allay her fears.

"What's your precinct number?" Tony asked through the closed door.

"The Thirty-Eighth. Now open the goddamned door."

He looked sidelong at Athena, who confirmed the precinct number was correct. He unlatched and opened the door. In the darkened hallway, a lieutenant and sergeant chafed, their sour mood betrayed by fingering their pistol grips.

The lieutenant had a pear-shaped face, a fractal of his pear-shaped body, with heavy, pendulant jowls and dark rings under his affectless eyes. In dramatic contrast, the sergeant, a rawboned rail of a man, lurched like a bony goblin with a narrow hawkish nose, pinched eyes, and dangling arms that seemed too long for his body.

The lieutenant did all the talking. "Is this the home of Athena Cruz?"

"Yes, it is," Athena said from beyond Tony's shoulder. "May we help you, officers?"

To Tony, her inflection rang comical, servile, and shiny from use. He studied the officers, who seemed oblivious to the overblown fawning.

The policemen tried to shoulder through the doorway at the same time until the sergeant gave way to the higher-ranking officer. Once in, they both toured the length of the living room like skeptical house buyers.

Athena headed into the kitchen.

"Where you going?" the lieutenant asked, short on politeness.

"I thought I'd fetch two kitchen chairs to make your stay more comfortable."

With a flick of his hand, the lieutenant signaled the sergeant to follow her.

Once satisfied the apartment was clear of god-knows-what, the officers flopped into their chairs while the couple settled side by side on the couch.

"What's your name?" the lieutenant asked, staring down Tony.

"Tony Marco. May I ask your names?"

Clearly favoring control over the thread of questions, the lieutenant's face changed from hard-boiled to surly. "I'm Klinger," he said, flicking a thumb to his chest. "This is Gorski," he added with a hitch toward the sergeant.

Tony pretended to smile. "Pleased to meet you, officers."

"You have any identification?" Klinger asked.

He failed to stem his eyebrows from arching. His identification was issued in the twenty-first century. Explaining that oddity would end in a one-way trip to the loony bin. "I'm afraid not, officer," he lied. "I was recently mugged, and the malefactor took everything." As soon as he said it, he knew "malefactor" was the wrong word to use.

"Ooh-wee," the lieutenant sang out. "Get a load of Mr. College Boy. A *malefactor* done you wrong. I just hate it when that happens. And now, here you are with all your fancy words but no identification." He clucked his tongue.

"No identification," Gorski echoed.

Cocking his head, the lieutenant stared at Tony from the corner of his eyes. "What kind of work do you do, college boy?"

"I'm a musician," he said, knowing he could prove that.

"A tootely-toot," Klinger said to Gorski with a snicker as he fingered an imaginary clarinet. "And where're you working?"

"I've been hired to play at the Cotton Club."

"Really," the lieutenant said, his pear-shaped face rotting on the vine. "I've been there. That's a boogie band. They don't allow no white musicians."

Detesting the cop's language, Tony would have taken great pleasure in popping him in the mouth.

The cops glared at him, daring him to do something stupid.

"They've made an exception with me," he said, trying to control his resentment. "They want to try something new."

Crooking his mouth to one side, the lieutenant gripped the sides of his chair and squirmed to settle in more comfortably. He reclaimed his cold, fish-eyed expression and laced his fingers over his paunch. "We don't like new things around here."

Hoping to disguise his brewing emotions, Tony was both silent and expressionless.

"We don't like troublemakers. We don't like people making waves, do we, Gorski?"

"No, sir, we sure don't. They're a mess of..." He let his sneer and bobbing head complete the thought.

Tony noticed Gorski stroked his pistol grip when he spoke.

"We like things as smooth as a baby's fanny," Klinger said, sliding his hand over the curve of an imaginary baby's rump, his swelling smile humorless.

The alarm clock from the bedroom ticked away the seconds.

Shifting his weight, Tony said, "I'm sorry. I'm a little confused. Are you here to talk about the man who fell from the rooftop yesterday?"

The lieutenant screwed up his face. "Oh, I don't think there's much to talk about. The whole neighborhood saw what happened. He was trying to hurt the negress here. Ain't that right?"

Behind a smirk carved from ice, Klinger glowered at Athena.

Her eyes didn't waver.

"Ain't that right?" the lieutenant repeated.

"That's correct," Athena said. "He wanted me dead."

Klinger sucked on his front teeth. "So I'm told." Pondering his left hand, the cop spotted a grain of grit under his middle fingernail, dislodged it with his thumbnail, and sanded his fingertips. "Now, I suppose it's natural you wanted him dead too. I mean, him working so hard to kill you and all."

"It was a question of self-defense," Tony said.

Wrenching his head, the lieutenant gave Tony a drop-dead look. "Was I talking to you, Mr. No Identification?" He affected befuddlement. "I don't think I was talking to you. Was I addressing this highfalutin college boy, Gorski?"

"No, sir, you sure weren't," the sergeant said as if dying of boredom.

"I didn't think so." Klinger spoke softly now as if explaining the danger of a hot stove to toddlers. "You see, I can usually tell when I'm talking because I can hear my voice. A little trick my mama taught me. I was definitely not talking to you." In apoplectic rage, he added, "So shut the hell up!" He tugged on the hem of his coat and smoothed the wrinkles down his chest. "Now, where was I?"

"You were saying this woman wanted him dead," the sergeant said.

"That's right. Thank you, Officer Gorski. You see how polite the sergeant is? You two could learn a thing or two from him."

Gorski coughed up a chuckle.

Exchanging a look of self-satisfaction with the sergeant, Klinger said, "Listen here, I'm willing to let bygones be bygones. We know this big fella was trying to kill you. We don't know why, but what the hell, people get killed every day in this city. I'm sure he was garbage. But I got this question gnawing at me. Who would want to kill a sweet little shine like you? Huh?"

With childlike innocence, Athena folded her arms across her waistline.

"Hey!" the lieutenant bellowed. "I'm talking to you. Who do you think would want to kill you? You must have some kind of idea."

After a still-eyed suspension, she shook her head no.

"Come on now," Klinger said, peeling off his cap and clawing his scalp. "You're not *altogether* stupid, are you?"

Tony lifted off the couch, but before he could straighten, the sergeant leaped to his feet with his hand on his pistol. "You better squat, mister." If his words had been mist, they would have shattered into particles of ice.

Tony sat. More from police browbeating than yesterday's car accident, he labored against a knot of pain at his side.

Adopting a singsongy tone, Klinger said, "I think you're getting this all wrong. We're the law here. We've come to protect you. And that's what we aim to do." He burrowed into Tony's eyes. "Now you tell me something. I don't generally talk about this much with the boys at the station, but I'm a student of human nature, see." His fingers pulsated before his face as if divining the future within a crystal ball. "It's important in my business to figure out how people think and all. So, I was wondering. You got some perverted sickness? Huh?" With drooping eyelids, he pooled his face into a frown. "You get some twisted kick out of hauling off to bed with burnt toast? Is that it?"

Athena stayed Tony's fist with a light touch. Although he unfurled his fingers, the gesture didn't escape the lieutenant.

Klinger smiled churlishly, the kind of grin that conveyed satisfaction in vexing a shackled rival, and turned to Athena. "And you. What the hell are you doing? You got a taste for white bread? Don't you like the jigaboos in your neighborhood?"

Tony unclenched his teeth to get the words out. "That's enough," he said, one heartbeat chasing another. "What we do in private is none of your damn business."

After a long hush, Klinger opened his mouth and howled. "Now, there you go again. Being impolite. Here we are trying to be real sociable and you behave like... What would you call these people, Gorski?"

"Troublemakers," the sergeant said. "I'd call them goddamned troublemakers."

"Yeah, that's exactly it." The lieutenant leaned forward and placed his hands on his knees in a vulturine pose. "So, this is how we work with troublemakers. We keep an eye on you. You step out of line, I mean if you even spit on the sidewalk, we'll come down on you with a bellyful of hurt. You'll wish your mama would tuck you in and kiss you good night."

"My mama's dead," Athena said without expression.

"Then let me put it this way," Klinger said with a cold-blooded huff. "You'll wish you was never born. Do I make myself understood?"

Tapping Tony's hand, Athena signaled her time to speak. "Officers, you're right," she said serenely. "You want the best for all of us. I see that. Like they sing in church, you're 'the tie that binds.' You keep us safe and secure, the entire neighborhood, and we don't tell you that nearly enough. But we promise to do the right thing. We want to make you proud."

Hatching a live-and-learn smile, Klinger opened his arms, clapped once, and dusted his hands. "Now that's what I'm talking about. You finally get it. You help us, and we'll help you. It's that simple. I'm glad we understand each other."

"So am I," Athena said, one hand cupped in the other. "Now, may I offer you gentlemen a cup of coffee?"

"That's awfully kind," Klinger said, "but we got a heap of calls to make today. A lot of folks in the city need protecting, you understand. You be safe now."

The lieutenant boosted himself out of his chair, adjusted his belt, and lifted one grudging knee after the other. "On the move, Sergeant."

Tony and Athena saw the men to the door.

"Thank you for coming," Athena said.

Although he gnashed his teeth, Tony hoped his expression would pass for a smile.

When they closed the door, they listened to the officers' footsteps peter out.

Tony swept Athena into his arms. "You're the most amazing person on earth," he said as he turned over her hands and bent low to kiss each palm.

"Well, thank you," she chortled. "I've been doing this a long time."

"But how? How do you do it?"

She collected his hands, stacked them, and held them against her chest. "It's like this. I know who I am. Their words don't define me."

"But they're so vile."

"I know that, but I'm not responsible for them. I'm only responsible for me."

"Yeah, but what they're doing is abhorrent."

"You're repeating yourself. Yes, they're vile and abhorrent, but we're better than that." She released his hands. "Now, let your arms drop to your sides."

He did so.

"This is something Isabella taught me." With a gossamer touch, she feathered her fingertips across his shoulders and down his biceps, forearms, and hands. "Breathe," she said, skimming the length of his arms a second time. "Now let the anger drain out of your body. Let the fury go."

"But—"

She put her finger over his lips. "No buts. You have to choose your battles carefully. Evil can't be swept away with a single swipe. It has to be chipped away in little chinks. You can't let the grinding pace break your heart."

His eyes dreamy, he said, "Do that thing down my arms again."

As Athena traced the length of his arms, he closed his eyes and imagined his hands were colanders that strained and purged his bitterness. When she'd finished, he opened his eyes and murmured, "I'm staggered by your strength."

"What did you expect? 'There is prodigious strength in sorrow and despair.'"

"Charles Dickens, *Great Expectations*."

"Close. *A Tale of Two Cities*."

He laughed. "You're too smart for me, in so many ways. I want to grow up to be like you."

"Don't say that. You're the person I love now, exactly as you are, with the exception of a few rough edges," she added, tickling his ribs. "For now, I need a long hot bath to scrub away the stench of cop-talk. Care to join me?"

Although his eyes said "yes," his heart fretted. The cops were dangerous, and his instinct warned there was more to come. "Absolutely. Got any pumice?"

## 32

Their normal heart rates had nearly recovered when a second knock at the door sounded. If the timid tap was a reliable predictor, the guest was friendly. Still, Tony questioned the visitor before opening the door. "Who is it, please?"

"I'm sorry to bother y'all."

The deep, rumbling voice was indisputable. It belonged to Buddy Jefferson.

Heaving a sigh of relief, Tony flung the door open and shook Buddy's hand. "Come in, my friend. What a great surprise to see you."

Athena threw herself at Buddy with such vigor a lesser man would have toppled.

"Uh…hey, M-Miss Athena," he stammered. "I'm real happy you okay. I hear what happened." He lowered his head and fisted his trembling hands. "And I knows the man that done it."

When they huddled to talk it out, Buddy's straight-backed chair groaned under his weight, his girth flanking both sides.

Athena asked how he knew the assassin.

Buddy's words were animated but with an undercurrent of affection for the couple. "I seen him at The Nest."

"What was he doing there?" Tony asked.

"He talking to Mr. Craven."

Athena covered Buddy's hand, which rested on his knee. "How do you know it was the same man who tried to kill me?"

"He talk real funny."

"Like a Russian?"

"Maybe so. Funny like."

"That's good," she said, clasping her hands. "Can you think of anything else?"

His face compressed. "Yes'um, he carry a big knife like this," he said, measuring the length from mid-forearm to the tips of his fingers.

"Anything else?"

After a long beat, Buddy said, "He got a tattoo on his neck like lightning. And something else. He big. Not big as me, but big."

Athena and Tony exchanged a confirming glance.

Shaking his head like a caged lion, Buddy said, "Miss Athena, I'm so sorry I weren't here to help you."

Tony glanced at Athena and noticed her lips tighten as if suppressing the urge to sob.

For his part, Buddy looked away in sympathy and heaved a breath that expelled in fitful spasms.

Athena rushed to the backside of Buddy's chair, hooked her arms around his neck, and kissed him on the cheek. "Oh Buddy, don't you worry your sweet heart. You had no way of knowing. We're glad you told us." Returning to her place on the couch, she added, "Aren't we, Tony?"

Touched by the tenderness shared by Buddy and Athena, he closed his eyes before responding. "Of course. It just seems we're surrounded by people who want to hurt Athena."

Buddy raised his head and peered at Tony, his brow sewn into a seam of turmoil. "Who else? Who else wants to hurt her?"

Grimly, Tony highlighted the bitter interrogation with the local police. When he mentioned the names—Sergeant Gorski and Lieutenant Klinger—Buddy's eyes got big.

The bouncer pounded his thighs in time to his words. "No, no. They're bad men. They working for Mr. Craven, and they always asking for more money." Buddy stuttered to get the words out. "Uh-uh, they bad. You don't want nothing to do with them. Y'all hear what I'm saying?"

"I hear you," Athena said. "But I'm not sure there's anything we *can* do."

Buddy's back straightened and expanded. "If that true, I gotta help you. I gotta help you real good this time."

## 33

Visions of Cal Craven and the Russian killer kept Tony turning through the night. In the morning, he had a job to do. It wouldn't be easy, and worse, it began with an unspoken lie.

At eleven o'clock, he said he was taking a walk to clear his head.

"Do you want company?" Athena asked.

"I always love your company," he said truthfully, then added, "but this time I need some time to think. I'm a doctor puzzling over the symptoms before I can make a proper diagnosis." What went unsaid was his plan to twist the dragon's tail.

"Okay." Although she didn't whine, there was a tinge of disquiet—an undertone that jolted his heart.

When Tony left the apartment, he noted Mack trucks loaded with booze lined both sides of Swing Street, their drivers relaxed, even jovial. They were as carefree as the familiar milkman or iceman on his route.

Impervious to the flurry of commerce, two youngsters wearing knickers and newsboy caps perched on a stoop and quarreled.

The scene delighted Tony—a snapshot of his boyhood growing up in the city. Although he had more urgent conflicts in mind, he stopped, leaned against the balustrade, and set one foot on the first step.

"Shouldn't you boys be in school?" he asked with teasing humor.

The boys stared back with fearless eyes. They were, after all, on the front stoop of their home. "We don't have to go to school if we don't want," the taller of the two boys said. "Besides, Jimmy here is sick, and I don't feel so good myself."

As proof of his perilous condition, Jimmy offered two dry, unconvincing coughs.

"I see," Tony said, arms folded in doctoral fashion. "What's your name?"

Tugging on the bill of his cap, the older boy, clearly in charge, said, "They call me 'Sneakers' on account of me being so fast."

"Nice to meet you both," he said without shaking their hands. "So, what are you boys arguing about?"

The response from Sneakers was more snarky than brotherly. "Jimmy here says Rogers Hornsby's the greatest baseball player of all time. I say it's Babe Ruth. Gee whiz, Ruth hit forty-one homers last year. Hornsby only hit seventeen." For emphasis, he repeated the number louder in Jimmy's face. "Seventeen."

With narrowed eyes and quivering lips, Jimmy hammered a rebuttal. "Yeah, but… Hornsby is the best because he plays second base just like me."

"That's dumb. What kind of argument is that?" Sneakers looked to the stranger for support. "What do you think, mister?"

Both boys raised their faces, waiting in silence with hopeful eyes.

Cocking his head upward, Tony searched the sky for a diplomatic response. "That's a tough question. They're both legendary players and always will be for as long as baseball is played, which will be forever."

A new speaker interrupted the conversation. "Boys, come in and get washed up."

"Okay, Ma," the boys said as they turned and scrambled into the brownstone without fanfare or farewell.

A handsome woman with a bird's nest of morning hair and a plain housedress leaned out of a first-floor apartment window. Her face was a portrait of suspicion. "Whacha doing talking to my boys?"

New York City-born and army tempered, Tony immediately detected meanness in her words. She was a woman itching for a fight. "I'm sorry, ma'am. I didn't mean any harm. We were talking baseball."

With a scowl that sharpened the lineaments of her face, she studied him as if scrutinizing a worrisome insect. "You're not from around here, are you?"

"No, ma'am. Least sake, I'm brand new to this part of town."

She took a harder look at him. "Wait a minute. I know you."

He rolled out his killer smile, which carried no weight with the woman.

"You're the guy who shacked up with that tramp piano player." Her face turned old and ugly. "We don't need the likes of you and your spade floozy in our neighborhood."

A surge of adrenaline chased through his body.

"Yeah, and somebody got killed at your place a couple of days back." Her eyes fluttered. "Jesus, I heard it was tied up with the mob."

Although he wanted to say something, anything to persuade the woman he was not a monster and Athena not a tramp, he knew his words would fall flat. He retreated two steps in silence.

Breaking the plane of the windowsill, her neck craning and deepening her jugular notch, she shouted, "Yeah, you better back off. And don't show your face 'round here again."

Tony knew that mixed marriages were not illegal in the State of New York—never were, never would be—but laws were unenforceable where morality was wanting. In 1924, racism was as prevalent as cockroaches. In 2019, racism was not dead by any means (covert bigotry was no virtue), but it was better.

Approaching The Nest, Tony braced his heart for conflict. *You can do this.*

The front door was open. He eased across the threshold and padded forward until the door swung shut behind him. Now the room fell as dark as a crypt. Motionless, he let his eyes adjust to the blackness.

Clutching his breath, he detected a sound. A soft shuffle or the light brush of fabric.

"Buddy?" he whispered.

"Buddy ain't here."

Tony spun and peered into the dark reaches of the room. "Mr. Craven?"

As in a nightmare, he heard the metallic clink of a dead bolt. He spotted the club owner's face illuminated by the flame of a lighter igniting a cigar tip. Although the light was scant, it scarfed a few of the shadows huddled in the gaps.

"Are we alone?" Tony asked.

"Does it matter?"

"Only because I have a private matter to discuss with you."

"We're alone."

Another flame sprang from Craven's lighter. He turned a stubby candle sidelong, stroked the wick with the flame, and set the candle on a small table.

"Have a seat," Craven said, his invitation a thin veneer of contempt. "I'm curious to hear what's on your mind."

They both sat.

Tony studied the man beyond the flickering candlelight for virtually the first time. Beneath his shaped brows, Craven's dark eyes glinted in the up-shooting glow. He sported an expensive navy-blue suit with chalk pinstripes that draped perfectly off his shoulders, though with a slight bulge under his left arm.

He was not homely. Some might call him handsome. His features were angular and hollowed, giving his face a sculpted topography. It was a face that reminded Tony of Egon Schiele's *Self-portrait with Lowered Head*—the image of a gaunt and angry man with menacing eyes and cadaverous fingers.

A slight scent of lemon, lavender, and cigar smoke caught a current of air and drifted into Tony's nostrils, each whiff nudging him toward the edge of nausea. "I know it was you."

"I beg your pardon?"

He'd known vile characters before—especially drill sergeants drunk with power—but compared to Cal Craven, those blowhards were candidates for the next Dalai Lama.

"Is that the way you're going to play it?"

"I can't play anything unless I know what you're talking about."

"How much did you pay the assassin to kill Athena?"

Though skinned in shadows, Craven's face was perfectly placid. "Still don't get you."

Tony had never been in a scrap and hardly a squabble. But he felt different now. A primal instinct had awakened—a burning protective nature, at once surprising and reassuring. "Right. Here's the thing you need to know. If you or any of your goons try to hurt Athena again, I will kill you." He let the threat penetrate. "Did I say that out loud?"

"Yeah, you did."

He squinted to ensure a more perfect read of the club owner. "For the record, what did I say?"

Craven spiked a conman smile. "You'll kill me."

"Good, you understand. I wanted to be sure. Trust me, I'm capable of doing it."

Craven's lips parted before speaking. "Now, let me tell *you* something." He pointed his pinkie and forefinger of his right hand at Tony's heart, both fingers saddled with a ruby ring. "When I set my mind to something, I always get what I want. And you're in my way, bub." Showing the tip of his tongue, Craven swiped it with two fingers, examined a particle of tobacco, and brushed his fingertips clean. "And when a rat's in my way, I crush it." He lingered, his head tilted away, and quoted Tony. "Trust me, I'm capable of doing it."

Craven whispered his right hand under his suit lapel.

In a fury, Tony lunged to his feet, sending his chair skidding backward. He drove the table into Craven's solar plexus, carried him five feet, and pinned him against a concrete column. The candle tumbled to the floor, which, still lit, spat an eerie under-light.

He knew Craven's diaphragm clutched in spasms. Shoving his hand under Craven's jacket, he unholstered the nickel-plated revolver and tucked the pistol under his belt.

Helplessly trapped, Craven panted for stingy spurts of air.

Tony leaned over the table, their faces separated by twelve inches of rancid air. "Relax. You're not going to die. Now that I have your attention, don't come near Athena or me again. That's your first and last warning. Nod if you understand."

Craven nodded, his assent barely visible in the dithering candlelight.

"Your gun is mine. I don't like guns. But if you force me, I'll turn it against you."

Soundlessly working his mouth, Craven's racked expression earned little sympathy.

"I know you want to say something, but we'll leave that for another time."

Finding his way in the dark, Tony reached the door, retracted the dead bolt, and cracked it open, which cast a strip of light across Craven's body. Before exiting, Tony turned for a final word. "By the way, you need to look for another singer. Athena doesn't work here anymore."

Once in the sunlight, he shook his head in mockery of his tough-guy performance. Before taking the first step homeward, he patted the handgun and gave his heart a moment to rachet down.

# 34

On his return to Athena's apartment, Tony hoped to avoid the angry woman. Although the boys were absent, their mother stood guard at the window, her hands on her hips. When he passed, he tipped his head and managed a troubled smile.

She responded by slapping her hand over her bicep and thrusting her fist skyward, holding the gesture as if posing for a shock-artist. A master painter would have doubtless captured the flaring rage in her eyes—the look of fear and bigotry.

As soon as Tony entered the apartment, he ached to come clean. He found Athena in bed, under a crocheted throw, rereading *David Copperfield.* "Hi, honey."

"Back so soon?" she asked, keeping her eyes on the page.

"It didn't take long," he said, unable to conceal his anguish.

She laid the book across her lap. "What's going on?"

Neither able nor willing to deceive her quick eye, he sat on the bedside, took her hand, and struggled to find the best words. He circled his fears but fell short of nailing the crux. Part of his turmoil was about Craven but also about his visit with the boys and their angry mother. *Where to begin?* He pinched the bridge of his nose.

"You're scaring me. Whatever it is, we can work it out."

"I had a talk"—he stumbled to get the words out—"with Cal Craven."

"Lord help us."

While pressing her hand, he edged closer. "It's not as bad as you think. Or maybe it is, I don't know."

She pulled herself higher. "What? Tell me what happened."

In a soft, measured rhythm, he explained everything.

When he confessed her sudden retirement from the club, he imagined she would cringe, but she said, "It's about time. In fact, it's long overdue." As her face sombered, she added, "Did you mean it when you said you would kill him?"

His stomach unsettled, he brooded on the question. "Yes. It wouldn't be easy. I have the skill and the motivation"—he laid a hand over his heart—"but there'd be damage to my soul."

Athena slowly dusted her palms. "Explain."

"Life is precious. To end a life is a terrible thing." He fidgeted. "Damn, this is hard. All I know is…neither cleverness nor hard times excuse depravity. Only goodness rules." More for his own sake, he allowed his words to settle. "But that's a decision for someone with a pure heart. A heart like yours."

She threw her arms around him. "I love you so much."

"Even after I told Craven you were through with him?"

As she eased away from their embrace, she stroked his face. "You're sweet. Stupid but sweet."

He puffed out his cheeks. "I'm not sure I like the sound of that."

"Look, you can't bully a bully. His ego won't allow it. He'll double down before giving in. This thing won't get easier. It'll get harder—a lot harder. And it may end ugly."

"Of course, you're right"—he stiffened his expression—"but I won't let him hurt you, whatever the damage to my soul."

"I know you mean that. But there may be more at risk than the health of your soul."

"I'm listening."

She hesitated long enough to smooth the throw that lay over her legs. "Craven's an evil man, and he may get to you or me or both of us. We have to be ready for that possibility."

He detected a curling in his gut. The most important decision of his life was now clear. "I have an idea. You don't have to say anything right away. You can wait a week or a month or even a year. It doesn't matter. Maybe waiting would be better so—"

She gave him a shove. "Will you please get on with it."

"Okay. Here it is. This may sound crazy. It probably *is* crazy—"

"Tony," she scolded.

"Okay." He straightened his back, the words capering to get out, hoping her response would be yes. "I'd like you and me"—the silence was palpable—"to leap to twenty-nineteen."

The alarm clock ticked away the seconds. "It's weird. I know you're from the future—I've always known it—But…"

"But what?"

"But time travel is so fantastic, I never even considered it. I knew you were from the future. My heart told me so, and Isabella confirmed it. But I… I don't know what to say."

Chattering now, he took Athena's hands. "Listen to me. Your piano got me here. It can get us back. I remember exactly what I did when I made the leap. I've gone over it a thousand times. It's burned into my brain. And I can do it again. I know I can."

"But *you* traveled in time. Not both of us."

"I know. I've been thinking about that too. Then it hit me." He seized her arms. "My trumpet came with me. It was sitting on top of the piano."

"So?"

"So, I think that anything—or anyone—that touches the piano will jump forward."

He studied her. At first, she sat huddled as if seeing her bones disassemble in flight, her head tucked under her arm. Then, on a slow accelerando, her body lengthened, and her gaze radiated like a full moon against a darkened sky.

*She sees it now.* "Huh? Huh? Remember, you don't have to decide now. We've got time. We're in no hurry. Besides—"

"Yes!" she said, her feline eyes aglow.

"What?"

Her chest was heaving. "Yes. Let's do it. I'm ready. Let's make the jump."

Although spurred by her excitement, he wanted her to be sure. "Wait. I haven't told you what the future's like."

She raised her eyebrows. "Is it better than now?"

"Eh, yes and no. There are good people and bad people. That part hasn't changed. Sometimes—"

"Are cops still corrupt?" she interrupted, seemingly more intent to dream than reason.

"There are some bad cops—we hear about them in the news—but I believe most try to do the right thing."

"Does racism still exist?"

Too many headlines from 2019 soured his stomach. "Yes, there are still lunatics in the world, but it's not as bad as your time."

"Are there speakeasies?"

"Don't need them. Drinking is legal."

She jerked her head. "Wow. When did that happen?"

"I think it was nineteen thirty-two."

When Athena questioned her place in the new world, whether there would be venues where she could perform, he said, "No question. I have the perfect club for you."

She grinned. "What club is that?"

"The Vanguard in Greenwich Village."

She frowned. "I haven't heard of it."

"That's because it won't open until nineteen thirty-five." As he envisioned Athena in the future, his mind spun out the possibilities. On a brain flash, he smacked his hands. "How would you like to play Carnegie Hall?"

She snickered. "Carnegie Hall. All they play is classical music for rich white people. I'm a black jazz singer. I'd never play there in a million years."

His cheeks dimpled. "Don't be so sure. Louie Armstrong played Carnegie in nineteen forty-seven—I mean *will* play in nineteen forty-seven. It's not out of reach for Athena Cruz, the best torch singer I've ever heard."

Perhaps Athena heard her own music. She rose to her knees and began to sway her hips, her torso, her arms and hands. In the next moment, her rollicking bed-dance ended with a jerk. "Hold on. How expensive is it in the future? Can we afford it?"

It was Tony's time to shine. "Sweetheart, I'm a surgeon. I make a good living. We'll have health insurance and an IRA and—"

"An IR what?"

"An IRA. Individual Retirement Account. It's a nontaxable way of saving money throughout your career."

Feeling embarrassed, she shook her head. "I've never saved money before, not one penny."

"We'll be able to do it in my time." Another happy idea came to mind. "Oh, and get this. We'll even have enough money to jet to England. Imagine, we'll see where Charles Dickens wrote all his masterworks."

"What's a jet?"

He laughed. "A lightning-fast passenger airplane. They can fly six hundred people from New York to London in five hours."

"Uh-uh."

"Oh yes, but that ain't all. Are you ready for this?"

As her eyes widened in childlike anticipation, he looked over both shoulders and whispered, "The United States sent a man to the moon and back in nineteen sixty-nine."

Looking askance at Tony, she said, "Come on. You must think I'm right off the boat. That's one big fat lie, and you know it."

He opened his arms to her. "I kid you not, babe."

She leaped into his embrace. Now both of them were bouncing like toddlers on the rickety bed, the compressed bedsprings twanging their grievances.

"Hold up," he said. "We're going to break this thing."

"Who cares?" she squealed. "We're going to have a brand-new bed. A brand-new everything."

"Yeah, who cares?"

Their bouncing settled into a gentle rocking motion.

"So, are you ready?" he asked.

"'Procrastination is the thief of time, collar him,'" she quoted.

"*Oliver Twist?*"

"*David Copperfield*. But it doesn't matter. What's true is true."

"Translate."

She trailed her fingers down his chest. "Neither one of us will be right all the time. It's human nature to make mistakes. But one thing will *always* be true. We'll be there for each other, no matter the time or place. Bring on your new world. I'm ready."

Although hopeful and certainly tickled by Athena's enthusiasm, there was a rawness in Tony's brain that forecast danger. *We have to be quick about it. Before Craven makes his next move.*

## 35

Later that night, Tony worried about leaving Craven's pistol in the apartment. Who knew when the cops might show unannounced again? Having the gun would be hard to explain. Besides, he didn't want to risk a stint in jail before Athena and he jumped in time. No, tossing the weapon in the Harlem River was the prudent choice.

At four o'clock, he slipped into Zalo's hand-me-down trousers and white long-sleeve dress shirt.

He explained his thinking to Athena, promising to return within the hour.

"Be safe." She grinned. "We've got a lot of planning to do for our ninety-five-year trip."

"I love you."

"Love you, babe."

Tony planned to walk midway onto the Madison Avenue Bridge and drop the revolver and cartridges over the railing.

Contusive clouds from the west spackled an otherwise blissful sky. A storm was on its way, but for now, the heavens were benevolent and ideal for daydreaming about his future with Athena. He chuckled to himself. Maybe they'd have children. They hadn't talked about that, but why not? With Athena's beauty and intelligence, they'd be sensational.

He recalled his first leap. It had taken him several hours to recover, although Athena's knockout punch may have thwarted a quick recovery. *Would the trip be harder on Athena?* He shook his head. *Probably not. She's a powerhouse. Is there a risk? Sure, there's always a risk. But isn't a new life safe from harm worth the gamble?*

As he considered the possibilities, he sensed someone trailed him. He turned. There were children, a couple here and there, but nothing seemed extraordinary. *Just jittery after that sit-down with Craven. Besides, the scumbag wouldn't have the nerve to face me on the street.*

Still, when he turned onto East 138th Street, a feeling of dread gnawed at him as if an insect skittered across the back of his neck.

A convertible roadster cruised by so leisurely he alarmed. It was nothing—a guy in his new car out for a spin in the late afternoon air.

*Relax. You're as jumpy as a cat.*

*Bam.*

A Model T touring car jumped the sidewalk curb and cut him off. When the passenger door slung open, Tony slammed into the door's edge. A tall man leaped out. *Damn. Sergeant Gorski.*

"Hold on there. Where you going so fast, college boy?" Gorski said.

Looking to his left, Tony expected to see Klinger in the driver's seat. *No one. He must be circling the Ford.*

"Look at me," Gorski demanded.

Tony turned to face the sergeant when a thunderclap sundered day into night.

***

Because time ticked to a stop, Tony could not judge how long he'd been out. His head pulsated like a jellyfish. He tried to move his hands. Impossible. They were tied behind his back. He was roped across his chest, legs, arms, and feet.

As he struggled to open his eyes, he made out a gray surface like a featureless slate sky. Concrete, he guessed. A pair of shoes. *Are they mine?* When he tried flexing his toes, nothing moved.

"Douse him," someone said.

The voice registered. *Shit, it's Craven. It all comes down to this.*

Someone emptied a bucket of water over Tony's head.

It helped.

As his eyelids raised, a hazy world unveiled. He was lashed to a straight-backed chair, Craven standing in front of him with one foot on a three-legged stool, his hand draped over his knee. Although he'd shed the suit jacket, he looked as steam-pressed as ever. He wore the pistol harness, which holstered the pearl-handled .32. The fat lieutenant stood to Tony's right, while the spindly sergeant lurched at his left, the empty water bucket still dangling from his hand.

As his throbbing head picked up tempo, Tony said, "Officer Klinger, what the hell did you hit me with?"

"Your standard two-foot nightstick. But I do know how to put some snap on it."

"That's a fact."

Klinger snickered.

"So, what's the game, and what're the limits?" Tony asked. It was a stupid gumshoe-detective wisecrack, one he immediately regretted.

Craven leaned closer to his face. "Here's the thing. There are no limits in this game."

Snagging the stool, the club owner swung the three-legged chair between his legs and under his butt. "It's simple really. The game is you give me whatever I want, and you walk. Or you play it stubborn, and you die—along with everyone else you love."

Although Tony's head still simmered, he tested the ropes biting into his chest, wrists, and ankles. They gripped like steel bands. *Someone had been one hell of a Boy Scout. Wait a minute. Did they have scouts in 1924? Must have. Teddy Roosevelt was a big scouting fan. When was he president? Around the turn of the century, right? Or was it later?*

His mind was boggling, and he knew it. *Have to keep focused.* His eyes flitted. *Looks like a warehouse. Was that the wail of a tugboat? Could be the Hudson River.*

They were encircled by stacks of crates and barrels. Three drop-ceiling lights yielded meek tendrils of amber glow. Despite the monitor roof windows, most of the warehouse perimeter was encased in hard shadows.

"All right," Tony said. "What do you want?"

Seemingly relaxed, Craven had his arms folded and his legs crossed. His tone was casual, but his words stinging. "I don't know where you come from. I don't rightly care. It makes no matter if your mama was a whore and your papa a drunk. That don't do me no mind. All I care about is business. And that's all these good officers care about. Am I right?"

"That's right," Klinger and Gorski said.

Uncrossing his legs, Craven drew a handkerchief from his back pocket and dabbed his mouth. "Now, I admit, I let this whole thing get personal. Fact is I don't like being disrespected—not from you and certainly not from no Jane, no matter how swell she looks."

Although his mind flailed in murky waters, he had to stay awake. He made conversation. "How did I disrespect you?"

"You're white, ain't you?"

"Yeah."

"And Athena is colored."

"Your point is?"

"That's disrespectful. A colored girl belongs with her kind. You get me?"

"No, I don't get you."

The exchange didn't help matters. Craven's words were edgy, caustic, and, beneath a thin facade of self-control, seething. He was in no mood to negotiate.

"It don't matter. The point is I let it get personal. I wanted you dead. Then I thought, no, I want *Athena* dead. That way I get the respect I deserve, and you get nothing but misery. Kind of poetic, right?"

"It didn't work out the way you wanted."

"No. But you did me a service. You got me thinking. I asked myself, 'Why flush good money down the crapper? That's not good business.'" Leaning into Tony's face, Craven jutted his jaw, which revealed a row of overlapping lower teeth with yellow ridges and valleys. "And you're getting in the way of my business."

While recovering from Craven's breath, Tony dropped his gaze to the pearl-handled pistol.

The club owner stood tall and pulled the revolver from its holster. "I'm so rude. I forgot to thank you for taking care of my Colt .32. She's a beauty, don't you think?" He waved the pistol about as if directing traffic.

Tony sat transfixed, unflinching, barely allowing his heart to beat.

"But don't let her beauty fool you. She can blow a nasty hole in your head. They'll be finding brain chips from here to Hoboken."

Time stopped as Craven pressed the cold muzzle against Tony's forehead. Then, on a slow growl, he straightened his back and holstered the Colt. "You see what you've done? You got me all bothered. Where was I?" He turned to Klinger, who answered Craven's questioning eyes with a how-should-I-know shrug. "Oh yeah, I was talking about business. So, here's what I propose. I want to invest in Athena. She's a fine piano player and a damn good singer. I think she's going to be a big star. Maybe even the movies someday. You never know. Besides, she's got one terrific ass, as I'm sure you know firsthand."

Twisting his wrists under the ropes only resulted in ripping his flesh.

The club owner continued. "She'll sign an exclusive contract with me. Everything she does goes through me. I'll promote her and make sure she gets good work. Whether she sings, tinkles the piano, or entertains important people like, say, the commissioner of police"—he turned to the cops and shared a snarky laugh—"I'll get sixty percent of her dough."

Heart quickening, Tony's blood sloshed through his veins and into his brain where his rancor stewed. "In other words, you want to be her pimp."

As if dodging jabs, Craven's head bobbled while his right eye twitched. Stepping close to Tony, he slapped him hard across both cheeks. He grabbed the scruff of Tony's shirt. "I don't like that word. Don't be using that word with me or anywhere near me."

He straightened his frame, placed his hands over his kidneys, and arched his back, which sounded the sharp *snick* of vertebrae. Retrieving a handkerchief from his back pocket, he dabbed his forehead as if blotting a tender wound. "So now that we understand each other, what do you think of my idea?"

On searching the inside of his mouth with his tongue, Tony tasted blood. "You're one malodorous piece of shit."

The club owner's face caved as if emotionally wounded. "He thinks I'm malodorous."

"He's a college boy," the lieutenant said with a smirk.

Craven hitched his head toward his captive.

On a pompous, humorless grin, Klinger edged toward Tony's right as he slipped out the nightstick from his belt.

Tony tracked the cop until he vanished behind him.

There was a whiff of displaced air as the baton landed with a heavy *thwack*—followed by a deep, troubled sleep.

# 36

Later that evening, Athena battered her brother's door. When there was no immediate response, she pounded again.

"Okay, okay, I'm coming," Zalo said from inside the apartment.

"It's me," Athena shrieked. "Please, open up."

When Zalo opened the door, he was shoeless and bare-chested. Bursting into the room, Athena's eyes loomed large and unfocused, her lids pinned spring-taut. She clutched her hair and rocked herself. "Tony's in trouble. Right now."

Although Zalo embraced her, she refused to be consoled and pushed him away with both hands.

"You don't understand. Craven'll kill him." She rubbed her forehead as if expunging the images. "Maybe he's killed him already. He wants him dead. I know he wants him dead."

Her words gushed, one phrase spilling into the next until her meaning pooled into oblivion.

Zalo held her face with both hands. "Look at me."

As if searching for the meaning of life, her tear-blurred eyes gazed into space.

He shook her with enough force to rattle her senses. "Thena, look at me! Don't think. Look at me!"

Awakened, she peered into her brother's eyes.

"Now, tell me what's happened. I can't help you if you don't talk to me."

In a cacophony of words, images, and emotions, she unraveled the events of the day.

Zalo let her speak without interruption. When he understood, he asked, "Okay. What time is it?"

"It's seven thirty. He said he'd be home by five."

In a single move, he snatched the shirt draped over the rocker and slipped it on. "We can't do this alone."

A voice drifted in from the bedroom. "That's why I'm coming."

Athena's spun, her body in a twist of knots. "Who's that?"

"I'm sorry. I didn't mean to scare you."

Athena discovered the face and silhouette of Johnny Mangum leaning against the bedroom door casing, wearing a silk wraparound robe that clung to the swell of her hips and breasts. With her hair down and her arms folded, she dazzled with an aura of contentment and self-assurance.

Even in her frenzied state, Athena dropped her jaw and gaped at her brother.

"What?" Zalo asked. "You're the only one allowed to get some sugar?"

Athena rushed into Johnny's arms. "You don't know how glad I am to see you. You're the person I need to dig out of this…"

"Helluva mess?" Johnny offered.

Athena answered with a worrisome scowl.

"She's the right person, all right," Zalo added, moving to the two women and kissing Johnny on the cheek. "She's one kick-ass dame."

"Oh, you say the nicest things," Johnny said, squeezing his cheeks with one hand, "but we've got work to do. Let's find Athena's man."

Johnny threw on a sweater, a pair of checkered wool knickers, and knee-high socks, which at once rendered her boyish, capable, and scandalous.

Lacing his shoes, Zalo said, "We've got two things to do. First, we have to find out where Tony is. Second, we have to get more help."

"What kind of help?" Athena asked.

"I'll explain on the way."

"Where're we going?"

"To The Nest," Zalo said. "If anybody knows where Tony can be found, it's Buddy."

"That's right," Athena said. "Why didn't I think of that?"

"Because your brain's on fire."

The Nest was a five-minute sprint away. All three were strong runners, but Athena's passion pushed her to the lead with long athletic strides. By the time they arrived at the club, the twilight had already hardened, and a storm brewed from the west under the cowl of night.

As usual, Buddy guarded the front door. Jolted by the torment in Athena's eyes, he ignored the long line of people waiting to enter. "What? What's going on?"

Holding the stitch that crimped her side, Athena stumbled over her words. "B-Buddy, you... We need your help."

"I do anything you want, Missy."

"Is Craven here?"

"No, he ain't."

With her hand raised to catch her breath, Athena said, "We think he kidnapped Tony, and we have to find him before something awful happens. Do you know where he might be?"

Buddy pounded his fist into his palm and leaned into Athena's ear. "I know exactly where he at," he whispered. "At the harbor warehouse where he keep all the booze. Has to be."

With a snap of her fingers, Athena kissed Buddy on the cheek, spurring him to examine his shoelaces.

Zalo dug into his pocket, retrieved a nickel, then escaped into the club while Athena worked at boot-tapping a hole in the concrete. When he returned, his eyes dazzled.

"We can't bust into the warehouse without backup," Zalo said. "He's sure to have thugs with him, maybe even dirty cops. So, I got us some help."

Talking around a lump that had formed in her throat, Athena asked, "Who... who'd you get?"

Pride overtook Zalo's face. "New York City's finest police officer, Samuel James Battle."

Although Athena had never met Samuel, she knew his reputation as a man of honor. "Yes, he's perfect."

"And I told him to bring an extra gun for me."

"Will he do it?"

"He said he'd think about it."

Zalo turned to Buddy. "Big man, do you have a baseball bat in there?" he asked, tilting his head toward the club.

Before the bouncer could answer, Johnny asked, "Do you have two?"

A wave of light brightened Buddy's face. "I sure enough does."

When he turned to enter The Nest, Athena snagged his arm with both hands. "Buddy, are you planning on coming with us?"

He sobered his regard. "Course I is."

"But what about your job?"

He ripped off the despised skimmer that read WHERE ALL THE BIRDIES GO TWEET, TWEET, TWEET, turned it upside down, and punched his fist through the crown. His mouth turned down into grit and moxie. "I don't work here no more."

For the last time, he slipped through the crowd to enter The Nest. When he returned, he gripped two baseball bats—one for Miss Johnny, one for himself.

"Hey, when do we get in?" a young man shouted from the front of the line.

Buddy turned and waved him off. "Do what you want."

Hunching his shoulders, the man barged into the club, followed by a stream of other patrons.

Five minutes later, a police car shimmied to a stop in front of the club. It was a windowless four-door touring car with a canvas top. Behind the wheel sat Samuel Battle in full police uniform.

A cold, menacing wind blew as the starry sky flickered out.

# 37

Tony revived, not all at once but in broken bits of awareness. With a physician's instincts, he counted the return of his senses. Feeling was the first faculty to return, most incessant the throbbing at the lower-left cerebral hemisphere. He placed the injury over the occipital lobe. Naming the lobe was a good sign. *I must be alive.*

The acrid tang of Craven's cigar and the rank scent of his cologne evidenced the second and third senses. *Sickening but encouraging.* Now, he heard the paradiddle of rain on the warehouse roof, which verified his fourth sense. *At least I'm not deaf.*

But the fifth sense, the miracle of sight, lagged. Even with eyes shut, he should have detected a faint penumbra of light through his translucent eyelids, but there was none. Maybe it was self-preservation. Maybe the brain took mercy and blurred a malevolent world to grant his eyes time to heal. It could be that. Or it could be the occipital lobe was hemorrhaging, and he was blind. To have eyes without vision tormented him like a dream that spiraled on a mindless question. It was simple. He was either blind or sighted. Replaying the question was insane.

His eyelids unsealed. Thank god, he could make out a dappling of dim radiance and murky shadows, but the color had bled out. He'd stepped into a film-noir stage with shadowy strands of ashen light, which fell over the eyes of the actors. Lifting his head, he gaped at Klinger's face. It was shrouded in hues of gray.

The nightmare was real. He was color-blind.

Something else was different. His arms were no longer tied behind his back. Maybe he was freed. *Hardly.* His chest and ankles were still bound. But his hands were now lashed to the arms of the chair, palms up. *What the hell is that about?*

"He's awake," Klinger said.

Craven glided into Tony's line of sight, the dandy's face painted in a darker spectrum of grays. "Did you enjoy your nap?"

Klinger expelled an unvocalized laugh.

Snatching the three-legged stool, Craven sat and crossed his legs like a woman. "I made a decision while you were asleep. I think we've been going about this all wrong."

As he compressed his eyelids, Tony hoped color would tint Craven's face the way early photographers brushed in pigment over a black and white portrait. *No chance.*

"You see," Craven continued, "I think you're too tense. Don't you think he looks tense, Lieutenant?"

"Tighter than a barrel of booze," Klinger said.

"Like I thought." Craven adopted a sarcastic, saccharine tone. "You see, trumpet man, when you're relaxed, you're agreeable."

"I can do that," Tony said, his words reverberating in his skull like loose change clinking in an echo chamber.

"Good," he said. "Gorski, give me the kit."

The sergeant lifted what looked like a cigar tin. "Got it right here."

Craven stood, flipped the lid open, and fished out a lighter, which he passed to Klinger. Drawing out and uncorking a brown-tinted vial, he tapped a level of white powder into a tablespoon. Now, to Tony's muddled mind, the cops standing alongside Craven appeared as two unhallowed acolytes assisting the last rites.

"Heroin," Tony said as if announcing his death sentence.

Craven cut a thin smile as sharp as the arched blade of a mezzaluna. "Well, it ain't sugar."

Two beads of sweat chased each other down the nape of Tony's neck and troughed into his spinal spillway.

He disliked needles, but, far worse, he despised being out of control, the victim of a madman's caprice. When he moved freely, he could always wrangle a solution. But this was different. His hands twitched, powerless under the knotted cords. "You don't have to do this."

"Oh, I think we do," Craven said. "Otherwise, you ain't going to listen."

"I'm listening."

"Dry up." He glanced at the bony cop. "Gorski, cut open his shirt sleeve."

Setting the open cigar tin on the stool, the sergeant fished out a folding knife from his pocket, opened the blade, and slit Tony's right sleeve from the elbow to the cuff. He pressed too hard and left a two-inch slice of blood on the captive's forearm. "Sorry about that, old man."

A familiar nightmare invaded Tony's consciousness. Twelve years old. A night when his drunken father missed a stoop tread, split open his chin, and crawled through the front door on his hands and knees. Swiping his muzzle with the back of his hand, which only smeared the blood across his jaw, he dragged into the apartment, retched, and vomited on the flowered living-room carpet. Watching, first from his bedroom window, then from his open door that framed the living room, he made a pledge. "I swear to god, I'll never be like him." The promise was sacred. He'd never be enslaved by madness. He'd be a man of discipline and restraint. But now, stripped of control, he was skewered like a pig on a spit. An opioid trip was as hideous to him as losing the gift of color.

Craven handed the loaded spoon to the lieutenant. "Take this. Fire it up."

Reveling in the unholy sacrament, Klinger bared his teeth as he flicked open the lighter, ignited the wick, and set the flame below the spoon's bowl.

Well versed, Craven slapped the inside of Tony's elbow. "Good veins. This is going to be nice and easy." He turned to the cigar tin and picked out a glass-barreled syringe by the tips of his thumb and middle finger—a gesture too delicate, too refined for the infamy to come.

Even in black and white, the syringe looked unclean.

Once cooked, Craven directed the lieutenant. "Hold the spoon steady."

"Yes, sir."

Setting the needle to the spoon, Craven extended the plunger. "Think of this as a persuader." He held the syringe to the light and ejected a thin line of the drug. "Give me what I want, or we'll do this all week long until you're hooked and begging for another hit."

"Do what you—"

Cutting him off, Craven sounded hellishly mordant. "Enjoy the ride, fucker."

Tony considered his options. *Who am I kidding? I have no options. I'm tied to this damn chair and surrounded by three thugs. Wait it out. Wake up. Then lie like hell to get free.*

"Hold him down," Craven told the officers.

When the cops pinned his arms, he didn't resist—not that resistance was possible.

He found Tony's artery on the first try and emptied the syringe.

His first reaction was a ripping urge to vomit. He gagged but pushed against the spastic contractions. In less than five minutes, a deep and languid heaviness migrated to every extremity. Drifting into a netherworld of half-sleep, half-wakefulness, all worries vanished. Only bliss remained.

As his eyes closed, he floated into a hypnagogic state. He could see Athena's silhouette sprinting toward him—not in a summer meadow with a low-hanging sun and a rolling sea of wildflowers but against a midnight backdrop relieved by roiling wafts of smoke.

Not a love scene. A vision of rescue. Athena, Zalo, Buddy, and a towering black man in a policeman's uniform bounded four abreast. *Was that Zalo's mentor, Samuel Battle?* They charged ahead like the four horsemen, their breath steady, their eyes shining and unwavering.

They raced to his rescue. He was sure of it. He only had to hold on…if he could.

# 38

Athena liked the way Battle took charge. His size carried a physical authority while being the first black New York City policeman lent a *moral* authority. Even though he gentled his tone, an undercurrent of confidence fortified his words.

Battle spotted Zalo as soon as he pulled in alongside the curb at The Nest. "Get in, y'all. We got work to do."

"Yes, sir," Zalo said, piling in the back seat with Johnny on his left and Athena on his right.

Buddy joined Battle in the front seat. Because the Model T cabin set inside the fenders, the fit crimped the broad-shouldered men. Buddy shrugged off his brass-buttoned doorman's coat and placed it on his lap.

Zalo made the introductions.

"Glad to meet y'all," Battle said but with a distinct trace of urgency. "Now, where're we going?"

"Chelsea Piers," Buddy said.

"Which one?"

"Pier Fifty-Nine at the end of Seventeenth."

As Battle shifted the Model T into gear and juddered off, a long thunderclap rumbled over New Jersey like a distant doomsday drum roll. He drove toward the Hudson River, then turned south. After a while, he shook his head. "I don't like this. This is outside my precinct."

"Is that a problem?" Athena asked without bothering to conceal her angst.

"It doesn't help, but we've got no choice." The policeman fingered the throttle lever. "We may get a break. I have connections with the precinct that covers the waterfront. I worked there before assigned to the Thirty-Eighth."

"I'm sure glad you're helping us," Athena said. "I don't know what I'd do if anything happened to Tony. He's—"

When her voice broke up, Battle came to her rescue. "Don't worry. We'll do everything we can. I wish I had another officer from the department, but, frankly, there's no one I can trust. I hate to say it, but that's the way it is."

As they pulled into the pier, Battle turned off his headlights. He pointed out a patrol car from the Thirty-Eighth Precinct parked near the front door of a warehouse that ran the length of the pier.

The warehouse was like all functional buildings. Uninspired. It had length, width, and height. However, to its credit, it did feature a band of high, narrow windows that encircled the gently pitched monitor roof.

They could see a tugboat tied to the end of the pier, the bridge bathed in a hazy golden bloom. Beyond, the lights from Hoboken piers and tenements danced across the Hudson River like fireflies against a tarry sky.

Turning his body sideways, Battle faced the team. "They're here," he whispered. "Now listen. I'll take a look around the entire warehouse. Then, I'll come back and tell you the plan." What he said next was punctuated with space between every word or two. "Don't move from this car until I get back. Is that clear?"

No one said a word.

"Is that clear?" he repeated, his whisper more strident.

Everyone murmured assent.

"You're our leader," Zalo added.

"Good. Don't talk unless you have to and then in a whisper."

With a brass-encased flashlight in hand, Battle paced the entire perimeter of the building.

Upon his return, he reported. "There's one three-foot and one twelve-foot door on each end." He put his forefinger to his lips. "I'm going to check out the front door."

The police officer moved to the three-foot east door and pressed his ear to the doorjamb. After cranking the door handle and confirming it was locked, he drew a picklock from his coat pocket and jimmied the keyway. He cracked the door open, peered inside, and eased the door closed. Soft-stepping to the car, he stood on the windowless passenger side next to Buddy in the front seat and Athena directly behind.

"There are—"

"Is he alive?" Athena interrupted.

He stepped back to Athena and placed his hand on her shoulder. "I could make out voices, but that's all." Although he was cool and measured, compassion tendered his eyes. "Right now, I don't know if he's dead or alive. That's what we're here to find out."

"Yes," she said, repressing an urge to sob. To be of any value she had to tame her emotions.

"I know," Battle said, squeezing her shoulder. "Please, we have to press on."

She squeezed her eyes shut, letting the expression speak for her.

On a deep breath, Battle continued. "Zalo, I want you to guard the front door. That's how they came in, and if they make a run for it, they may try to exit by the same route." He gave Zalo his nightstick. "Use it if you have to."

"Only a billy club?"

"That's all you need. It's the safest way."

"Okay," Zalo said with a noted mix of obedience and disappointment.

Turning to Johnny, Battle said, "Zalo has already told me about you. I know you can handle yourself"—the couple exchanged a private smile—"so I'm placing you at the *back* door, but only as an observer. I don't want you in the line of fire. You'll find a lot of crates and heavy equipment to hide behind."

"I've got a bat," Johnny said, slapping the potential cudgel into the palm of her hand.

"I see that, but I want you safe. You're a witness, not a cop. Keep hidden. Clear?"

"Yes."

When Battle turned to Athena, her eyes steadied. "I think you're too close to this. I want you and Buddy to stay in the car."

All the sweetness and charm dropped out of her face. "That's not going to happen."

"What do you mean?"

"I'm not staying in the car. I can be useful."

The policeman jagged his brow. "How's that?"

She lengthened her torso. "I'm not a child. I know when men want me, and Craven wants me badly. He may have tried to kill me, but if he thinks he can have me for his own—no strings attached—we can play on that, and no one'll be hurt." She locked onto Battle's eyes. "I'm going in."

"I don't like this idea. It's too dangerous." Snapping off his peaked cap, he swiped the sweat from his forehead with his coat sleeve. "All right. But I want you to stay behind me. And I want you to wear this." He unlaced an ankle holster that held a Remington double-barreled .41 caliber derringer.

With eyes locked on the holster, the Russian assassin flashed before Athena's eyes, his fingers slipping from the rooftop ladder, his arms and legs mauling the sky, the awful smack of his head hitting concrete, and the deep-red blood oozing from his shattered skull. The scene had haunted her from the start. She now understood what Tony meant when he spoke of "damage to the soul."

"I don't want to shoot anyone."

"Neither do I, but that's the price of admission." Battle moved a step closer. "Listen. Don't shoot unless your life or the life of one of us is at risk. Now, lace it up or stay in the car. Your choice."

In that instant, Tony's words echoed. *Only goodness rules.* She extended her open hand.

Samuel gave her the holstered derringer. "Are you right-handed?"

"Yes."

"Lace the holster to the inside of your left leg."

"Why?"

"Watch this." He knelt alongside the car with his right knee on the ground, his left foot planted, and emulated drawing the pistol from the inside of his left ankle. It was a natural move.

"I get it." Although a large holster, it laced snugly over her tall boots. Once attached, she drew the derringer. "How does this thing work?"

Taking the gun in hand, Battle flipped the release lever forward and raised the barrel over its hinge. He extracted both cartridges, closed the barrel, and handed the unloaded derringer to Athena. "Now, pull the trigger and see what happens."

She squeezed the lever. Nothing. "It doesn't shoot."

"That's right. It has to be manually cocked. Pull back on the hammer."

Tugging on the hammer with both thumbs, the derringer clicked, fully cocked. "Got it."

"You have to do the same thing to discharge the second cartridge. Understood?"

"Yes."

After reloading the handgun, he returned it to Athena and pivoted to the team of liberators. "Are we ready?"

"Mr. Battle," Buddy said. "Is Miss Athena going in?"

The officer scowled. "You heard what she said. It looks like she is."

Although he spoke softly, apologetically, his conviction was clear. "If she going in, I'm going in. I'm here to keep her from getting hurt."

Athena could see the operation was becoming complicated and, consequently, more dangerous. It clearly unsettled Battle, but she kept her thoughts to herself.

The officer stared a long time at the bouncer, and, atypically, Buddy held his gaze. "Damn, I don't like this. It breaks all the rules." Buddy didn't twitch, hardly breathed. "Okay. But if there's shooting, I'm in charge."

Although silent, Buddy nodded.

Sliding forward in the back seat, Athena placed both hands on Buddy's shoulders and whispered in his ear. "I love you, Buddy."

He opened his mouth and closed it again.

"What is it?"

Shaking his head, he ducked away.

Battle turned to Johnny. "You'll go first. Find a good hiding place near the back door, and be quiet about it. We'll give you two minutes to get set." Circling to Zalo, he said, "You're the front-door guard."

"Right."

"Buddy and Athena, you stay behind me. The warehouse is dark with lots of crates and barrels for good cover. Ready?"

Everyone nodded, their solemnity captured by a flash of lightning over the Hudson Harbor.

# 39

Rain spattered as the team slipped silently from the Model T. Battle pointed at Johnny, then in the direction of the back door. Johnny responded by winking at Zalo, turning with spirit, and edging into the sludge of night.

Battle then eased to the front door and placed a hand over Zalo's heart. "Let's do this," he whispered.

Rolling his shoulders back, Zalo struck a boxer's pose.

Finally, Battle squared off on Athena and Buddy. Placing both palms forward and chest high, one behind the other, he indicated they were to follow him.

They gave him a thumbs-up sign.

After unsealing the door, the policeman followed a winding path of crates at the back of the warehouse. Over his shoulder he signaled Athena and Buddy to join him, which they safely executed, all three now crouched behind two side-by-side double-stacked crates.

They listened to Craven and the cops.

"How much did you give him?" Klinger asked.

"Enough to keep him happy for the rest of the night," Craven said.

"You're sure he's not dead?"

"No, he's in dreamland."

Athena thrilled, every nerve ending bristling. *Tony's alive.* She placed her hands over Buddy's ears and, eyes welling, kissed him on the cheek. *He's alive*, she mouthed.

Both beaming with equal fervor, Buddy took Athena's hand, kissed it, and pressed it over his heart.

Battle turned to Athena and Buddy. "Stay here," he whispered. "I'll try talking to them."

Pushing to his feet, Battle unsnapped the strap that fell over the hammer of his Smith and Wesson .38 revolver. He unholstered the gun, held it with both hands against his chest, and stepped to the side of the two crates that towered above him.

"Police!" Battle bellowed. "Hands up."

Craven and the cops craned their heads toward the sound of the booming voice. Klinger raced for cover on Battle's right while Gorski dove behind a crate on Battle's left. Meanwhile, Craven drew his handgun, fell to his knees behind Tony, and jammed the barrel under the captive's chin.

Falling back, Battle leaned sideways against the stack of crates. "It doesn't have to be like this," he shouted. "No one's been hurt. Don't make it any worse."

"Battle, is that you?" Klinger bellowed.

"Yes, sir."

"What the hell are you doing here? This don't involve you."

"It involves me now."

"We can work this out. If you want a piece of the action, we can cut you in."

"I don't like the smell of that."

***

Crabbing his way to the front exit, Gorski bolted for the open door, burst into the night, and was met in the chest by the blunt end of Zalo's nightstick. Although the blow dropped him to his knees, he managed to lift his pistol and point it at Zalo.

"Back off."

Zalo retreated a step.

Gorski flinched from a poke in the center of his back.

"Yoo-hoo," Johnny said.

When Gorski turned his head, his arm followed, whereupon Johnny pounded his gun hand with the Louisville Slugger, pitching the revolver onto the deck. Jumping forward, Zalo kicked the gun to the side as Johnny's second blow fell hard over Gorski's shoulder, driving him facedown.

Zalo snagged the gun and held it on Gorski. "Stay right where you are." Eyes trained on the cop, he told Johnny, "Get his handcuffs and cuff him. Make them snug."

With Gorski pinioned, Zalo turned to Johnny and kissed her. He held her at arm's length to take in her beauty—her hair and face bejeweled by raindrops. "I'm never giving you up."

"Not unless you want a taste of this," she said, slapping the bat into her palm.

With a spank to her backside, Zalo said, "I want you when this is over." After making a hungry growling sound, he added, "But we need eyes on both doors. Back to your post, babe."

*** 

Convinced her time had come, Athena stood, shook out her hands, and stepped into the open. "I know what you want, Craven."

"Get back," Battle whispered.

She dragged a hand through her hair. "I'll give you whatever you want. You want to be my man, you've got it. Just let Tony go."

"I don't believe you."

When she took two more steps, Craven panned the gun in her direction. "I could take you out right now with—"

"—a single shot, but you won't."

"Why's that?"

Although his sinister inflection made her doubt her wisdom, she said, "Because it's too easy and unripened. Deprived of torment and play." She took another step forward.

"That's close enough."

To ease his mind, she raised both palms. "That's fine. I want you to be happy. Tell me what you want, and you have it."

Sensing movement at her left, she risked a glance. It was Battle, frantically waving her away. She looked back at Craven, who chased the direction of her glimpse.

Battle stepped into the light, his pistol pointed at Craven's head. "Drop it," he shouted.

In a single move, Craven whirled and fired a shot.

The blast pitched Battle against a crate. At once, his gun slipped out of his hand and hit the concrete with a *clack*. He slumped to the floor...dead still.

Athena bellowed. *"Samuel."* She took a step toward Battle but stopped when she heard a shuffle in the darkness at her right. Spinning around, she spotted Klinger on an even plane with her.

As a blaze of lightning flared the monitor windows, she sighted the long foreshadow of Klinger's extended arm. She traced the shadow to the physical barrel of the policeman's revolver.

Bat in hand, Buddy lunged forward and placed himself between Athena and Klinger's pistol. The first bullet nicked his right temple, sending the bat clattering to the floor. The second bullet ripped through his side.

Although Athena screamed at Buddy to stop, the big man staggered toward Klinger.

"Go down," the cop howled as he shot again.

The third bullet tore into Buddy's gut. Now, two patches of blood swelled into each other, turning the bottom half of his white shirt an unholy crimson.

"Buddy, no!" she wailed.

The big man lurched forward, his arms outstretched, his hands scrabbling the air.

In unison with booming tolls of thunder, Klinger shot three times.

Buddy fell to his knees, his lifeless arms dangling like sad tresses of Spanish moss. Blood pooled everywhere. His body twisted, his head wrenched, his eyes searched for Athena. On finding her, he let go and collapsed, contorted and crumpled, onto his side.

Racing to Buddy, Athena rolled him onto his back and knelt alongside his bloodstained torso. Tears were in her cry. "Don't go, Buddy, don't go." She held his face in her hands and pleaded for some miracle of life.

When Buddy parted his lips to speak, Athena placed a light hand on his chest, arched over his body, and lowered her ear to his mouth. "What, Buddy? What is it?" she asked, her sobs ragged, her tears stinging.

He fumbled for her hand, found it, and wrapped his mighty mitt around her fingers. "I... I loves ya."

Thunderbolts cannonaded over the warehouse, burst through the narrow bank of overhead windows, and illuminated Buddy's last, endearing smile saved for Athena.

Buddy Jefferson was gone.

Tears spilling, Athena slumped back onto her heels and rested her cheek on his silent chest.

"You've caused me enough grief," Klinger said from the shadows.

Looking up, she faced the lieutenant, now a step closer. He pointed the gun at her head and pulled the trigger.

A hollow click.

She uncoiled her body, and, with her right knee still rooted, stepped forward and planted her left foot. Drawing the derringer, she cocked the hammer with both thumbs.

"What're you going to do with that?" Klinger mocked. "It takes a special kind of person"—he extracted a cartridge from his belt but fumbled it—"to be a killer." Drawing a second cartridge from his belt, he hammered it home into a chamber, closed the cylinder, and took a single step forward. One more stride and he'd be able to snatch the derringer and turn it on her.

White-knuckling the handgun to keep it steady, Athena hurled the words at him. "Not another step."

"Go ahead, shoot me. Make me bleed—if you have the stomach for it." In one move, he lifted his revolver and pulled the trigger. It *clicked*—the sound of a firing pin striking an empty chamber.

With eyes closed, Athena squeezed the trigger.

The bullet punctured Klinger's chest, throwing him to his knees as if impelled by prayer but without a penitent heart. His revolver slipped from his grip.

Nearly blinded by fury and grief, she again cocked the Remington, stood, and stepped over Buddy's legs that separated her from Klinger.

The cop teetered on his knees, glugging for air in walleyed frenzy. "I'll be goddamned."

"Exactly," Athena said as she jammed the derringer into the fat man's skull. For five seconds, she considered her next move. She watched as his eyes rolled up, showing mostly white.

Expressionless, she pointed the barrel straight up and uncocked the hammer.

Klinger fell dead, his face lodged between Buddy's knees.

Sickened that the cop and Buddy lay intertwined, she holstered the derringer, straddled Klinger's shoulders, bent over to lace her fingers under his jaw, and swiveled him to one side.

Trembling in shock, she returned to Buddy's side. His eyes were open but spiritless. She feathered her fingertips down his eyelids, closing them for eternity. Hot tears streaming, she leaned over and kissed both eyelids. "Good night, my sweet prince."

Anger-riddled, she drew the derringer from its holster and turned to face Craven.

# 40

Craven scowled as he pulled a nine-inch dagger from his boot and cut through the ropes binding Tony's feet, hands, and chest. Sheathing the knife, he drew his revolver and hoisted his hostage from the chair. Although his prey was still delirious, Tony's eyes began to animate. The captive managed to shuffle his feet, which eased Craven's task.

\*\*\*

All the shooting drew Zalo into the warehouse. Even before he got his bearings, he heard Johnny's frenzied call and dashed back through the door into the rain-veiled night. With a pounding heart, he searched all directions and located Johnny running full speed from the west end of the pier.

Zalo sprinted toward her. "Are you okay?"

"Yes, but the bull escaped."

He scanned the length of the pier over Johnny's shoulder.

"No. That way," she said, pointing east.

Spinning to face the terminus of West Seventeenth Street, Zalo squinted into the murk, at first saw nothing but then spotted a shadowy figure. It was Gorski. He was sure of it. The cop scurried like a crippled bird toward the city lights, his arms still cuffed behind his back.

"We've got to get him before he stops a car." Zalo sprinted toward the reeling policeman, Johnny following a few strides behind.

\*\*\*

"Stop," Craven warned Athena as he shambled toward the back door with Tony as his shield. "I'll shoot your goddamned lover."

"You shoot him, and I'll shoot you"—the speed of her retort provoked a smirk from Craven—"because I've already killed once. I can kill again."

Straggling backward with Tony in tow, Craven opened the door and trudged into the storm, the rain slanted in sheets. He half-shuffled, half-dragged his hostage toward the end of the pier, keeping his eye on the warehouse door. When Athena's head appeared, he shot, but his aim was wide, the bullet zinging into the doorframe as she ducked into the warehouse. Roused by the blast, Tony squirmed under his captor's clutch.

As Craven neared the tugboat, he shot again at the warehouse door and dropped Tony onto the pier deck. He unraveled one line from the tugboat's bow, a second from its stern. Scrambling now, he jumped on board, scaled the bridge ladder, and barged into the wheelhouse.

He faced a gnarled old man sprawled in a captain's chair, guzzling a long draft of whiskey straight from the bottle, oblivious to all the gunplay.

Everything about the blowsy, untidy captain was gray. His beard, his thick drooping mustachio, and now his complexion.

He pointed the revolver at the shipman. "Start this tug or die."

The captain promptly obeyed.

"Head upriver," Craven commanded.

Bent on pumping a few bullets into Tony's delirious heap of flesh, Craven left the wheelhouse and descended onto the tugboat's deck. His hostage had disappeared. Through the driving rain, he surveyed the warehouse doorway, detected what might have been Athena's profile and fired until the last cartridge was spent. As he turned toward the wheelhouse, he sighted Tony with his right leg and arm slung over the portside gunwale.

"Damn you," Craven said as he took a running leap and kicked Tony across the ell of his shoulder and neck.

With a grunt, Tony tumbled back over the gunwale.

When Craven peered over the side, he discovered Tony, his left hand and foot hooked into tire fenders. Before he could react, Tony snagged the club owner's shirt and hoisted his right leg over the gunwale for a second time.

Dipping into his boot, Craven snagged the dagger and plunged the knife to the hilt into Tony's thigh.

***

Undone, Tony toppled into the icy water and sank, seemingly held under by a greedy leviathan, his barbed claws tearing into his flesh. He had little strength or will to wrestle with death.

*This is it. Thirty-five years old. Ninety-five years back in time. Ends like this. On the bottom of the Hudson River.*

Like a burial shroud, the frigid darkness slipped over him. In a final gasp of hope, he looked upward and saw Athena's face in rolling wraiths of currents against a deep devouring chasm. He searched the skin between sea and sky. But the surface was elusive, and Athena disappeared. Nearly spent, unconsciousness would follow. *Sleep. Let me sleep.*

# 41

Athena was soaked to the bone as the storm crowned in a fit of rage, throwing lightning and torrents of lashing rain. A bolt of lightning ripped into the Hudson Harbor and flashed across the river, followed by a peal of thunder so vicious it seemed to quake the earth's crust from surface to molten core. The pungent chlorine scent of ozone scorched the night.

Athena screamed, the howl purging from deep within.

Never having learned to swim, she searched for a life ring—anything that floated—but barring crates that scaled ten times her weight, there was nothing.

The choice was unequivocal. Swim or let Tony die.

She'd seen people splashing in the water at Coney Island. Although the beach was segregated, she could make out the frolicking swimmers from the propriety of the boardwalk. Maybe she could *pretend* to swim.

She wildly unlaced the holster and boots, tore off her clothing down to her slip, stared one last time into the kaleidoscopic curtains of rain where Tony submerged, and leaped into the Hudson River. Though braced for the cold, the water cut with such fury she yelped the most obscene word she knew.

One arm after the other smacked the water's surface.

After four strokes, she gulped and gagged on a wave of brine and thought she'd drown right there, twenty feet from the pier's end. In one final, desperate push, she envisioned how skilled swimmers glided across the surface. *I can do that. Throw arm, pull back.*

A shaft of lightning slashed the sky and spiked the New Jersey side of the river. However distant, electricity pinpricked the length of her body.

On a frantic breath, Athena tucked her head and stroked downward into the deep, the pressure on her ears singing a requiem. Blinded and starving for air, she turned for the surface but the freezing water was a swirling topsy-turvy abyss, darker than a cavernous sky, a skein of misdirection. She was a frail leaf in a street gutter, surging toward the jaws of a storm drain.

Crazed and nearly undone, she felt a tug, a propulsion, a sense of being lifted as if a benevolent spirit had taken possession of her body. However strange, she was not afraid. She was exhilarated. She was going home.

***

A volley of light slashed overhead. Tony followed that radiant rupture, impelled by whatever nameless power battles the dispassionate whims of death. It was not a struggle without consequences. His lungs bursting, his mind an armada of spiritless galleons, he opened his mouth for air a second before breaking the surface, sucked in the sour river water, and retched. When he breached the surface, his appetite for life rollicked—but no less celebrated than by Athena, whose body was tucked under his arm.

She gagged and wriggled.

"Relax," he said. "You're safe. I've got you."

"B-but how?" she sputtered.

"Relax."

Flanked over his rib cage and hip, her head on his shoulder, he felt Athena's body unwind as he sidestroked to a ladder at the end of the pier where Zalo and Johnny were waiting, their expressions torturous.

With one arm around her waist, Tony carried her midway up the ladder. Zalo and Johnny fell on their bellies, their shoulders and arms dangling over the pier's edge, and lifted Athena onto the deck.

Taking a breath to refill his lungs and clear his head, Tony waited for his body to unravel.

***

Although the eye of the storm had passed, a scurry of clouds shed a dwindling spray of rain. Athena shivered violently. Johnny unfurled Buddy's brass-buttoned overcoat and draped it around Athena's shoulders. She then stripped to her waist, gathered Athena into her body, and stroked her back.

Though Buddy's overcoat hung like a carpet over Athena's slender frame, the coat was dry and warm. She immediately recognized it. Although the coat reminded her of the last horrific moments with her sweet prince, she loved the smell of it and imagined Buddy's embrace, even in death.

Johnny drew back to capture Athena's eyes. "Are you okay?"

Over tottering knees, Athena pitched at the waist and coughed up a spate of river water.

"Hey, girl."

Although her eyelids were heavy, Athena collected herself, squeezed Johnny's arm, and nodded. "Where's Tony? Have you—" She broke off when she made out Zalo—or the ghost of Zalo—in the mist at the end of the pier, muscling something or someone onto the deck. She swiped and blinked her eyes. Although his back was to her, she was now sure it was her brother. Strangely, he stripped off his jacket in the rain. Then, stepping aside, he wrapped his coat around...a man. *Tony.*

Reeling forward, Athena flew into Tony's arms. "I love you so much."

He stumbled back a step. "I love you, my courageous girl."

They clung together, their passion rushing, pulled away to look into each other's eyes, and, unbelieving, embraced again.

Taking hard gulps of air, Athena buried herself in his arms and felt the weight of ecstasy burning within.

Zalo and Johnny followed the reunion, grinning after them, but not for long. Zalo stepped forward and turned to his sister, whose face and neck were shades of blue. "Are you sure you're okay, Thena?"

"Yes, I'm sure," she said, wrapping her arms around herself. Her memory returned, and she asked, "Where were you?"

Zalo's face transformed from tenderness to guilt. "I'm so sorry. We had to chase the cop down."

"Did you get him?"

"We did."

"Where's he now?"

"He's cuffed to the Ford axle," Zalo said with visible pride.

Athena turned again to Tony and held his face in her hands—a sallow, drained, and buffeted face. "My god, what did they do to you?"

"I'm fine. Just dazed and dead tired. And there's this," he said as he examined his right thigh, blood from the knife wound seeping into the wool legging.

She sucked air. "What is that? Were you shot?"

"Stabbed," Tony said with a grimace. He asked for Zalo's shirt, furled it by the cuffs, and wrapped and knotted the makeshift compression over the wound.

"Is it serious?" Athena asked.

"It'll be okay. He missed the femoral artery. We need to get home and clean it properly."

"Not yet," Zalo said, "You have to see my friend Samuel Battle."

"Then he *is* here. I thought I dreamed him up."

"He's here, but wounded. The bleeding has slowed, but I'm worried."

Athena clutched her brother's arm. "Samuel's alive? Thank god. I was sure he was dead."

Fighting off the seductive languor of heroin, Tony hobbled toward the warehouse.

When they found Battle, he was woozy but conscious and propped up against the crate where he had been shot. They all knelt in a semicircle around the officer.

Tony examined the wound. Although the bullet had ripped through the fleshy part of his shoulder, the blood had already begun to clot. "You're okay, but we have to get you to the hospital."

"Gorski?" Battle asked.

"In cuffs."

"Good. Klinger?"

"Dead," Zalo said.

Battle's expression darkened. "Send someone back for him."

Zalo rested a light hand on Battle's shoulder. "I'll take care of it. You rest now, Samuel. You can depend on me."

Although his eyes were mere slits, his speech slurred, Battle managed to ask, "What about Buddy?"

"We have to send someone back for him too," Zalo said, stumbling on the words.

Tony's jaw unlatched. "Buddy's dead?"

After a beat of silence, as if no one dared say and make it real, Athena answered with a single word, which was all she could muster. "Yes."

His face flagging, Tony dropped his head and moaned. "Not Buddy."

Athena took Tony's hand.

Turning to her, he spoke haltingly as if from lack of air. "Your prince is gone."

Athena parted her mouth but, too moved to speak, lashed her arms around Tony's neck and wept.

# 42

Levi Goldstein was not a happy tugboat captain. Unlucky in life, he was wallpaper at school, invisible to women, and hapless in business. When alone and honest with himself, he deemed his life an afterthought.

As years advanced, he managed the pain of failure by numbing his brain. His drug of choice was whiskey—any brand would do. A living corpse, he'd long ago checked out from the human race—didn't even know what the race was all about. No matter. When existential questions breached his wall of protection, he silenced the noise with another drink.

One day, the rabbi from his family synagogue insisted on sobriety, railing that Levi disgraced the will of the Almighty.

Levi listened politely and said, "Rabbi, you're a cruel master—one who is either ignorant or heartless. You advocate torture. You cannot or will not conceive that whiskey is the only solution that quiets my torment."

***

The wheelhouse was strewn with dead soldiers, clink-clanking when the boat pitched, the overhead light hurling prismatic pennants through the brown and olive-green bottles and onto the walls and deck.

The captain knew himself. He was an alcoholic caricature—his eyes rheumy, his face blotchy and bloated. The alcohol his liver had failed to process seeped through his pores. He noticed the stranger recoiled from the stink, but he didn't give a damn. "Where're we going?" Goldstein asked.

The stranger shoved his hands into his pockets and stared straight ahead. "Any pier in Harlem."

The two were silent as the storm drew from the last full quiver of lightning bolts and loosed them to the east to fizzle and die over the Atlantic Ocean.

Despite the shadow of the mean-eyed stranger, the captain's thirst trumped all distractions. "Would you like a nip?" Levi asked, fumbling for a half-empty bottle.

"Nah."

"Mind if I help myself?"

"It's your life."

The captain took a long pull and savored the hit. "What's your name?"

"Cal Craven. What's yours?"

"Levi Goldstein."

"You're a Jew boy then."

Levi polished the helm with both palms. "I was born in the Lower East Side. But, yeah, my parents were Jewish. I guess that makes me a Jew."

"I take it being a Jew ain't important to you."

"No, I guess not."

"Then, you don't stand for nothing. I mean look at you." He scanned the ragged wheelhouse. "How can you live like this? You reek of failure."

The captain hardly blinked. Having heard all the racist slurs, endured all the accusing stares, shame held no sway over his sensibilities. Insults were no more threatening than the waves that slapped against the tug's hull—dull and constant, like the years of self-loathing he had bucked and hushed. He took another swig. "Yeah, that's about right."

Craven sneered. "I don't like kikes. But I despise frauds, and that's what you are. You've abandoned your faith. And you've turned your body into a heap of garbage. You're an embarrassment—occupying space and sucking up good air."

"Uh-huh."

He surveyed the cabin. "Where do you keep your money?"

Without hesitation, Goldstein pointed to the locker below the forward bridge window. "In there. Take what you want."

When Craven found the captain's roll of bills, he coughed up a laugh. "A lot of kale for a rummy. There must be a couple of hundred bucks here."

"I make a living."

Approaching the pier opposite 142nd Street, Craven said, "Pull in there. Park this thing at the end of the pier."

Levi was adept at ignoring condemnation from disagreeable people. But this time it was different. This time, he was sickened by the bilious taste of failure, by the heartache of being invisible. With clenched teeth, he picked at the scab that shielded his soul and retrieved a particle of pride in being a New York Harbor tugboat captain. "You don't *park* a tug," he said. "You *dock* it."

"Well, la-di-da. Then dock the goddamned boat and tie it down."

***

Craven had decided the captain's fate. While Levi eased alongside the pier, descended, and wrapped the bow and stern lines to cleat hitches, Craven searched the wheelhouse for anything useful. He selected a black watch cap and a short-waisted Mackinaw jacket in a blue and ochre plaid.

He looked out the bridge window. "I'll be damned."

Stumbling helter-skelter across the length of the pier, Levi threw a wild-eyed glance over his shoulder.

Craven started after him. He scrambled down the bridge ladder, hurdled the gunwale, and sprinted down the pier. His heart jolted like a jungle cat in chase. "Don't make me run after you," he shouted.

The captain lurched along the sodden pier, each clumsy footfall shattering the mirrored splashes that dappled the deck. He tumbled to one knee, gathered himself, and careened forward again, his course ever more serpentine. When he screamed, the feeble cry made Craven's eyes glint with bad blood. *He's mine.*

At mid-pier, he grabbed the captain by his collar and threw him sprawling facedown. "You made me run, Jew boy."

Levi gasped for air.

"You gave me a ride, so I'll make this quick."

Craven unsheathed the dagger from his boot, cupped his left hand under the captain's chin, and slit Levi Goldstein's throat.

The captain gurgled something incomprehensible.

As if evil had poured into a human-shaped vessel, Craven belched a hollow laugh, clenched Levi's hair, and exposed his blood-washed throat. He hunched over the fallen man. "What's that, Jew boy?"

Although Levi's mouth was seething with foam, he steeled himself to pronounce his epitaph. "You...dock a boat."

Craven released the captain's head, which landed with a wretched *whump*. Arching his back, he straddled the captain's body and shifted his feet to avoid the expanding pool of blood.

"You should've believed in something. It might've saved you...but probably not."

After Craven swished his knife in a puddle and dried the blade on the captain's ass, he headed east, stopping at the first sleazy hotel on 142nd Street. With a strong scent of mildew, the lobby offered two straight-backed chairs and a splintered side table upon a tattered rug. Whether by irony or delusion, the hotel was called A Piece of Paradise.

Avoiding the night clerk's tired eyes, he took a room on the second floor that overlooked the street. There was a bed with a centered swale, a scarred dresser, and, down the hall, a yellow-stained sink and toilet with sticky floor tiles from urine oversplash— all an unwelcomed flashback to his childhood.

He snaked off the Mackinaw jacket, wiped off the watch cap, and flopped into the bed's trough. Lacing his fingers under his head, he let his vision blur and his mind scheme.

Although the mission failed, he suffered no regrets. His blood chilled dispassionate over Klinger's death. *What do I care?*

He held no reverence for cops. Ten years earlier, a bull had shot his younger brother, Josiah, in the face for being black in the wrong place at the wrong time—a twelve-year-old boy who only dreamed of becoming a fighter like Jack Johnson. No, cops were a tool to be used until they became annoying. When the time was right, they could be flushed into the sewer.

Nor did Buddy's death ruffle him. He was a cockroach—too stupid to play the white man for a sucker, too dense to become a predator.

The law of the jungle governed everything. *Kill or be killed.* Anyone—black or white—who disrespected his place in the city would know his savagery. *Goddamn it, I'm the bastard at the top of the heap.*

He despised Athena and Tony. Because their defiance pricked like a thorn burrowing into his brain, they had to be taught. He was the predator and they nothing more than a gaping silent scream. The natural law of survival gave him the right. He *had* to kill them— smash their pretty faces—even at the risk of being captured and caged like any other wild animal. *No. Won't happen. They'll be dead. And I'll be smoke.*

# 43

It took three days for Tony to heal. He began by disinfecting the knife wound, which was a clean entry on the outside of the femur—the best place to be stabbed if a stabbing was unavoidable.

Without the luxury of iodine or rubbing alcohol, he asked Athena to bathe the gash with soap and boiled water. Rather than stitch the laceration, he allowed the lesion to heal from the inside out.

As instructed, Athena boiled long strips of cloth, let the strips air-dry, flushed the gash, and bandaged the wound. "Is that too tight?" she asked.

"Perfect. You're the best nurse a man could have."

With limited movement, his body had repaired itself. Pink granulation tissue filled the gash. Although there was no infection, some soreness would linger, but only for a few weeks.

One condition remained unchanged. Although only a neuro-ophthalmologist could confirm, he was persuaded the occipital lobe could not repair itself. Klinger's blow had turned his world black and white.

Of all the colors washed out of his life, the greatest loss dwelled in the gold bands and yellow flecks of Athena's eyes. How he missed the sequin glitter of her gaze.

Because she still grieved for Buddy's death and the passing of her innocence, Tony waited until his third day of recuperation to reveal his loss.

They lay propped in bed, he bare-chested, she in a slip, enjoying the soothing heat of each other's body.

"There's something I haven't told you," he said.

"Oh?"

"Sit up so I can see you."

She pushed upright and turned to face him. "What is it?"

"Klinger whacked me hard on the back of the head."

She stroked his face. "Sweetheart, I'm so sorry. You poor thing."

"It didn't go well. He damaged the part of the brain that controls vision." He looked at the ceiling, then returned to Athena. "I no longer see color. I'm totally color-blind."

She looked as if someone had pummeled her belly. "Oh, Tony. I don't know what to say. Is...is it permanent?"

"I think so... I'm afraid so."

"How do you know?"

Stroking the curve of her cheek, he said, "I can't verify it with nineteen twenty-four resources, but that's my recollection from medical school." He let her process the news in her own way, her own time.

Looking into his blue eyes, she spoke in a measured cadence. "Do you see me clearly?"

"Perfectly. Only without color. Like a black and white photograph."

She spread her arms out to capture the entire room. "Then you see everything."

"Yes."

Troubled, she lifted her torso to its full height, revealing her short rayon chemise with slender straps and a tight centered bow at the yoke. "Then tell me, what am I wearing?"

"This is silly. I told you, I see perfectly."

She insisted. "Don't be like that. What do you see?"

"I see—" He tapped his most professional elocution. "You can't fool me."

"What do you mean?"

"It's a trick question," he said with a knowing smirk. "You're wearing nothing but the slight scent of Ivory soap."

She looked stunned...tormented.

Holding his deadpan expression as long as he could, his mouth turned into a slow, mischievous grin.

Her initial shock recast into reprisal. "Oh you," she said as she punched him in the chest.

"Hey, I'm wounded here. Nurses don't slug their patients."

"That wasn't a slug. It was a love tap. I'll show you a slug." She straddled his hips, tightened her lips, and pulled back her fist.

He raised both mitts to his temples and waited.

Dropping her fist, she lowered her chin and tilted her head the way she did when she wanted to be kissed.

He hauled her in, then suddenly pushed her away. "What's with these bib coveralls you're wearing? I can hardly feel you."

With sultry eyes, she slipped out of her chemise and wriggled across his torso. "Is this better?"

"I can almost feel you now. Could you get a little closer?"

Raising her head, she said, "I'll work on it. Unless you think your heart can't take the stress." With a concerned frown, she added, "I mean, given your weakened condition and all."

He caressed her face and with the lightest touch reeled her in. "I'll risk it."

## 44

On the morning of the fourth day after the warehouse rescue, Tony and Athena agreed it was time to visit Samuel Battle.

The police officer's hospital room was stark with a white tubular-framed bed, a metal side table, and a single window with a beige roller shade. In contrast to the grim setting, Samuel was awake, lucid, and propped up against two pillows.

"You're looking a lot better," Tony said.

"Compared to what?"

"Compared to death warmed over in the warehouse."

Pulling himself higher against the bed backboard, Battle said, "I feel better. The bullet went clear through. No bone chips. They say it'll be some time before I throw a decent right hook...but I'll be fine."

"Being a black cop creates enemies on both sides of the law," Athena said. "You put a lot on the line, Samuel—including your career. I don't know how to thank you."

"I think you just did," Battle said. "I only wish Buddy had made it. I could tell he was a good man."

"The best," Athena said, her eyes glistening with unshed tears. She quickly changed the subject to avoid choking up. "Do you know what'll happen to Gorski?"

"The case'll be reviewed. I don't know how it'll sort out. He may go free, and if he does time, it won't likely be for long. That's the way the system works."

Her eyes darkened.

"Both of you will be questioned—that's the way it has to be—but you won't be arrested. I can fully corroborate your stories. I saw it all."

"Thank you," Athena said. "I confess, I've been on edge about that."

"Don't be."

"Have you heard anything about Cal Craven?" Tony asked.

Restrained anger crossed Battle's face. "The police captain came in this morning and said Craven dropped out of sight. He thinks he's still hiding out in the city."

"Should we be worried?"

Battle let Tony's question hang. "I think so. He's a bad man. Treat him like a copperhead. Keep an eye on him and guard your distance." He raised himself higher against the headboard. "I don't want to exaggerate. But be careful."

Moving in closer, Athena took Battle's hand. "And how about you? Will there be any charges made against you?"

Battle advanced his lips as he speculated. "I can't say. Like Gorski, I'll be reviewed. I'll tell my story—no punches pulled. Hopefully, they'll believe me. Maybe I'll get a desk job, maybe a promotion. You never know. It's all about politics."

She patted Battle's hand. "Well, I believe in you. I'd testify for you in a minute."

"Me too," Tony echoed.

"I appreciate that." He looked away for an instant, then added, "I don't know if I want you testifying. That would make you public figures. Frankly, I wish you could disappear." He reviewed his own words. "Disappear and be safe."

Athena took Tony's arm. "We'll keep that in mind."

# 45

The time had come. After a full week of dreaming and planning, Athena and Tony were ready to make the leap into the future. Their disquiet was only outmatched by their anticipation—a life of great possibilities without the torment of Cal Craven.

Craven. They had neither seen nor heard from him, and that was terrifying. A man like him would not go quietly. He'd prowl in the shadows, bracing to ambush his enemies. With every tick of the clock, they felt he was lurking just around the corner or outside the door. Yes, it was time to go.

The most daunting task was saying goodbye to Zalo, Johnny, and Isabella. Although they understood the grief of separation, their destiny beckoned. They decided to break the news over dinner at Athena's apartment.

Athena and Isabella prepared a feast that included chicken, rice, and morsels of bell peppers, tomatoes, and mushrooms. To enhance the flavor and raise the heat, Isabella mixed her special Caribbean hot sauce. The savory aroma seasoned the entire apartment.

Memories and laughter animated the first half of the evening. Isabella recalled the days when she bathed Zalo and Athena together in the tub on Saturday nights. In those days, the apartment was a cold-water flat, the only source of hot water from a deep pot boiling over a gas stove.

"I remember," Zalo said. "Athena liked to lather her hands and blow soap in my eyes."

"That wasn't nice," Tony said with a cocky grin.

Athena raised both hands in defense. "Hold on a minute. That's not the whole story. Z used to make a funny face, tell us to listen, and push bubbles out his butt."

Although everyone laughed, Isabella hooted until she cried.

"Oh my," Johnny said, taking Zalo's hand, "you were a naughty boy, even then." With her bedroom eyes half shuttered, she added, "Too bad I wasn't invited to come over and play."

When the stories had waned, Tony tapped his glass. "It's been so much fun to be with you tonight. I'll hold you all in my heart forever."

"That makes for a heavy heart," Zalo quipped. "Have you lifted Isabella lately?"

"You better behave yourself," Isabella countered. "You're not too old to get a swat to your bony bottom. And you know I can do it."

Zalo leaped out of his chair, scurried around the table, and wrapped his arms around Isabella. "You know I love you"—Isabella grinned—"every ton of you," he added as he scampered back to the safety of his chair.

"Save me," he said to Johnny.

"Don't drag me into your tomfoolery. You can clean up your own mess."

Isabella looked sideways at Zalo, shook her finger, and laughed her musical Caribbean laugh.

Squinting at Zalo, Tony said, "I hope you're done."

With his palms pressed together in deference, Zalo offered a humble bow. "The floor is yours."

Pushing to his feet, Tony asked Athena to stand alongside him. "You have become my family, more precious than I could ever imagine. And I want you to know that wherever we go, you'll always be with us." He checked Athena, who smiled softly. "We're going back to my time. Twenty-nineteen. It's not a perfect world—I don't think we'll ever live to see that—but it's better. It's a place where we can live in peace."

Zalo looked stunned, as though he could not imagine his sister leaving—for any reason. In contrast, Johnny smiled knowingly, approvingly, or so it seemed to Tony. As usual, Isabella appeared neither surprised nor troubled but serene. Tony gave Athena a quick kiss. "Then, there's my work. I'm a twenty-first-century surgeon. I'd like to use my skills to help ease a small measure of human suffering. And finally, there's Cal Craven. We hate giving in to a thug, but frankly, we don't want to spend the rest of our lives looking over our shoulders."

The room quieted. Tony saw their sorrow in losing two people they loved to a strange portal of time. He turned to Zalo and Johnny. "We want to offer you the same opportunity. Would you like to come with us?"

Zalo took Johnny's hand. "God, we'll miss you so much, but this is our time. We're both excited to build our home together." When he glanced at Johnny, she lowered her eyes, a tell everyone read as "no." When he resumed, it was with heartache in his eyes. "We need to stay."

"And we approve," Tony said with a nod and a wistful smile. He turned to Isabella, who sat with her head bowed, her hands laced across her belly. She seemed at peace as if in the deepest state of meditation. "Isabella?"

She took her time. When she raised her head, her eyes shone sad but courageous. "I would like to share my deepest sorrow." Her lilt was so soft Tony leaned into her words. "My son's name"—a gentle smile graced her face—"was Cecilio. He was such a brave boy." When her words faltered, she waited to tame her emotions. "In eighteen ninety-eight, the Spanish-American War broke out. My son joined the African-American Tenth Cavalry." After a hushed moment, she added, "His decision was a pledge of loyalty to the United States and the Cuban struggle against Spanish rule." She took a breath and huffed on a sob.

When Tony glanced at Athena, her gaze lowered as if in honor of Cecilio's death. He rounded the table and placed a hand on Isabella's shoulder.

Patting his hand, Isabella raised her torso. "He fell a month after the war began at the Battle of San Juan Hill. He was twenty-one."

"Oh, Isabella," Tony murmured. "I'm so sorry."

She took Tony's hand and shifted to look into his eyes. "There is no greater heartache. Twenty-six years later, the pain still simmers below the surface." She tugged on his hand, and he dropped to his knees beside her. "Listen to me. I could never curse my son's decision. I might as well curse his nobility, which I will never do." She lifted her eyes to Tony. "You and my Athena have another quest—love, security, adventure. I will miss you, but I understand. Destiny is a two-sided talisman that gifts both sorrow and joy. You have your destiny, one that is no less honorable than Cecilio's choice."

Eyes watering, Athena covered her heart with both hands and mouthed, "I love you." Then, unable to restrain herself, she rushed to Isabella and knelt alongside Tony.

Isabella cupped their faces. "I am an old woman. Travel is for young people. You have your lives ahead of you. Good times, I'm sure." She caught Athena's eyes. "I'm so proud of you, child. You're such a powerful woman, full of vitality and promise. Imagine all the wonders you'll see. I think—I know," she corrected, "you'll become a great student of all the miracles a brand-new world can offer. And here at home, I'll think of you as my own children in another country, away but never forgotten."

Athena took Isabella's hand and kissed it.

"Remember," Isabella added, "if there is ever a time you are in danger, think of me, and I will be there. Both of you have sacred spirits. They will not be wasted."

They both kissed Isabella, slowly stood, and returned to the head of the table.

To settle the mood, Zalo asked, "When are you leaving?"

"Tomorrow night. I'm afraid this is our goodbye," Tony said, choking back his melancholy. "It's hard for me to express all the feelings churning inside. In times like this, I lean on music." His eyes flitted, his head lolled, giving him time to compose his thoughts. "As you know, Fletcher Henderson asked me to perform with his orchestra. In fact, he asked me to write an original ballad, which I've done."

Athena lifted her chin. "Honey, you never told me."

Smiling, he said, "I wanted to surprise you." He gave her a quick kiss and turned to the family. "I call it 'Athena's Song,' and I thought you might like to hear the premiere performance."

As everyone applauded, Athena made her way to the piano and scanned the lead sheet with chords and melody notated.

"We'll go through it twice," Tony said. "First time through as a vocal, second time with trumpet, and closing at the chorus with a vocal." After a four-bar introduction, he sang in a feathery baritone.

When will her eyes first meet mine?
When will our hearts and our souls intertwine?
No matter the right stage, no matter the right age,
Let love begin here and now.
When will the springtime be here?
When will she finally dry all my tears?
No matter the right stage, no matter the right age,
Let love begin here and now.
Coquettes may flirt, but they soon disappear.
Never a romance sublime.
Give me a love that is always sincere,
One that is true for all time.
Cherish the colors of love:
Black as a raven and white as a dove.
No matter the right stage, no matter the right age,
Let love begin here and now.

After his vocal, he played the melody on his trumpet, but was undone when he glanced at Athena. Her eyes were shining, her tears streaming and falling like raindrops on the keyboard. Even through his color-blind eyes, she glowed like an angel—radiant and fresh and wise. He could not play another note. Sitting on the piano bench beside her, he pressed her warm, responsive body into his chest as if they would become one if he could only hold her tightly enough. They both sobbed.

Zalo, Johnny, and Isabella joined them in a family embrace of unmatched tenderness—as though a sixth sense had been conceived and now bloomed within their spirits, forged and purified by love, a love Tony and Athena would never forget, no matter the year, no matter their fate.

# 46

Cal Craven had been holed up in the flop-house hotel for a week. He knew it was the right thing to do—cops would be hot on his trail—but now he was sick of hiding out. The job was unfinished and, consequently, maddening. On the night of the eighth day, he decided to make his move the following morning.

Before dawn, when night hovered still and deep, he dreamed Athena lay over Tony's body—both of them lifeless in a confluent pool of blood. He stared at the back of Athena's head, her hair an encrusted tangle, then at Tony's face, his eyes closed as if coffin-readied. Something irked, and he edged closer. A piece of lint? No, a minuscule larva writhed in the cadaver's eyelashes. Despite his contempt for the man, Craven gaped, revolted a maggot fouled his prey. He approached with thumb and middle finger to pluck the grub from its nest. The instant he brushed the lashes, Tony's eyes snapped open like mechanized lids on a wooden dummy.

Craven bolted upright, his skin glazed in a cold sweat. He hurled from the bed and clawed his face against a spectral foe. His chest heaving, he careened to the window and stared blindly at the crumbling tenement across the alley.

He waited for dread's hold to bleed out.

Finally, after blotting his damp hands on his shirt sleeves, after recouping the whiskey color in his eyes, after hushing his tremors, he said, "Today's the day. Today, I make the kill."

He could use a bath, but his mind rebelled. Although meticulous by nature, scrubbing the filth from his body seemed suddenly vexing and beneath his dignity as a killer. He slipped into the Mackinaw jacket and tugged the watch cap over his head. The garb would be warm, even sweltering for a New York City spring day, but he would likely go unrecognized.

When he glimpsed the small smoky mirror that hung over the dresser, he recoiled with a start. Was the glass haunted, revealing an uninvited double? He sidled toward the reflection and stole several side-glances at the mirrored doppelganger. Assured the intruder wouldn't crash through the glass and pounce for his throat, he faced the image straight on. The stranger stared back at him—eyes flared with a jackal glint, a ravenous nonman with chiseled bone structure, sharp and fierce.

When the beast skinned back his teeth, Craven relaxed. The graveyard reflection captured the man he wanted to be. The first glimpse at the new man had startled him. Not anymore. He *was* the new man; he was the jackal.

He paced the room. His heart was an empty drum with only a razon-sharp stone tumbling within—a juju with effigies of Tony and Athena. And when he walked, the amulet sliced and festered until his malice oozed.

With only nine blocks separating him from Athena's apartment, he had time to plan. He swiped off his watch cap, lay on the bed, and dozed off.

At midafternoon he awoke disoriented. But his senses returned when he pressed the Colt against his ribs. He reloaded the pistol and checked the security of the sheathed knife in his boot.

Nagging hunger pangs crowded his obsessions, insistent enough to jeopardize his mission. Not knowing how long the stakeout would last, he needed something to eat—anything, even a bite from a street peddler.

As soon as he left the dingy hotel, he spied an umbrellaed food cart at the corner of 142nd Street and Lenox. With his head down, his eyes tracking the contraction joints in the sidewalk, he strode toward the street merchant.

The vendor, who had a dark, sunbaked face and an ungroomed thatch of hair under a short-brimmed fedora, sold apples, oranges, and doughy pretzels the span and girth of a man's hand.

Craven took two apples and two pretzels.

Pegging the vender as Eastern European, he was rankled. When it came time to pay, he crumpled a dollar bill in his fist and let it fall to the ground. The vendor's glare wilted when the strange man swelled his chest and stared him down with beastly intentions.

Craven stuffed both apples and a single pretzel in his coat pockets. Munching on the second pretzel, he headed south toward 133rd Street, just nine short blocks away.

Arriving at Athena's apartment building, he scoped the neighborhood for the best lookout and selected the tenement rooftop on the opposite side of the street. He worked his way up the fire escape. A woman on the third floor stared at him when he slipped past her window, but he hardened his eyes, and she scuttled into the shadows. At the rooftop, he settled in behind the overhanging cornice and ate both apples and the remaining pretzel.

He waited for hours like a looming gargoyle on a cathedral parapet.

As gray light dusked the sky, the couple strutted out of their apartment building. They dared to laugh. *If they only knew their fate in the next few hours.* They skipped down the stoop steps and headed west toward Saint Nicholas Park.

Craven scampered down the fire escape, crossed the street, worked the front door latch with a picklock, and skulked upstairs to Athena's second-floor apartment. Pressing his ear against the door, he heard nothing, jimmied the keyway, and edged into the apartment.

He searched the flat for firearms. The most lethal weapon was a butter knife. Shaking his head in disbelief, he wandered into the bedroom. He tested the firmness of the bed, which was topped with an arabesque off-white throw of crocheted rosettes. Flopping on the bed, he waited, his heart trembling in raw anticipation of carnage.

Nightfall had occluded the sky when he heard muffled noises at the front door. He jolted out of bed, smoothed the throw, unholstered his revolver, and hid behind the bedroom door. A one-inch gap veined the hinged side of the door, more than enough space to accommodate the muzzle of his pistol when the time was right.

Athena and Tony were the first to enter. When Athena switched on a floor lamp, Craven feared a strand of light imprinted his eye and cheek, which impelled him to fall back into the gloom.

Squinting through the door crevice, he recognized Zalo and Johnny from the club. The fifth person—a meaty old woman in a garish Caribbean cape—posed no threat. If he had to, he could take them all. Still, five people would make things messy.

He waited for the guests to leave. If they didn't shove off within the hour, he'd turn the apartment into a charnel house. The puddled blood would seep into the oak floorboards, tarnishing them forever, each stain a medallion of his boldness…his mayhem.

## 47

Craven's gut soured when the five entered, cackling and hugging each other as if they actually gave a damn. The scene made him knuckle his brow.

Athena moved to the fat woman they called Isabella. "Let me take this," she said, removing the woman's blue-and-yellow cape. "This is so beautiful. Cuban I bet. I'll set it on the bed."

"Thank you, my dear. And, yes, it is Cuban," she said in what Craven took as conceit. "All things lovely are Cuban."

*So damn smug.* Craven disliked her immediately and later only thought of her as "the Cuban" as if the word were a curse.

When Athena moved toward the bedroom, Craven flattened himself against the wall and eased the door toward him. He watched her place the cape on the bed with two hands as if cradling a newborn. Pointing the gun at her, he fingered the trigger.

"Athena, I have a question for you," the Cuban said from the living room.

"I'm coming."

Craven raised the gun and tucked deeper into his hiding place.

When Athena reentered the living room, the Cuban asked, "Tell me, child, do you have everything you need?"

"What do I need? We have each other. I won't even miss my piano because it'll be there already."

*What does that mean? Where's she going? The Bronx? Brooklyn?*

Tony crossed the room and placed both hands on Zalo's shoulders. "I promise to take good care of your sister. I love her more than I love myself."

"I know you do, brother."

Craven grimaced.

"And it won't be long before she's performing in New York," Tony added, chirping like a goddamned warbler. "I've already told her she'll be a great hit at the Village Vanguard."

"The Village Vanguard," Zalo repeated. "I wish I could be there for the opening night."

Craven knew every club in town but had never heard of the Vanguard.

"You'll be with us," Tony said, "in every note we play." After glancing at Johnny, he added, "You're a lucky man, Z. Johnny's perfect for you—such a powerhouse. I just hope you can keep up with her."

"He better," Johnny said. "After all, he's not the only pebble on the beach."

Craven flinched. *Her mouth was always too strident for a woman.*

"Honey, you do me wrong," Zalo said.

Johnny plastered his cheek with a kiss. "You know I'm playing with you, baby."

The Cuban took center stage. Puffing herself up, she raised her arm over her head and snapped her fingers. Everyone quieted like cowering children.

*God, they're pathetic.*

"I have something I want to say." She moved to Athena and Tony and put her fleshy arms around their waists. "We've all witnessed wondrous things in the last few weeks. But the most important thing we've seen is a timeless miracle. These two children have created a spiritual child through the intermingling of their life forces. That child is greater than the sum of one plus one. It is greater than any number you can imagine. And it is forever."

*Jabber, jabber, jabber.*

"Some people are repelled by talk of love. They consider it too sentimental. They are wrong. Love is the act of being absorbed in the other, valuing their essence, and breaching all boundaries to satisfy their needs. It is the most glorious path any human being can pursue, and I am thrilled these children have taken the first step of this sacred pilgrimage—each step forward an affirmation of their eternal love."

*Wrong. If Athena belongs to anyone, it's me.* Itching to silence the old woman, Craven let his finger glide over the smooth nickel trigger of his revolver.

Athena ushered a loose strain of hair behind the ear of the yakking woman. "Thank you, Isabella. You're a wonder. We'll never forget you."

The Cuban clucked. "You better not. I will hunt you down like a hound dog."

Turning to Johnny and Zalo, Athena put her arms around both of them and pulled them into her. "I'm going to miss you so much," she said. *Christ, was she crying?* "Promise me one thing. Promise me you'll love each other as much as I love Tony."

"We promise," Zalo said, his oath trailing off into a dog's whimper.

Although she murmured when she took her brother in her arms, Craven caught she would miss him the most. *Where the hell is she going?*

Zalo hugged her back, then held her shoulders at arms' length. "Thena, you'll always be with us. We'll tell our children all the wonderful stories about Athena Cruz. And they'll tell their children. You'll never be forgotten. Never."

*What a blubbering child.* Craven's gut knotted, but his mind was clear. *Their deaths are my salvation. My liberation from a job undone.*

Tony slipped his arm around Athena. "Are we ready?"

"I think so."

*She looks scared. Why? What's so frightening about a trip?*

Tony faced the group. "All right. I'm going to do exactly what I did when I came. My trumpet is on the piano lid. I've loaded the piano roll of 'It Had to Be You.' There's only one difference. Athena and I will share the piano bench." He asked her to sit on his left side with one hand on the bench and one hand on the piano. "I'm going to play along with Athena's recording as best I can. Finally, I'll touch my fingers to my lips and then to her name's engraving."

Although the room hushed, the Cuban cocked her head as if listening. Craven held his breath. *What did she hear?*

"I love you all," Tony said as he started the piano roll.

His fingers seemed to be in sync with the recording, his head leaning over the keys as if in a trance.

When the music ended, everyone suspended like a lifeless row of bar stools.

The Cuban said, "Kiss her name…and leave now."

Seeming to awaken from his trance, Tony pressed his fingers to his lips and touched the last two keys on the keyboard.

They were all grouped around the piano. *I can take them now. I'll shoot the men first, then the women.* He eased the tip of the revolver into the break between door and frame.

But at that instant, a goddamned miracle happened.

Athena and Tony vaporized in slow motion. With the Cuban standing to one side, Craven could see their bodies crumble as if they were granular ghosts, increasingly transparent. Now a cloud of dust in the shape of human silhouettes expanded and fell away.

When Zalo held out his hand to touch the space where they had been, the Cuban held him back. "Wait."

They all froze until Isabella said, "They are gone. They are in the future now."

*In the future? What the…*

"How do you know?" Zalo asked.

"I know, and I am at peace," she said like some damn swami. "But we should leave."

Craven had long ago shunned all believers who spoke of harmony and serenity. The Cuban's mere mention of the word "peace" riddled his insides. If hell was a place of torment, he had crashed the gates. There would be no relief, no comfort in destroying those who remained behind. They were tripe and risky distractions from his true mission—the extinction of Tony and Athena.

*I have to think this through. The old woman said they're in the future. What does that mean? Is the piano a gateway to another time? That's crazy. But it's my piano. If it worked for them, it can work for me. I can follow them. Why the hell not? Imagine the possibilities.*

He considered the advancements made in the last one hundred years—the beginning of the industrial revolution, the making of oil, steel, and railroad barons. *What does the future hold for me? Fabulous riches! No modern man is smarter or more powerful than me. Cal Craven, the marvel of Harlem. I'll kick the new world on its ass.*

*But not before destroying Athena and Tony.*

Seething in bloodlust, he remained silent behind the bedroom door.

In a few minutes, Zalo and Johnny left the room like faithful laity leaving a church, washed in their precious reflections on goodness and hope. *Screw them.*

The Cuban stopped at the front door and turned. Coming straight at him, he wedged deeper into his niche. She trudged into the bedroom, gathered her cloak, and stood tall and still. At first, she seemed to be talking to herself. "Call on me, Athena, and I will be with you." Then, louder and in command, she added, "There is no place for you here or anywhere else on earth. You will not harm my family; I won't allow it. Be gone. The Prince of Darkness awaits your arrival."

*What the hell? She's talking to me. But how...*

She slow-stepped out of the room and escaped.

Although the Cuban's words bit sharp enough to cut, they were hardly deep enough to kill. She was peculiar, maybe even twisted, but not like him—not murderous.

After waiting for his heart to reset, he pressed his ear to the front door, listened to the silence, and slipped out with brewing plots of violence and greed.

He would return.

# 48

*Greenwich Village*
*2019*

Traveling ninety-five years into the future was not for the fainthearted. Their molecules atomized and stirred in a cosmic vortex of time and space—disembodied and dissolved. Both enthralled and petrified by the experience—one she wouldn't remember—Athena saw the future of her piano in a swirling haze.

As she peered more closely, she discovered Zalo and Johnny, older with gray in their hair and crow's-feet at the corners of their eyes, but still shimmering with life. At their feet sprawled two teenagers—a boy and a girl. She was an aunt. They all listened attentively, not to each other but to a grand louvered box with rounded corners, an illuminated screen, and a cluster of knobs. A stentorian voice emanated from the strange cabinet. "Yesterday, December seventh, nineteen forty-one, a date which will live in infamy…"

Seeing the misery in her family's eyes, she hovered over the scene, longing to comfort them. She could wish herself there.

As the time continuum turned the corner and her body slowly coalesced, Athena had a new sensation. She was now tethered to Tony as if they were twins, suspended in amniotic fluid without reason or sensation and, therefore, without angst. As her family had advanced in years, she now regressed. She heard her mother's heartbeat and the warm rush of her blood soothing her, and so her spirit smiled for her body remained amorphous.

When they neared their destination, Athena resisted rebirth.

\*\*\*

Tony revived first. Maybe it was easier for frequent flyers. Still, he awakened jelly-boned. When he had fully materialized, he discovered they were in his apartment on MacDougal Street in Greenwich Village. All the familiar pieces made him feel at home: the Turkish wall tapestry, the leather chairs, the glass-encased fireplace, and the accent lighting that spotlighted the eclectic paintings he loved.

He turned to Athena, who was hunched in a near fetal position at his side, her head prone, her arms tucked under her torso. He tenderly stroked her back. "Sweetheart, are you all right?"

She could not or would not answer.

With rising panic, he called again. "Athena?"

Placing one hand across her sternum and the other rounding her neck to support her forehead, he pressed ever so lightly. At first, she didn't respond. Then, as slowly as an unfolding flower, she enlivened. Her head lifted.

"Easy," he said, his hands still supporting her. "You're nearly home."

Ponderously, she raised her hands, rubbed the heels of her palms into her eyes, and let her arms collapse onto her lap. She was slow to open her eyes and respond. When she did, her words husked as if awakening from a deep sleep. "That was the strangest sensation. My memory is scattered but, from what I remember, not scary. In fact, I don't think I've ever felt so calm." She took a long, slow breath. "But I do feel used up…as though I've been run through a wringer."

"What's a wringer?"

She jerked a shoulder. "Huh? You know, rollers you crank to squeeze the water out of laundry."

On a chuckle, he kissed her cheek. "We don't have those here."

She looked at the piano, *her* piano, then swiveled to see the rest of the room.

"Tell me what you see," he said.

"Your apartment?"

"Yes."

"It doesn't surprise me." There was humor in her tone. "Fit for a man who is meticulous, discriminating, and accustomed to comfort."

"Guilty as charged."

"I like it. So elegant." She stroked her eyelids with her fingertips. "I still feel disjointed. What day is it?"

"Echo, what's the date?"

"It's Friday, April nineteenth," a pleasant female voice said.

Athena searched the room. "Who said that?"

He held back a laugh. "That was Echo." In an undertone, he mused, "April nineteenth. That's good. The same day I jumped to nineteen twenty-four."

Testing his balance, he stepped to an accent table and presented a black nine-inch column. "This is Echo," he said, displaying the device. "Echo, say hello to my friend."

"Hi there," the speaker said.

Athena hesitantly rose to her feet, tested her legs, and crossed to Tony. She took Echo from his hand, set it down, and put her arms around him. Leaning in for a kiss, she stopped. "Echo, look the other way."

"Look the other way," Echo said, "is usually defined as 'to ignore something wrong, to turn a blind eye, to connive.'"

"She doesn't get a joke."

"Just so she knows I'm the girlfriend here."

"Oh, she knows." He said in a whisper, "Echo, I love my girlfriend."

"You should tell her that," Echo whispered back.

Enfolding Athena into his arms, he said, "Good advice. I love you so much."

"Maybe she and I'll get along after all."

"She can be useful. For example, you can say, 'Echo, play "It Had to Be You" by Frank Sinatra.'"

Sinatra filled the entire apartment. Standing still, her eyes big, Athena tittered, chortled, laughed gleefully as she surrendered to the music's enchantment. "Heavenly," she said, her head keeping time to the music.

"The Chairman of the Board."

Because Tony's greatest desire was Athena's happiness, her laughter shook him to the core. And now he wanted her, more than ever. "Echo, set the mood."

Instantly, the fireplace burst into flame, and the lights dimmed to a warm afterglow.

Hugging herself, she wheeled around to take in the ambiance. "Oh, you're a bad man."

"Welcome to my world. How do you like it?"

She turned to Tony, stood on tiptoe, and crossed her arms around his neck. "I'd like it better if you'd kissed me."

"I don't know if I should. You're so beautiful right now, I'm afraid you might dissolve in my arms and slip back to nineteen twenty-four."

"I'm not going anywhere. My home is where you are."

He drew her in. When he claimed her mouth, the rush deepened and raised his blood. From her response—slinking into his body—she, too, had followed the call of desire.

"Do you want to see what it feels like to make love in twenty nineteen?"

Her eyes turned seductive, and her inflection misty. "It did cross my mind."

\*\*\*

Athena loved the way Tony scooped her into his arms, powered through the bedroom threshold, and threw her onto the bed. She was surprised how swiftly she rebounded, the mattress all at once caressing and grounding her.

She scanned the bedroom, which conjured a nineteenth-century hunting lodge. A nearly wall-to-wall Turkish carpet in muted shades of wine and gold covered a red-oak floor, the walls seizing a lighter shade of the carpet's maroon tone.

Bracketing the bed were two nightstands set in a warm glow by African-inspired table lamps, one of which revealed a copy of *David Copperfield*. The room seemed more like a sanctuary than a bedroom.

"Oh, I think I could get used to this." As she shimmied her body into a cloud of comfort, she outstretched her arms to Tony. Purring in catlike pleasure, she wiggled her fingers.

"I'm sorry, did you want something?"

"Come here and ravage me."

"I can do ravage." Not bothering with buttons, he peeled his shirt over his head, lay across the length of her body, and kissed her as though it were his last quintessential act on earth.

To her delight, he stripped and slung her clothing without regard for neatness.

His fervor burned through her, shocking her with pleasure. To make love in another room was a pleasant novelty like a bathtub soak with a flute of champagne. Nice but not earthshaking. But amorous play in another time was lustful and exotic and otherworldly, passion beyond all imagination—a forbidden sensual dance to the music of Grecian sirens, deep within the shimmering splendor of Atlantis. Warm and luxurious and enchanting.

The more his breath entangled with hers, the more she wanted all of him. It sprang from a tingle, a twitter centered in her belly, diffusing through her body, and seeping through her skin. Her spirit life mingled with his in perfect sympathy.

As the thrusts quickened, she dug her fingernails deeper into his hips until he groaned in either rapture or pain. She rolled him onto his back, mounted, and yearning to be closer still, she fell onto his chest and moved to feel the sweat of his body against her breasts and belly.

After the urging, after the chase, after the music of passion crescendoed, she nestled in his arms, awash in the lingering afterglow. She giggled when she spied the shoes that were flung, the socks that were pitched, and his briefs that were left dangling from an accent lighting fixture.

"What's so funny?" he asked.

"Nothing. I love your ambition." With a teasing lilt, she added, "Although I'm wondering about your stamina."

Turning onto his side, he ran his fingers down her middle and between her legs. "Let's take it out for another test drive. Give me a minute." His fingers were swirling circles in the crevice of her desire. "Don't start without me."

"Too late," she moaned. "Catch up if you can."

# 49

On their first morning in 2019, the world was bejeweled, as usual. The sun still rose, the sky still dazzled, and the air still nourished Athena's body.

And yet, she awakened aggrieved. Everything was the same, and everything was different. Although her heart still beat, Zalo, Johnny, and Isabella were gone—tender memories already paling by the dispassionate zephyr of time.

She rolled to her side and faced Tony, who slept, the soft morning light dappling his face and torso. He glowed so serenely and boyishly his image, reminiscent of Dutch Golden-Age portraits, prompted a rush of gratitude.

Running happy and sad—the yin and yang intertwined—she inhaled and let the used-up air expel into a new century. On that thought, she became the guardian, the peaceful shogun of her loved ones. All the charity and courage her family embodied must be instilled *in* her and modeled *through* her. If she honored them, she would honor herself, and that tribute would kindle her joy and temper her grief. She would not build a physical shrine in homage to her family, but their incense would always burn in her soul, and the spirit smoke would inspire every venture in the new world.

She eased out of bed, tossed her twentieth-century slip over her head, and stepped onto the fire escape. The buildings reflected her time but sheened by wealth.

The nearly whisperous motorcars flaunted curved windows, sensuous lines, shiny wheels, and color: magnificent hues of sky blue and champagne gold and a flamboyant red that dazzled in the sun like flecks of rubies. *Henry Ford finally discovered color.*

People were another matter—elegance seemingly scuffed by time. One portly man, with dark strands of hair unfamiliar with a comb, sported a tank top in a dizzy swirl of red, black, and blue, a pair of khaki shorts cut above his knees, and a weird set of rubber sandals, each with a thong wedged between two toes. The curious slippers made a comical flopping sound with each stride. Despite the man's unflattering costume, he appeared pleased with himself. He galumphed down the sidewalk as if royalty dressed in his finest frock.

A woman followed with a bushel of blonde curly hair with purple tips—*purple*—billowing translucent bloomers that revealed the shape of her legs, and a black sleeveless scoop-neck top that barely covered her spunky breasts. Most puzzling was a slogan in magenta scribbled across the width of her blouse. TOO HOT TO HANDLE.

She then glimpsed a chunky man—they *all* seemed weighty—dressed in business attire. He wore a dark blue suit, white shirt, and a red tie. Although he looked smart, she noticed another man who trailed in the identical costume. *The uniform must be required by law.*

Something struck peculiar. Every pedestrian escaped into his or her world, heedless of all others. They resembled robots, human in shape but mechanical in disposition. No one smiled. No man tipped his hat because no man *wore* a hat, excluding the khaki-shorts individual who wore a New York Yankees baseball cap. *But a cap isn't really a hat, is it? Where did all the handsome fedoras go?*

All the pedestrians seemed transfixed by another entity—something other than human beings. They strolled mesmerized by a thin rectangular surface they clutched in the palm of their hands and poked at with their thumbs and fingers—an unworldly device that sometimes drew a scowl, other times a laugh. Whatever its attraction, it eclipsed the charm of nature and the people who passed them on the street.

Adrift in her thoughts, she startled when Tony—shirtless and barefooted—stepped onto the fire escape, put his arms around her, and kissed her on the neck. "Good morning, sunshine." He stopped cold. "Honey, where's Zalo's necklace?"

Panicked, Athena patted her bare neck and saw herself in 1924. She'd taken the necklace off the day of the departure before taking her morning bath. Her belly twisted. "Oh no. I left it at home. I can see it on the small table by the sink."

"Honey, I'm so sorry. I know how important it was to you."

"I let Zalo down. He'll think I don't love him."

Turning her about-face, Tony stooped and searched for her eyes. "He would never think that. I promise you. It was a simple mistake. That's all."

"I hope you're right," she said with a long moan.

"We both know Zalo. His love is unconditional. No different than my love for Sophia."

Bravely, resolutely, she pecked him on the cheek. "Yes, of course."

She turned again toward the street, Tony standing behind her, his arms around her waist.

"So what do you think about Greenwich Village, twenty-nineteen?"

"I love it. But I also discovered something about myself."

"Oh?"

"I'm a creature of habit."

"Meaning?"

She described her world: the smokestacks and horse-drawn carriages and rambling cars with beeping horns. And children playing in the streets. "Where are the children?"

Tony remained silent.

"The people are different," she added.

"You know that already?"

Pointing across the street at a teenager striding with a jive swagger, she asked, "Do you see that boy? What is he? Maybe fifteen years old?"

He placed his chin on her shoulder and followed the direction of her finger. "That's about right."

"What's he wearing?"

He studied the teenager and crimped the corners of his mouth. "That's a tough one. He's wearing a sweatshirt with a hood. We call it a hoodie. As for the pants, that's harder to explain. You're looking at about seven inches of his boxer shorts on display above his pants."

Athena cocked her head. "Why?"

"It comes from prison culture. Inmates are not allowed to own a belt because they can be used as a weapon or a suicidal noose. As a result, their pants tend to sag. Somehow, that fashion seeped into the general population. The kids have the idea it makes them look tough."

"I'm not sure 'tough' is the best word."

"I understand. You're the most unique person in the world right now." He swirled his hand over her belly. "You leaped ninety-five years in time. You've missed all the transitions. The zoot-suiters, the beatniks, the hippies, the punks."

"What?"

He raised a hand of resignation. "It's complicated, I'll explain later. The point is a lot has changed in a century. Even for me, it's hard to keep up. Try this. Imagine you're living in a foreign land surrounded by strange customs. All of it may seem irrational or impractical or downright silly but—"

"—judging is not helpful."

He snuggled her. "That's my girl. Be curious. Observe. Try to understand. Ask me any question anytime."

Facing Tony, she held his steady gaze. "I want to understand. This is my home now. I want to be part of this brand-new world and maybe even make a difference."

"You will. This world will fall in love with you."

Reflecting on her early morning yin-and-yang mood, she said again, "I *do* want to understand." She placed a flattened palm over her chest. "But I never want to abandon my spirit or the spirit of my family. I have to keep them alive, including Buddy."

Moved by her goodness, Tony enfolded her into his arms. "We will. Always."

In silence, they scanned the street again.

"We have a big day today," Tony finally said. "We need to get you some new clothes...just none that shows off your underwear."

She turned and tugged on his ears. "Very funny."

"How about some breakfast first?"

Her body and face quickened. "Yes. I'm starved."

"Good. Echo, make coffee."

# 50

The new world dazzled Athena. At breakfast, she reveled in the aroma wafting from the automatic espresso machine and marveled at the rotating waffle maker that beeped when the breakfast cakes were toasty on the outside and fluffy on the inside. She'd never tasted coffee so rich, bacon so crisp, and waffles so sweet with real maple syrup and plump blueberries.

Wonders rolled out like a fantastic world's fair exhibition: the French-door refrigerator with a water and ice dispenser, an over-and-under front-loading washer and dryer concealed in a closet, a fifty-five-inch flat-screen television hung on the bedroom wall like a museum painting. Life in the twenty-first century staggered at every turn.

After breakfast, she took the first hot shower of her life. The black granite enclosure, featuring shower heads at both ends, seemed more like an exotic grotto than a place to bathe. Above, showerheads adjusted from a tropical rainforest to a pulsating massage. Below, water swirled and disappeared into the brass-covered drain. She shampooed, lathered, and rinsed, never before feeling so clean. *Nothing feels this good.*

As if to prove her wrong, she heard Tony turn on the second shower spigot before she saw his glistening body.

"May I wash madam's back?" he asked officiously as he glided his fingertips down her spine.

With another game in play, her insides tripped and stumbled. "So thoughtful of you to offer, kind sir." Placing both hands on the shower wall, she allowed the water to cascade over her hair and down her back. With pelvis tilted, she pistoned her hips.

"I'm sorry, madam, I'm a trifle confused. Precisely which detail of your anatomy did you wish me to cleanse?"

Turning about and drawing him into her cove, she nibbled his ear and whispered, "All of me."

After lathering his torso, he imprinted his body on hers, his force so primordial and she so pleasured her mind dazed as if she were Adam's Eve taking her first breath.

"Echo," he said, "turn on blue."

The LED lights recessed in the showerheads snapped on, turning the water azure.

With that color shift, Athena returned to the depths of the Hudson Harbor. She remembered now. She hadn't rescued him. Tony was *her* savior. He'd found her in the dark sea world, wrapped his arm around her, and guided her to the surface.

That realization set her passion on fire—fierce and frenzied. She ached to give herself to him—to be one with him and in that oneness tumble all barriers. Leaping onto his hips and locking her legs around him, she clawed her hands into his hair, thrust her tongue into his mouth and moaned—wanting to get under his skin.

\*\*\*

It was the power of her touch that awakened him—twice over. In 2019, her embrace threw him back to the instant when, exhausted, he surrendered to sleep in the cold arms of the brackish depths. In 1924, her nudge—forgotten to them both—resurrected him from an ocean grave. Only then, had he curled his left arm around her, thrust his right arm skyward, and swept for the surface. With the vision clear, he revived awash with grace—the sense of being blessed with modest merit in his favor. He aspired to be fully hers, pledged to her well-being but also devoted to her pleasure, for when she was pleasured, so was he.

"Now," she said, her desire clearly cresting. "Take me now."

# 51

Their sexual desires satisfied for the moment, Tony could hardly wait to guide Athena into the twenty-first century. For him, all beauty—a cerulean sky, a scurry of children, a colonnade of locust trees—beguiled more deeply when shared. He itched to introduce Athena to the outside world and see that world through her new-born eyes.

On their descent from the apartment to the first floor, he noticed Jessica Sweet at the bank of mailboxes. How curious. He harbored no apprehensions, not even a twinge of embarrassment or awkwardness. Neither brazen eyes nor innuendos held any power over him. In fact, the tall, green-eyed blonde quickened his step.

Before taking notice of Athena, Jessica greeted Tony with a hipshot stance.

"Hi there," she sang out. Then, upon seeing a woman trailing behind, the flaming extrovert befuddled and blathered in bursts. "I declare— Who is this gorgeous woman?"

"I'm so glad we ran into you," Tony said as if incarnated into the most polished man-about-town. "I'd like you to meet my fiancée, Athena Cruz. Athena, this is my friend and neighbor, Jessica Sweet."

"Fiancée," Jessica said on a gulp and a flurry of eyelashes. "That's... that's amazing. My, oh my, I near about peed my pants. I didn't even know you were dating." She turned to Athena. "Where're you from, sugar?"

"Harlem."

"I'll be switched. Harlem, you say," she caroled with genuine Southern hospitality. "And, eh, however did you meet?"

Glancing at Tony, Athena smiled coyly but said nothing.

"At the Village Vanguard," he lied. "I was playing there, and Athena came in to see the show. During a break, we hit it off, and... well, the rest is ancient history."

Slack-jawed and blank-eyed, Jessica looked as though she'd witnessed an armed robbery. "I do like ancient history. How long ago did this history begin?"

"Oh, I don't know," Tony said, looking at Athena. "How long has it been, sweetheart? Three or four weeks?"

She let her eyes lower as if searching the calendar for a date. "Something like that."

"Three or four weeks," Jessica repeated, her drawl more pronounced. "Imagine that. And already engaged." She glimpsed Athena's left hand. "But I don't see an engagement ring on your—"

Tinting a light shade of crimson, Tony topped Jessica's sentence. "We were going to look for rings," he said, turning to Athena. "Weren't we, honey?"

She tilted her head and grinned. "We sure were."

"We should be going. Lots to do today."

They were nearly out the door when Jessica sang out, "Hey, hold on a minute before you skedaddle."

The couple turned to face her.

The flirtatious neighbor tapped Athena's arm. "I'd like to 'fess up." She took her time composing her next sentence. "I'm sure it's no surprise to Tony, but I've had a crush on the boy for over a year. He's a lovely man, as I'm sure you know by now."

Athena smiled sweetly and glanced at Tony, who shrugged innocently.

Jessica wrinkled her nose. "I reckon I made the doctor a little nervous."

"Not really," he protested.

Jessica glared sideways at him. "You know it's true." She clucked her tongue and turned to Athena. "He'd have no truck with me, darling. But he's plumb crazy about you and as happy as if he had good sense. I'm good at reading people"—on a quick glance at Tony, she waved him off—"and it looks to me you two are made for each other. It could never be me or anyone else. It had to be you."

Jessica spoke so honestly, Athena's eyes brimmed with tears. She embraced Jessica, and the Southern belle stalled for only an instant before hugging back. "You're so precious. I know you and I are going to be the best of friends."

"I would like that. And listen, girl, if you ever need help planning your wedding, I'm your gal. I've got organization skills from here to Tallahassee."

Athena's face brightened. "I'll take you up on that. I'm sure to need someone to help me pick out the perfect corset."

When Jessica looked puzzled, Athena added with a tattered chuckle, "Or whatever's in fashion in this part of town."

Tony stepped in. "Thank you, Jessica, for wishing us the best," he said, giving his neighbor a light peck on the cheek.

Jessica flashed her eyelashes and jammed her words. "You're... you're welcome. Eh... really you are."

***

It was a seven-minute walk to Washington Square Park. During those long minutes, they strolled hand-in-hand in silence. Stonewalling their real history from Jessica pricked Athena's conscience. *Honesty counts.* She weighed the word "fiancée." Maybe Tony had simply dodged his neighbor's questions. *Maybe it's nothing, maybe it's everything.*

Bristling with Saturday-morning brio reminiscent of her time, the park popped with tulips and dogwoods in bloom. While parents swung their children behind a decorative wrought-iron fence, street musicians played, skateboarders skated, and dog owners struggled for control with pups who strained at the leash.

The cross-century lovers strolled to the center of the park and watched the youngsters wading in the fountain, sometimes squatting to cup their hands in the water and douse their friends who squealed with the kind of delight that evaporates when children become teenagers.

Tony then directed Athena toward the towering Washington Square Arch.

Fronting the arch, a jazz alto saxophonist played "Round Midnight." He wore a brown collarless chiffon shirt with three lengths of pendants suspended from his neck. When he'd finished the jazz standard, Tony approached him, slipped him a bill, and whispered something Athena could not make out.

On his return, he led Athena under the arch with Fifth Avenue to the north and the fountain geyser to the south. He gestured to the saxophonist, who sailed on a tender rendition of "It Had to Be You."

Tony moistened his lips and took her hands. He squinted at the sky, settled, and gazed into her eyes. "Athena, angels are by nature true believers. Wild beasts are slaves to their desires. Only human beings have freedom of choice. It's the most precious and tender gift we possess."

With every word, her world narrowed and quieted. The park and its patrons all but disappeared as the chatter-clatter-yip-yaps faded and hushed. All she saw and heard sprang from her man.

"Athena, I choose you, only you." In jazzman style, he grabbed the lyric from the sax solo. "'Nobody else gave me a thrill.' The fact that I traveled back in time to find you makes our love all the more sacred. 'It had to be you, wonderful you. It had to be you.'"

New Yorkers were beginning to circle the arch, some framing photos or recording video.

Athena's chin was trembling.

As Tony slipped his hand into his pocket, he knelt. "My great-grandmother was a Greek immigrant. Her name was Sotira Kostikos. She married my great-grandfather, John Marco, in nineteen thirty-eight." He opened his hand. "This was her wedding ring. I offer it to you with all my love and the love of three generations before me. Love of my life, will you marry me?"

Her belly fluttered, her eyes teared. Caressing his face with both hands, she coaxed him to his feet. Their breath tangled. She enfolded him into her body and kissed him again and again.

As the crowd cheered, Tony asked, "Does that mean yes?"

"Yes, yes, always yes."

He placed the diamond heirloom on her finger, turned to the onlookers and shouted, "She said yes!"

The New Yorkers whooped and applauded.

He swept and cradled Athena into his arms and twirled her under the grand arch. Although she was off her feet, every fiber in her body was dancing. New York and her people were all a blur, but Tony's blue eyes were clear and pristine—eyes that would caress her, protect her, challenge her. Eyes she would adore for the rest of her life.

# 52

At midday, Athena was laden with smiles when they headed north on the subway to the Herald Square Station and on to Macy's flagship department store.

She could tell Tony was equally absorbed as he gushed about the outing. "This'll be fun, like creating your trousseau," he said.

But the more he chattered, the more Athena wished to rein him in. She'd always made do with hand-me-downs or simple dresses she could make herself. The idea of going to a grand department store to be outfitted was intimidating. *What do I know about modern clothing?* But mostly, she fretted about spending so much of Tony's money.

"This is going to cost a fortune," she whispered.

"Don't worry about that. I have a great job, and my bank account is padded." He brandished a just-relax smile. "And I can't think of a better way to use it than with you, *for* you."

Fidgeting, she winced at the idea of being spoiled. "So long as you know you don't have to buy my love. I give it to you freely. Remember, I loved you when you didn't have two cents to buy me a flower."

"I know that," he said, his plea wrapped in tenderness. "But, if for no other reason, you can't live in one dress from nineteen twenty-four for the rest of your life."

She gave him a haughty stare. "What? You don't like my dress?"

"It worked for Mary Pickford. I think you could use a backup or two from my century."

"Fine." But her expression said she was unsure.

"Athena, I want you to know something."

His manner of speaking was so earnest, she shifted to face him.

Shards of light spangled his eyes. "I didn't go back in time to save you. You don't need saving. You already have your family's wisdom and toughness. I'm just tagging along for the ride."

A tear pooled and careened down her cheek. She caressed Tony's face, started to speak but stopped to calm her quickening heart. Rather than sob like a child on the subway, she dragged one hand down his chest and stilled her breath.

At their station, but before climbing to street level, she pulled Tony to a vacant sidewall.

She spoke quietly, privately. "My god, how I love you. Thank you, sweetheart, for saying all that on the subway. You've made something clear for me."

He was captured.

"I'm an uncomplicated girl from Swing Street. My name will never be on a social register, and I'll never be invited to a fancy ball. But you're right, I do have my family." She took his hand and traced the contours of his fingers. "And I do have you. If there's any goodness in me, it's by the grace of everyone who has ever truly loved me. *That's* the heart of me. *That's* my character. Everything else is window dressing."

He shouldered off the tile subway wall and turned to face her straight on. "I understand. You're talking about your spirit, which I adore. But you're also an entertainer. The audience will always be moved by your spirit, but the first thing they see is your dress, your beauty, and the way you hold yourself and take them in with your eyes. You're both *spirit* and *image*. The image—what you call window dressing—is not the most important part, but it's the gateway to your spirit."

Punch-drunk by his love, she straightened her back, embraced his arm, and drew in closer. "I'll make a monstrous sacrifice, Tony Marco. I promise to spend your money without feeling *unbearably* miserable." She squinched her face. "Can you live with *mildly* miserable?"

As if closing the deal of the century, he pumped her hand. "You've got a deal. And I promise, if your misery ever becomes insufferable, I'll happily return your old undies."

Upon kissing his ear, she whispered, "Good. Now can we stop talking about my bloomers? Unless, of course, you prefer panties optional."

He waggled his head. "There you go again. Now I'll be fantasizing about that for the rest of the day."

# 53

They began their Macy's shopping spree on the third floor in women's casual wear. The first thing that caught Tony's eye was a mannequin in dark purple jogging shoes, lavender leggings, and a violet off-the-shoulder dolman top.

He stood in front of the model with one hand around his waist, the other propping his chin. "I can see you in this."

Eyebrows arched, Athena laced her reaction with disbelief. "Come on."

"Oh, baby."

Tracking her fingers down the sheer legging, she said, "What would I wear it for?"

"Well, lounging to start with. Add a windbreaker and you could use it for jogging or bicycling. I'd love to cycle with you."

She showed the palms of her hands. "I know as much about biking as I do swimming."

"It's a cinch. I'll teach you both. It'll be fun."

"Hold on a minute."

She spotted a woman close to her size who glanced at her mobile phone with one hand and sorted through a rack of blouses with the other. Looking to be in her early twenties, the woman wore a fitted pink dress with spaghetti straps and a hemline hovering neatly below her cantilevered rump.

Athena threw her shoulders back and marched directly to her. "Excuse me? May I trouble you a moment?"

"No prob," the woman said in a perky voice.

Guessing that "prob" was short for "problem," she said, "Oh, that's good. I didn't want it to be a problem," she said politely.

As if offended, the woman's head twitched. "Huh?"

Detecting her reaction, Athena scrambled to ease the tension. "Please excuse me. But I could use a woman's opinion right now, especially from someone as lovely and well-dressed as you." Visibly pleased, the woman rolled her shoulders. "You see, my fiancé—" She broke off and waved at Tony. "That's him over there."

Although Athena knew he was going for debonair, his smile came off as adorably shy.

"Shut up," the woman in pink said.

"I'm sorry. What did I say?"

The woman ogled Tony. "OMG, he's a total snack."

"Uh-huh. Well anyway, he and I are trying to build a wardrobe for me. This is our first stop. He likes that purple outfit over there for jogging or bicycling."

Overworking a stick of chewing gum, the woman glided her hands to the back of her hips. "Oh, that's sick."

"Okay," Athena said, sounding the word with a string of extra vowels. "I was wondering if it's...well, too daring."

The woman pursed her lips. "Not for a hottie like you. Kid you not. You'd look totally dope."

"Dope?"

"Word."

The fog rolled in. "Word?"

"Sure. You know, smoking, screaming, lit."

"Then, it would be all right, you're saying?" she slow-talked.

"For real, girl. Go crazy," she said as her phone made a mosquito sound. Raising one finger, she took the call. "Wassup?" She listened and spun her forefinger, indicating that the conversation would be lengthy. Evidently, their exchange was over.

*Thank you*, Athena mouthed and returned to Tony, rubbing her temple as though it ached.

"She says I'd look 'totally dope.' Is that a good thing?"

He chuckled. "That's a *very* good thing."

Tenting her mouth, she whispered, "I wasn't sure. I hardly understood her. I think she's a foreigner."

\*\*\*

They shuttled from floor to floor. Two for shoes, five for dresses and suits, eight for jackets and coats, one for sunglasses, handbags, watches, and jewelry. They carried a few items—a silk robe, a floral spring dress, the purple jogging outfit—and requested home delivery for the rest. Their last stop was the sixth floor for lingerie, what Macy's called "intimate apparel."

"This makes me feel squirmy," Tony said.

Athena giggled. "You travel ninety-five years in time but can't bear the sight of panties?"

Shrinking, he waved a hand in surrender. "Panties. I don't even like saying the word. It's like speaking in French with nasal vowels and puckered lips. It's not natural."

"Then you better step back and let a woman take charge." She shimmied her shoulders, a movement she adopted from the strange-talking woman in pink. "I've got this."

Parading to the counter, she waved to a youthful clerk dressed in a stylish black shirtdress.

"May I help you?" the clerk asked.

She read the clerk's name tag. MADISON, INTIMATE APPAREL MANAGER. "Hello, Madison. My name is Athena. I wonder if I could be honest with you."

"Why of course."

Murmuring, as if speaking normally would make the lie even more abhorrent, she said, "You see, I'm not from the United States. I'm from a small village in South Africa, and I have never been to a magnificent store like this before. I certainly have never seen such beautiful lingerie. Would you be willing to help me find what I need? I don't even know my size."

Seemingly charmed, the clerk said, "I understand completely. I'd be delighted to help you. Why don't we start with bras?"

The two women moved to a long display of brassieres.

While Tony trailed behind like a pistol-whipped puppy, Athena learned all the virtues of wireless bras (contouring your shape), comfort bras (with soft and seamless cups), push-up bras (offering a curve-enhancing lift), and sports bras (for an active lifestyle).

When she caught a glimpse of Tony, he flicked his fingers at her.

Athena asked if she could try on the push-up number.

"Certainly," the clerk said.

"Would it be all right if my fiancé stepped into the dressing room with me?"

Glancing at Athena's engagement ring, Madison smiled and said, "Of course."

Against his visible reticence, Athena asked Tony to sit near the hall of dressing rooms.

Although she took three brassieres into the fitting room, the first bra she tried fit perfectly, which, indeed, lifted her breasts and displayed a brazen cleavage. It was the strangest thing. All the bras in her time were designed to flatten the bosom, making women appear more boyish. In dramatic contrast, this brassiere was a celebration of breasts, as if to say, "I am a woman, and these are made for more than nursing babies." She liked what she saw. It excited her.

After ten minutes, she called for Tony, which prompted a tentative tap at her door.

"Athena?" he whispered.

She peeked out and chuckled at his ridiculous expression of relief.

Plunging into the dressing room, he found Athena stripped to the waist, except for the push-up bra in a color called "totally tan."

"Man alive, you'd look stunning in winter gear designed for Mount Everest, but this... What do you call it?"

"A Wonderbra."

"This Wonderbra is...well, wonderful on steroids." He blew out a puff of air. "Oh man, did the temperature rise about twenty degrees?"

Placing her hands on her hips, she splayed her fingers across the small of her back and rolled her shoulders forward.

"Don't do that." He raked his scalp with both hands. "You could stop a freight train with that look."

Whether by pretense or genuine dithers, his reaction both tickled and boosted her confidence. Unmercifully, she puckered her lips. "You like what you see?"

"The color is perfect for you."

She perplexed. "What do you mean?"

"The color. It's a shade lighter than your skin tone. I'd call it teak."

Cupping his face, she asked, "Sweetheart, can you see color?"

The question stunned him. He looked at his long-sleeve dress shirt. "Blue," he said in awe. "French blue." He lifted the hem of Athena's new skirt with a slit on the side that revealed the length of her leg. "Peach." Chuckling now, he announced with authority, "That is definitely peach."

"What are the colors of my new bracelets?"

"Two gold and one silver."

"And the color of the stone in my engagement ring?"

He took her hand. "Blue diamond with a hint of green." Passion-driven, he cradled the nape of her neck, gazed into her eyes, and grinned. "Golden with flecks of yellow fireworks. Your beautiful, beautiful eyes."

"I thought you said the damage was permanent."

Laughing outright, he caressed her face. "I thought it would be. I guess I was wrong. Maybe the occipital lobe *can* repair itself with time. Or maybe I'm one lucky guy."

She kissed him. "We're both lucky."

Wonderment turned to laughter.

"Is everything all right in there?" Madison asked officiously from the dressing room corridor.

"Everything's fine," Athena said. "Perfectly fine."

"Very good," Madison said, her heels clicking away into a slow decrescendo.

Now, in a spunky mood, Athena struck her seductive model's pose. "Then, it's fair to say you like it?"

"Don't be alarmed. I'm a doctor." He cupped her breasts with both hands. "I love this bra. And I love this caramel mama"—he added as he kissed her breast—"and this caramel mama"—as he kissed the other.

"I can buy it?"

"In every color."

He gulped and turned to leave.

"That's all you have to say?" she asked with steamy eyes.

"Eh. Wrap them up before I get arrested?"

With one final glance at Athena, he swiped the back of his neck and burst out of the dressing room.

On a contented smile, Athena said, "How I love that man."

\*\*\*

After several other stops, including dresses and suits, they were ready to leave. But on the first floor, Tony noticed a display of smartphones. He reviewed the benefits of the device. "You can make phone calls anywhere in the world. You can also listen to music, take pictures, and make movies."

Athena shook her head. Although the device was clearly useful, her guilt was chattering again. "But if we buy this, will I lose you?" she asked with questioning doe-eyes. "I've already seen how people are attached to these things." She crimped her fingers. "I don't want my hand becoming a claw in the shape of a screen."

Tony passed his fingers down her arm. "I promise you'll never lose me. We'll put limits on how much time we spend on them—especially at home. I want to be *with* you when we're together, not *near* you."

"Okay," she said warily, "but on two conditions. First, this is our last purchase and, second, we promise we'll never let these things own us. Fair enough?"

With a beguiled smile and a long gaze, he said, "That's why I love you so much."

Athena selected a smartphone encased in silver to match a new silver clutch bag. After the clerk programed the device, Tony added his phone number.

"Oh, let's try it," she said, unable to dampen her excitement.

After showing her how to make a call, he slipped away and out of sight.

Athena called, Tony answered. She giggled, they talked.

After two minutes of patter, she said, "You sound so close."

"That's because I'm right here," he whispered in her ear.

On a squeal, Athena whirled and threw herself into his arms.

As they left the store, the remnants of the day lengthened the shadows that crept over sidewalks and city towers. Athena was wearing a navy midcalf pencil-dress suit. The one-button jacket had a slender white trim that traced her collar and center front. Both jacket and dress were fitted, which accented the curve of her waist and hips. She loved the contoured shape—vastly more flattering than the straight-line dresses from her time.

She carried her new silver clutch bag, which held her smartphone, a blush compact, and two new shades of lipstick that promised to make her lips kissable. On her wrist twirled the trio of silver and gold bracelets.

Tony admired her figure. "Mm-mm. I don't know if I should eat you or make love to you."

Taunting him with her gaze, she said, "If you have to ask, I need to get you home right now."

***

When they arrived at Tony's building, they were too exhausted to prepare dinner. They crossed MacDougal Street to Minetta's Tavern, a swanky Italian bar and restaurant with angled black-and-white checkerboard tiles, cotton tablecloths and napkins, and a panel of village frescos in sunbaked yellows and oranges that wrapped the room.

They both ordered the filet of trout *meuniére* with crabmeat and brioche croutons. As Tony had previewed, their dinner presentations were only outmatched by the lingering savors of each bite.

Their eyelids were beginning to droop when they left Minetta's. By the time they'd crossed the street, climbed the stairs, undressed, and lay in bed, they were already half asleep.

Athena curled into the dreams that washed over her from one century to the next and back again. Like the modern world, her dreamscape promised peace and boundless love.

## 54

They slept in late on Sunday morning, finally nudged by the rustling city. When her eyes cleared, Athena volunteered to make breakfast with a little help from Tony on the marvels of kitchen technology.

She pranced barefoot as she assembled the ingredients for a cheese omelet, wearing nothing but Tony's short apron that was bibbed in the front and bare in the back. White letters over a black background read THIS IS A MANLY APRON FOR A MANLY MAN DOING MANLY THINGS WITH MANLY FOOD.

For the first time, she spoke to Echo. She requested a singer who, according to Tony, was born Eleanora Fagan. "Echo, play music by Billie Holiday."

An open-throated trumpet led into Billie's yearning version of "The Man I Love."

"Sing it, Eleanora," she said as she swayed in time. "That's my girl."

With a lopsided grin, Tony leaned against the kitchen doorjamb, his arms folded. "What a silly apron. A gift from my nutty friend, Harlan Lowe. But I love how it looks on you."

She twirled about and flicked the apron's skirt to tease a glimpse of her thigh.

"Ruff." Slipping a wooden spoon from her hand and setting it on the counter, Tony gathered her into his arms, dipping and whirling about the kitchen until the song ended. He kissed her hand in princely fashion, thanked her for the dance, then roguishly patted her bare tush.

"Hey, no distracting the chef," Athena said as she plucked and brandished her spoon with scolding eyes.

When she turned to the counter, he came up behind her, slipped both hands under the apron to cup her hips, and hauled her in.

She tilted her head, opening her neck to his kisses. "Yes."

"Is it too early?"

"Never too early."

The breakfast ingredients lay idle as they satisfied their lust for each other.

In the bedroom again, Athena loved the way Tony explored her body. A slow, gentle search as though an ear or a cheek or the curve of her neck could ignite an explosion of pleasure for him—as it did for her.

As his breath mounted in time with hers, she was on top of him, he on top of her, both moving with such rapture her head dizzied and her body quaked out of pure, unbridled pleasure.

\*\*\*

After preparing and having breakfast in bed, Tony said, "I have a treat for you."

She smiled impishly. "Please, I'm sorry I ever questioned your stamina."

"Not that kind of treat." When he set the breakfast tray aside, he commanded Echo to "play movie." The bedroom wall monitor flicked on, and the adjustable bed hummed into its programmed viewing position with back raised and knees lifted.

As they ensconced under a duvet, the opening credits of *Avatar* rolled.

All in as the story unfolded, Athena whooped, chortled, and cooed. When the villain appeared on screen, she hurled twentieth-century insults. "Oh, what a cad."

Midway through, when the hero and heroine took flight on the mountain banshees, the music soared. The characters flew with grace on the backs of the giant birds, swooping from the rookery, flashing past waterfalls, gliding over and through arches. With elbows akimbo, Athena flew with them, leaning into the dips and bends.

When the movie ended, she snatched Tony's hand. "That's how I feel with you. Flying above the earth where no one can hurt us." She fell silent, drifted off, returned. "You know what it makes me think?"

"Tell me."

"We should explore *everything*." She lifted off the bed's back support, shifted toward Tony, and pretzeled her legs under her. "Is it possible to make our dreams come true? To discover the limits of all our gifts? I mean what's to stop us?"

"Nothing at all."

All the great novelists she'd ever read swirled in her head. Twain and Hawthorne, Austin and Kipling, and, of course, Charles Dickens.

Unable to contain the glee that shivered through her, she said, "I want to see the world. Do you know I've never been outside of New York? I want to see everything. Peer into the Grand Canyon…stroll along the cobbled streets of Paris…ride a bicycle in Denmark…swim in the South Pacific.

"Oh yes, I want to go to Mooréa. Do you know about Mooréa? I read about it once in the high school library." Her speech started to rush. "It's a lush volcanic saw-toothed island near Tahiti with natural bays and whales and stingrays and mangos and watermelon and sweet potatoes." She paused for air. "We've got to go there. I want to swim in that lagoon."

Swept away by her excitement, Tony searched Athena's eyes. "You know, that's the first time you've ever asked for anything."

She let her sail flutter and still. "I know. I'm so selfish. I'm sorry."

With a calming touch, he rested his hand on her thigh. "Don't be sorry. I agree with you. So does our friend Mr. Dickens. Let's see, how does it go?" He silently rehearsed the quotation. "'My meaning simply is, that whatever I have tried to do in life, I have tried with all my heart to do well; that whatever I have devoted myself to, I have devoted myself to completely.'"

"*A Tale of Two Cities?*"

"Ha. I finally got you. *David Copperfield*." He turned the duvet back and sat cross-legged to face her. "Let's do it. We know we want to be devoted to each other. Done. But let's also devote ourselves to a life without regrets. You want to see the world? So do I. Let's make it happen."

Her eyes widened, her lips rounded. "Are you sure?"

"Absolutely. New York's a great city, but it's not the *only* city. For Pete's sake, I'm a surgeon. I can practice anywhere. And you're the brightest, most talented person I know. Nothing can stop us. Pack your bags. Let's take this world by storm."

Athena swiped a tear away. *What a wonder. This is our life. Passionate, engaged, together. No sleepwalking. No regrets. No fears. Nothing to worry about.*

*Nothing at all.*

## 55

Athena paid attention when Tony told her about his favorite psychiatrist, Harlan Lowe.

"He can be trusted," he said. "Our adventure has been fantastic. Much of it we'll keep to ourselves. But to be fully enjoyed, some of it needs to be shared. Harlan's the right guy for the job."

Athena could see the confidence Tony placed in his friend, and it pleased her. She too wanted their family to grow. "I'd love to meet him."

"Good. I'll set an appointment for Friday at 6:30 P.M. I'll meet you at the front door of the medical center if that works for you."

"I'll be there."

Because Harlan was Tony's best friend, Athena wanted to look pretty for Tony's sake. Three days before the appointment, she asked Jessica Sweet if she would help her pick out something special for the meeting.

"Honey, I'd *love* to get you gussied up," Jessica drawled.

Their first stop was Marcus on West Thirteenth Street. Jessica picked out a pair of cropped skinny jeans—in white no less. The top was a black stretchy V-neck tank top that revealed cleavage. Scampering through the racks, she then discovered a long, silky, black-and-pink floral jacket with breezy side-slits. "Perfect," she said, as she snatched a pair of white open-toed four-inch heels that strapped in place more by magic than physics.

Athena looked askance at Jessica's choices, her eyes dubious. "Are you sure?"

"No sass, girlfriend. You can trust me. I know fashion."

On a shrug of concession, she escaped into a dressing room. Ten minutes later, she reappeared, leaned a shoulder against the dressing-room doorframe, and placed one hand on her hip, the other arched over her head like a flamenco dancer. She looked both sexy and classy.

"Well, I declare. Tie up the boys and cage all the men. Athena Cruz is in the house."

"What does that mean?"

Jessica sashayed full circle around her friend and hummed. "You are definitely ready for prime time, darling."

"What does *that* mean?"

She stared at Athena with admonishing eyes. "Honey, it means you're as pretty as a peach."

Athena looked at herself in the mirror. "I feel, I don't know, naughty." She giggled. "Which is exactly why I love it so much."

"Now you've got the feeling, girl."

\*\*\*

The next stop was an hour-long manicure, ending with Athena tapping out a syncopated rhythm with her new French-tip nails. "How did I not know about this?"

"Maybe you missed the lesson on pampering yourself," Jessica teased.

Next, Jessica schooled Athena in modern makeup essentials. Foundation, blush, eye shadow, eyeliner, mascara, and lipstick. No need for a concealer. The makeup didn't change her beauty. It *enhanced* it, pumping up the shadows and light, the way a painter defines and enlivens a dull portrait by darkening the edges and illuming the chin, cheekbones, and bridge of the nose.

Playing her final card, Jessica introduced Athena to her favorite hairdresser who layered, feathered, shampooed, and styled Athena's short black hair, creating an image that was at once elegant, youthful, and spunky.

Athena gazed into the mirror, shook her head, and her hair fell back in place, perfectly lofted and layered. "Unbelievable."

At the end of the day, the two women stood side by side in front of a full-length mirror. Appraising her friend from under her eyebrows, Jessica piped a long wolf-whistle.

"Oh, stop that," Athena said.

"You're ravishing."

Hardly recognizing herself, Athena had to remember she was still the coltish and free-spirited girl from Harlem's Swing Street. "I feel a little funny."

"Now you hush up, darling. There ain't one lick of funny about the way you look." She bent at the knees and slowly rose, casing Athena's full length. "Dazzling? Yes. Sophisticated? Sure. Funny? No effing way. Not even in the same rodeo."

"Do all women look like this? Dress like this?"

Jessica folded her arms and raked one leg to the side. "No, sugar, not *all* women. Only women with your kind of natural beauty and grace. So get used to it. Believe me, there are worse attributes." She grumped her face and waggled her thumb at herself. "Like having one big impertinent mouth."

Athena was still unconvinced.

Jessica pinched the corners of her mouth. "I swear, you could make a preacher cuss. I know you're a sweet kid. Anyone with both oars in the water can see that. And that sweetness ain't going away. It's who you are. You hear me, girl?"

On a slow shrug and big eyes, she said, "I know you're right. I just have to remind myself."

"I promise you, Tony'll love it. You'll have to hog-tie him to get some rest."

Athena giggled. "I could live with that. I mean, a woman does have to make a few sacrifices." She slow-twirled. Then, with more attitude, she took a wider stance and swayed this way and that.

"Adorable," Jessica said. "If he doesn't gobble you up like shoofly pie, you march him right down to my apartment, and I'll reshuffle his teeth."

She wobbled a double-take and laughed. "And I think you're the girl to do it."

"You better believe it, sweetheart."

Taking a long look at Jessica, Athena was struck by how much she enjoyed her company. The Dixie belle was unfiltered, which made Athena laugh, but she was also smart and perceptive and sensitive—exactly the person she wanted as a friend. "Tell me something. Why are you so kind to me?"

Jessica kindled a smile. "I have to tell you, I'm a simple country girl. Sometimes a little outrageous, sure, but serious when it comes to the important things in life."

"Like?"

"Like loyalty and integrity." She gazed at Athena as if admiring an exquisite painting. "You are such a lovely person. Beautiful, of course, but also bright and kind and awfully charming. When it comes right down to it, I cotton your friendship."

Her face aglow with emotion, she embraced Jessica. "You're my friend—my best friend. In fact, I'd like to ask you to be my maid of honor."

Out of character, Jessica sobered, took a step back, and lightly touched the base of her neck. "Darling, I would love to be your maid of honor, but I have a confession."

Catching sight of a different Jessica—one who was more stayed, more deliberate—Athena searched her friend's eyes. "Yes?"

"This is not the first time I've been a bridesmaid. And I'm always tickled pink to oblige, but—"

Athena cut her off. "The tune is getting old."

"Exactly. I'm looking and I'm ready. All I want is a man who is bright and accomplished and a little rough in the saddle."

Eyes welling from empathy, she said, "I understand." Then, with a playful nudge, she added, "I'm not sure I know what 'rough in the saddle' means, but I can guess." Canting her head to catch Jessica's gaze, she said, "I want the same thing for you. And I believe it'll happen before you know it."

Although slow in coming, her smile was real. "Bring it on."

Athena grabbed her up in a hug.

When they separated, Jessica knuckled a fresh tear. "Lordy, I'm gonna blubber here in a second. I've never had"—her breath snagged—"a best friend to kick with before. I'm so glad it's with you."

Turning away, Athena said nothing for a beat, collected herself, and returned with conviction. "Me too...me too."

# 56

Athena scanned the menagerie of subway patrons on her way to the medical center, their barren faces as expressionless as moonscape. She was tempted to sing "Ain't We Got Fun," but nixed the idea, even as a whimsical glockenspiel rendition belled in her head.

When she exited the subway, men secreted a glance when she passed, which prickled her spine. She was pretty, but her beauty was not her doing. Her mother's adage came to mind. "A kumquat doesn't boast because its skin is orange and its taste is tart. It just is." For Athena, the attention didn't inflate her ego, but it did swell her gratitude, especially for Tony and the intimacy they saved for each other.

Her body tingled when she spotted Tony seated on a textured concrete bench in front of the medical center. He was hunched over his knees reading the *New York Times*. With style and attitude, she sauntered within a half step and posed with one foot angled out, the other on point—letting him discover her inch by inch.

*** 

Tony's discovery didn't take long.

Over the newspaper's top edge, he followed an exquisite line of long-stem heels, white skintight jeans, a floral three-quarter-length jacket, a woman's glowing face with smoky eyes and feathered hair. Not recognizing her, he smiled politely and went back to his paper.

In double-take fashion, he crumpled his paper and snapped his head to her eyes.

Athena imitated a pouty Clara Bow.

"Oh my god." He jumped to attention and leaned side to side to catch every angle.

"Well?"

"Excuse me, miss, are you *the* Athena Cruz?"

"Why, yes I am. And who might I ask are you?"

Unfurling a handkerchief from his back pocket, he comically fanned his face, which made her laugh. "Just the luckiest man in the world. In fact, if I were any luckier, I'd be 'faster than a speeding bullet.'"

Confusion drifted across her face. "I'm not following."

Tony threw both hands skyward and spoke evenly. "You know, 'able to leap tall buildings in a single bound.'"

Her confusion faded into outright bewilderment.

"You've never heard of Superman, have you?"

She shook her head.

Charmed by her innocence, Tony laughed. "That's okay. I'll explain later, but no superhero has anything over you." Despite a growing number of amused onlookers, he tugged her in at the waist and tasted her lips. "Hmm-hmm. You are—" he drew back to take in her ensemble—"definitely 'more powerful than a locomotive.' I'd love you in a trash bag, but this is…" He clutched.

"Yes?"

His mouth softened. "I'm… I'm sorry, I don't have the words."

She dipped her chin and raised her eyes. "It's not too much?"

Rolling his shoulders on a shiver of delight, he said, "Oh, you're too much all right. I think I may have to boost my vitamin intake, but I love it."

She took his arm, looked up at him, and, in a style surprisingly businesslike, said, "Good. Because if you disapproved, you might have to readjust your thinking."

He shook off the thought. "No adjustment needed here."

She wet her lips and regarded him from under her brows. "Good. Now, are you ready to see your friend?"

"I suppose we should. I hope he has a strong heart. He's going to need it."

\*\*\*

When they entered Harlan's office, the psychiatrist sat with his back to a full-length window, his head bent over a short stack of documents. He snapped to attention and met them halfway.

Tony always appreciated Harlan's professionalism, but on this occasion, the psychiatrist was hard-pressed to curb his fascination for Athena.

"Oh my, who is this lovely woman?"

"Harlan, close your mouth," Tony mock-scolded. "You look ridiculous."

"It's only right," Harlan said, adjusting his bow tie. Then, with his boyish smile, added, "On an occasion like this, I should look meticulous."

"I didn't say *meticulous*"—Tony punished Harlan with his eyes—"I said *ridiculous*."

"I know what you said, bunkie." Offering an apologetic grimace to Athena, he added, "Sometimes orthopedists are a little slow on the uptake. Try to ignore him." With his gaze still on Athena, he said, "For Pete's sake, introduce me."

Puffing his chest, Tony said, "I'd like you to meet my fiancée, Athena Cruz."

Harlan was shaking Athena's hand when his sparkle vanished. "Wait a minute." He looked at Tony. "Did you say Athena Cruz? The jazz singer and pianist? *That* Athena Cruz?"

"The very one."

The psychiatrist released her hand as if suddenly learning she had leprosy. "Okay, this is going to take some work. Please, both of you take a seat."

Tony led Athena to the sofa as Harlan took the leather lounger at a right angle to the couch.

Shaking his head, Harlan began. "First, whoever you are, Miss…"

"Athena Cruz," she said with precise diction.

His eyebrows crested. "I hope you'll forgive me. I never talk about appearances in this office, certainly not with clients, but I must say you are"—he hesitated, his gaze flitting—"sensational. You should be arrested for looking this good."

She smiled and whispered a shy thank-you.

Shifting in his chair, he turned to Tony. "Now, enough with the gags. Tell me what the Freud is going on."

After an internal review of the last month, followed by a sigh of contentment that jagged in his throat, Tony squared off on his friend. "Only Athena's family knows what I'm about to tell you. In the end, you may think I'm insane, that we're *both* insane, but every word is true."

Considering the dire consequences from a *National Enquirer* exposé, Tony's eyes turned grave. "I trust you, Harlan, but our story can never go public." He shifted his weight and resettled. "I hate bringing this up because I already know your answer. Whether you believe us or not, you must never repeat what we're about to tell you. Can you make that promise?"

Without a twitch, Harlan said, "I wouldn't be much of a psychiatrist if I couldn't. Yes, I promise. Nothing will leave this room."

As the couple related their history, Harlan listened, his gaze unwavering.

"So that's our story," Tony said. "What do you think?"

Stroking his chin, Harlan dithered to the window behind his desk, stared at the skyline, and returned. "Tony, you're my best friend. And Athena, I have a feeling you and I'll become great buddies too. Frankly, I'd like to hang out with you and watch people watching you. Maybe some of your stardust would fall on me."

"Please," she said with the flip of her hand.

The psychiatrist laced his fingers over his chest. "And I do want to believe your story. But it's so—"

"Wacky?" Tony offered.

"I was thinking delusional, but that'll do. Look, I'm a scientist. I need evidence." On a burst of moon-eyed inspiration, he said, "Hey, I've got an idea. Athena, would you mind if I quizzed you about your time?"

"Sure, go ahead, if you think that'd help."

Harlan went to his desk, retrieved his laptop, and returned. "I'm going to ask you some questions about nineteen twenty-four, questions someone from your time could answer. I'll verify the answers online."

"Works for me," she said.

Tony chuckled. "Me too. This should be fun."

Harlan typed something on his laptop. "Okay, first question. This one's easy. Who was the president of the United States in nineteen twenty-four?"

"Calvin Coolidge," she blurted.

"I suppose a good history buff might know that one." He scanned his laptop. "Okay, how about his vice president?"

She contrived an oh-you-little-devil smile. "You're trying to trick me. He didn't have one. Frank Lowden was nominated, but he declined." In playful get-back, she added, "So there, Mr. Hooligan."

Glimpsing Tony with elvish eyes, Harlan undid his bow tie, popped the first shirt button at his neck, and said, "Whew, she's good." He nibbled at the laptop keyboard. "How about this? What's your favorite movie from nineteen twenty-four?"

"That's easy. *Girl Shy* starring Harold Lloyd. I love it because it reminds me of how shy Tony was when we first met. Harold gets the girl in the end." She arched her eyebrows. "So did Tony, by the way."

Speed typing, Harlan said, "That's right. *Girl Shy* did star Harold Lloyd. And it did open in nineteen twenty-four."

"That's what I said."

The questions were flying now.

"Who won the World Series in nineteen twenty-four?"

"I don't know. The season just started when we left."

"Okay, nineteen twenty-three then."

"The New York Yankees, of course. Babe Ruth hit three home runs in game six. It was all the city could talk about."

Harlan shook his head and expelled a slow, soundless whistle. "Who did they play?"

"The New York Giants."

"She's right. Absolutely right."

"That's my girl," Tony said.

The psychiatrist closed his laptop, pondered, and on a brainchild snapped his fingers. "Tony, you told me earlier this Craven fella stabbed you in the leg."

"That's right."

Harlan crossed his arms. "Show me."

Tickled by his friend's spirit of investigation, Tony raised an eyebrow. "You mean you want me to drop my pants right here?"

"I'm a doctor. I can take it."

Tony stood, lowered his pants, and showed Harlan the scar.

The psychiatrist dipped his head and squinted at the wound. "That does look fresh."

"May I put my pants on?" he said with playful sarcasm.

Lost in thought, Harlan dallied. "Look, I want to believe you, but believing would drive a hole in my profession. I'd have to rethink my entire understanding of schizophrenia, delusional psychosis, and shared psychotic disorder. Ludicrous and yet—"

"Real," Tony capped with heartfelt meaning.

"Yeah." Harlan sat on the edge of his lounger. "I can't say I'm a hundred percent convinced. I don't know I'll ever be. And I'll probably want more proof as time goes by, but at this point, it doesn't matter. You're both so doggone adorable. And I can see you're mad about each other." He paused long enough to add drama. "It would make me proud if you called me your friend."

A wave of pleasure crested in Tony's chest. "We want a little more than that. You're already my best friend. And now that you've seen me with my pants down, I'd like you to be my best man."

Turning away, the psychiatrist looked at the couple from the corner of his eyes. A goofy grin bushwhacked his face. He stood. "Come here, both of you."

He extended his hand to Tony and pulled it away. "Clinical correctness requires a professional handshake but"—he rocked his head—"what the heck." He embraced them, one after the other.

"Welcome to the family," Tony said.

"You're such a sweetheart," she said.

Color flooded Harlan's cheeks. "I'm a skeptical psychiatrist"— he raised a finger and tilted his head—"but also open-minded. I mean, what could go wrong? Other than losing my license, turning to drink, and ending up on skid row selling yellow pencils for a nickel apiece."

Always amused by Harlan's imagery, Tony chortled. "That's your problem. Your profit margin is too low. Make it a dime apiece, and you'll be living high on the hog in SoHo before you know it."

Harlan looked like he'd swallowed a fistful of live bugs. "Yeah, right."

As they turned to leave, the psychiatrist snagged his friend by the arm and stepped in close to his ear. "Does she know about Sophia?" he asked as if he were the only person in the room.

Tony sported a wry smile. "Yes. You can speak freely."

Including Athena in the conversation, he said, "Tony, I can see you're at peace. And I don't think it had anything to do with our sessions."

Tony held up a fist and tapped Harlan's chest. "I loved our chats. You always got me thinking. But in this case, Athena was the therapy I needed. And Buddy. They taught me the nature of unconditional love, even in death." Feeling his eyes watering on the edges, he took his friend's hand and gave it a firm squeeze. "I'll always love Sophia. That'll never change. But love is not a zero-sum game. There's always enough to go around. I think Sophia would agree."

"Man alive, when did you get your psychiatry license?"

Tony grinned. "Let's see, that would be nineteen twenty-four."

# 57

*Harlem*
*1924*

Craven had brooded and plotted for days. Now the time was ripe for killing.

It was eight-thirty. The New York pigeons glided to their nightfall resting places along rooftops, bridges, and window ledges while the blackened sky gloomed all the city curbs, doorways, and stairwells. He picked the building entry and apartment lock and slipped unnoticed into the flat.

As soon as he entered the apartment, the air in the room compressed heavily on his chest. He wilted—not out of fright from the normal but the paranormal—as if condemning eyes wished him dead. Spider-quick, he crouched and whirled in defiance of the raiders before they struck.

He was alone.

Only the afterimage of the woman they called Isabella darkled his mind.

As a cold chill skittered his spine, he quaked like a dog shaking off a sodden coat. "There's no one, not a damn soul, and I'm in power."

*Should have killed them when I had the chance. Especially the old woman. I'd be free now. Only had to pull the trigger. What spooked me? Even if they fried me in the electric chair, I'd be famous. Envied. Respected.*

Standing in the middle of the room, he listened to the rushing beats of his heart and the soft whirr of airflow. *Should I do this? Is it reasonable to go to god-knows-where?* Three times he thumped his head with his fist. *Stuff reason. Vengeance counts.*

He sat at the piano and reviewed the steps he would follow to face his adversaries one last furious time. First, he confirmed that the piano roll was clipped in place. It troubled him that he was not a pianist, but what difference could it make? He'd simply place his hands over the keys and *wish* himself gone.

With the brass knob tugged, "It Had to Be You" filled the room. He shadowed the keys with his hands. At the end of the song, he placed two fingers to his lips, then to Athena's scrimshaw inscription on the keys. *Did her name glow?*

"Shit." He gawked at a ghostly image of the keys *through* his hands. The room was swirling now and he a whirligig within that swirl.

Descending deeper and deeper into a ravenous maw, he detected a child's rueful mewling—a sound spawned from his own desiccated larynx.

Within a ghostly cloud, he spotted a gun. He drew closer to the weapon. A blast. A wisp of smoke. He looked aside and, to his horror, watched his brother, Josiah, fly backward into infinity. Craven opened his mouth to scream, but only ash escaped and molted into the darkness.

Although his arms rested immobile at his side, his hands on the keyboard, in the mirror of his mind, they swirled overhead like tall reeds whipped by a frigid wind. The vault faded darker into blind-black—the thread of his existence seeming to bow and fray until his skin crumbled into flakes. A madman's scalpel scraped his brittle bones, flensing them until they splintered and pulverized into ossein.

Boneless, sightless, mindless, he spilled into an abyss of nothingness—without heavenly hosts or a pinpoint of light in the distance—*simply nothing.*

Time lapsed.

A wave of nausea was his first revived sensation, followed by a tingling in what must have been fingers.

He waited.

He sensed he now had eyelids, closed but with a flicker of dull light scrabbling to enter.

He waited again.

When he dared to unseal his eyelids, he spied a dusky dreamworld—neither real nor fantastic.

*When will the dark give way to my destiny?*

He distinguished a splash of light—a blur of black suits wavering against a slate sky until the figures materialized into ebony and ivory keys. Athena's piano.

As his body assumed substance and the veil of gloom lifted, he peered from side to side and viewed a strange new room with dark green walls and unfamiliar paintings.

Commanding his head to quiet, he stilled and waited. He boggled as if rousted from a dream and lay confounded by time, space, and the remembrance of his name. He needed to rediscover his mission. *What was it? Tell me.*

Whatever the source—an unnamed demon heeding his call or the heart of the beast revived—his memory awakened. *Yes. Stalk and kill.*

His mind still defogging, he caught a soft murmur from another room—no more defined than the chittering of insects.

# 58

*Greenwich Village*
*2019*

Athena lounged in bed, increasingly at ease in her new jogging tank top, leggings, and matching running shoes (goodness, those shoes were comfortable). It was nine o'clock, and Echo had closed the window shades for the night as programmed. Tony called for the second time to say he'd be late. There was a smash-up on Route 9A, but he had only one more patient, an uncomplicated case. He promised to be home soon.

Nestled in bed with a copy of Dickens's *Oliver Twist* resting on her lap, she crooned, "Do what you have to do. I'll be waiting for you. I'll meet you at the door in my new lace panties, push-up bra, and high-heel shoes. Can you picture that, babe?"

"I'm busy now. I'm trying to pick myself up from the floor. I think I tore my medial patellofemoral ligament."

In a husky voice. "Ooh, I love it when you talk dirty."

"I'm just getting started."

His words tremulous, he confessed his love so tenderly the nape of Athena's neck creped with gooseflesh. But when his name was called over the intercom, his tone became professional. "Honey, I've got to run."

After smooching the receiver, she set her new smartphone on the nightstand.

Like a flash flood, she was swept away by the anticipation of being with her man, but anticipation was little comfort when sexual desire overpowered. Imagining him in bed with her now, cocooned under a blanket of silk, she rose and fell as his hands discovered the curves of her neck, her breasts, the inside of her thighs, the—

She contracted and sucked air. *What's that?*

At first, she thought it was a gale clawing at the seams of window frames as if the wind were jealous of newfound love.

*It's crazy. Why should I be spooked?* Her gaze fell to the open pages of *Oliver Twist*, and she simpered. *That's it. I'm haunted by the murderous Bill Sikes.*

She heard a muted creak like the sound of a heavy foot over a loose board. Lurching, she sat straight up, her body taut, her ears piqued. Detecting labored breathing, she imagined it must be her own gasp. No, the wheezing was outside her body, muffled but no less terrifying than a banshee shriek announcing impending death.

# 59

Her heart skidding, Athena eased off the mattress, lifted the silk robe pooled at the foot of the bed, and slipped it over her jogging suit. Tying the drawstring around her waist, she crept to the bedroom door, stared with tapered eyes, and staggered back. She placed both hands over her mouth and silently screamed.

Facing the length of the room, a stranger hunched at the piano bench. He resembled a dockworker in his Mackinaw jacket and black watch cap pulled over his ears. Peering into his dark, grim eyes, her senses returned.

*That's no stranger. It's Cal Craven!*

Her heart beat against her ribs, her fear running as deep as the river Styx with no coin to pay the ferryman. *How can that be? Is he real? Or a murderous ghost?*

She glared at him from the shadows—her nose flared, her mouth turned down. A waft of his pungent body odor drifted across the room. *He's not a ghost. He's real.*

Strangely, as if no longer in command of her own will, she succumbed to a storm of condemnations. As her eyes glazed, she surrendered herself to the inevitable. *Who am I kidding? There are no happy ending. I was a fool. It was lunacy to think it could last.*

She would allow Craven to have his way with her.

She opened her mouth to give herself up. Not a word, not a syllable sounded. It was as though the gift of speech had been ripped from her throat. Unnerved, she clawed at her neck.

The dead air was her salvation. In that instant, her delusions fell away like a glacier cracking and crashing into the sea. In exchange, her eyes turned steamy, steadfast, and tiger-sharp—her courage now sluicing through her veins. She thought about Tony, her family, and her own independent will. *Hell no, I won't yield to a bastard. Not now, not ever.*

*I have to escape. But how?*

Exhaling a ragged breath, an idea flashed. She stepped back to the nightstand and lifted the small Echo satellite. "Echo," she whispered. "Turn on shower."

"Okay," Echo whispered back.

She sidled moth-quiet to the door.

Taking the bait, Craven shambled to the bathroom on the opposite side of the living room. He clutched a knife, surely the same blade that punctured Tony's thigh.

With her hand on the doorknob, she waited for him to cross the bathroom threshold. When he did, she exploded into the living room, but the robe's closure snagged on the L-shaped door lever. Mouth open but silent, she eeled and escaped from the clinging wrap.

Craven stepped back into the living room. For a second, they froze, she with her biting stare, he with his cut-stone face and molten eyes glinting from shadowed sockets.

She shouted. Thank god, her voice had returned. "Echo, lights off."

The apartment snapped to black.

As she bolted for the front door, Craven lunged for her in the dark, tripped, and fell.

She turned the doorknob lock and yanked. *Nothing.* Damn, a second latch above the door handle was engaged. Hands shaking, she fumbled at the thumb turn.

Craven reached with both hands, grabbed and wrenched Athena's left ankle, and slammed her to the floor. She landed on her hip with a crushing *thwack*, a blitz of pain lancing the length of her leg. Although she wanted to kick in his teeth, she couldn't make out the outline of his head or the menacing knife.

"Echo, lights on."

The apartment sprang aglow.

His knife lay at his side on the carpet. As the monster reached for the dagger, she battered his face with a single ferocious kick. His nose *crackled.* With a barbaric howl, he released his grip on her ankle.

Clambering to her feet, she retracted the dead bolt, ripped the door open, then stumbled when the woolen welcome mat rucked under her foot. Balance recovered, she groped for the newel post and flung herself down the first flight of stairs, screaming for help.

Craven swiped at her at the first landing and caught air.

Careening down the second flight of stairs, she screamed again.

*** 

Jessica Sweet opened her door and sighted Athena running pell-mell. A stranger with wild eyes clawed at her from behind. Flinging her apartment door open, she grabbed the straight-backed wicker chair at her entry, retreated two steps into her apartment, waited for Athena to pass, and heaved the chair into the hallway.

The timing was perfect. The chair ensnared the savage and toppled him to the floor, baying like a wounded jackal. He peeled back his lips and scorched Jessica with a furious glare. Terrorized but not beaten, Jessica slammed and bolted the door. She snagged her phone and dialed 9-1-1. As soon as she entered the numbers, she screamed into the doorframe, "I'm calling the police."

*** 

When Craven untangled himself from the wicker chair, he hobbled through the front entry. As he scuttled down the stoop, a heavyset couple who had knocked back too many beers blocked his passage. Craven shoved his way through them, but the man was sturdy and shoved back, throwing the club owner to the ground. Although his spine sagged over his limbs, he drew out his revolver, levered to his knees, and pointed the gun at the burly man. They raised their hands and backed away and down the steps to the basement alehouse.

As Craven checked his bearings, he stiffened and for an instant delayed the chase. The lampposts cast a muted dreamlike glow on a city laden with mist so thick he could barely make out the buildings across the street. Still, there was the familiar scent of beer and pasta in the air. The world was at once bizarre and familiar.

*I'll make it here. But where the hell is she?*

## 60

Craven raised the tip of his nose as if tracking Athena's spoor. Nothing. He crossed the street toward Minetta's Tavern, barged in, and stood at the head of the bar with his gun in hand, his eyes a fired glint.

After shooting once at the ceiling, he detected a dull gasp before the echo decayed. Craning his neck, he spotted Athena at the end of the bar, hunkered down on the floor, her arms pinning her knees, her mouth sealed shut.

"Come on out," he blared.

She tried to make herself smaller.

A broad-shouldered steward stretched over the bar, cocked, and hammered a baseball bat across the shooter's hand. As the gun clattered to the tile floor, Craven slumped over in pain, exposing his back to a second blow that sent him sprawling facedown.

Athena charged for the exit. When she hurdled over his draped body, he swiped at her but only brushed her shoe, allowing her to escape into the night.

Despite the agony of a pummeled spine, he retrieved his gun, rolled onto his back, and pointed the pistol at the steward. Horsing himself to his feet, he kept the gun trained on the bartender. It would be satisfying to blow a hole in his square face, but Athena was slipping away. *First things first.* Backing out of the tavern, he double-gripped the revolver, his left palm supporting his battered shooting hand.

Six patrons called the police.

\*\*\*

When Athena charged out of the tavern, she turned left onto Minetta Lane and scuffed to a stop. A road bicycle leaned against the corner of the building, stripped of its front wheel. The bare front forks would make a wicked weapon. Glimpsing Craven through the tavern's window as he struggled to his feet, she swung the bicycle onto its rear wheel, pressed her shoulder against the side of the building, and waited for the killer to round the corner.

When she peered again into the tavern, Craven crashed through the front door, tramped two steps to the right, and reversed course. In five seconds, he'd be on top of her. Lifting the bike off the ground by the handlebar, she retreated three paces for a running start.

She spotted his advancing shadow, waited, and stormed with a primordial shriek as Craven rounded the corner. Ramming the bicycle forks over his clavicle and into his throat, the blow toppled him like a felled tree. With hardened fury, she turned the frame lengthwise, lifted it over her head, and pounded the bike into Craven's face. The pedal crushed the root of his nose, which at once splattered blood into his eyes, over his lips, and into his mouth.

When he clutched his punctured throat, the blood seeped through his fingers. He expelled a sputtering, guttural cough, but he was not undone. Though his eyes were filmed in blood, they were vicious—hungry for revenge.

Athena turned and raced west on Minetta Lane. Although her hip was aching, it didn't feel like a break. Thankful for her new running shoes, her pace was swift.

She could hear his stumbling footsteps behind her, and then his voice, hoarse but full of fury. "Stop or I'll shoot."

On the run, Isabella's words invaded Athena's mind. *If you are in danger, think of me, and I will be there.*

"Now, Isabella, help me now."

A gun blast rang out.

With acid rising in her throat, she zigzagged the misted street with long-reaching strides.

A second shot. The bullet zinged past her head. She whiffed a wraith of burning sulfur and, with trembling fingers, felt the frizzled strands of her singed hair.

She heard Isabella's voice. *Talk to him.*

Although it defied her instincts, she skidded to a stop and faced the demon—ready to quell the frenzy, the dread, the crushing fear.

They were separated by fifteen yards. Craven swiped the back of his hand across his blood-swept mouth.

She unclenched her teeth to get the word out. "Why?"

"Because you have no respect," he barked, flecks of red spittle flying as he spoke.

"Do you want respect or reverence?"

"Does it matter?"

"It does to me. Put the gun away and talk to me."

"Sure," he said, staring at his left hand gloved in blood. He opened the pistol's cylinder and replaced the spent shells with live cartridges. "I can take you whenever I want."

Reloaded, he holstered the revolver and approached.

She stood sentry tall, an arm's length away, and bore into his bleeding eyes. Though appearing calm on the surface, she felt his villainy reaching into her bone marrow.

The next voice came from behind Craven. It was Tony. And ten yards beyond Tony was Jessica, just barely in view through the mist, her eyes wide, her hands over her mouth.

"Step back," Tony commanded, the two words charged with fury.

Craven sprang toward Athena, his fingers reaching for her neck, but she sidestepped his attack, threw out her leg, grabbed his jacket, and used his momentum to trip and throw him to the ground. His revolver skittered beyond his reach.

Tony sprinted toward the killer.

Lying face down, Craven pawed at his gun as Athena juked for cover in the crevice of an arched doorway. Despite his bloodstained eyes, he edged forward, snatched the handgun, and squeezed off a shot into the fog. The bullet splintered the doorframe above her head.

With the echo of Tony's steps rising, Craven scrabbled to his feet and, holding the revolver with both hands, trained the weapon on his nemesis. He blinked wildly and shot.

The bullet gouged the asphalt at Tony's feet. Thirty paces separated the two men when a second discharge boomed.

Tony stopped so suddenly Athena screamed.

Mouth agape, Craven pitched, his cold, wolfish eyes filled now with shock and frenzy. His left arm hung slack and lifeless at his side. On a cluster of gags, he turned and spotted an obscured sniper framed by a first-story window.

"Drop the gun," the shooter commanded.

Craven's eyes were defiant, bestial, his mouth contorted into a Doberman's offensive pucker. With fading strength, he raised his revolver and fired an errant round at the gunman.

The shooter curled behind the window casing. "Drop it."

After three blundering steps toward the sniper, Craven squeezed off another round. The bullet ripped into the shooter's window apron.

"No!" Tony bellowed.

Craven whirled and faced Tony who, three paces away, hunched ready to strike. "Uh-uh," the beast snarled, his handgun no more than ten feet from his prey's chest. "I got you now, trumpet man."

Grinding to a halt, Tony stared at Craven with hard eyes, his jaw granite.

Seemingly indifferent to the sniper's threat for now, Craven whorled the revolver's muzzle in small coils as if drilling into Tony's heart. His words disgorged in a throaty rumble. "Welcome to Armageddon. Someone has to lose." He crumpled his face. "Sorry it has to be you, dogmeat."

Thumping her chest as though to steel her heart from leaping out, Athena stepped from the recessed doorway. "Craven!"

The killer half turned and pointed the pistol at her.

A gunshot bark fractured the night and thundered in her ears. She tumbled back into a huddle.

Standing stock-still, Tony's face was drawn and void of illusions.

# 61

Craven's head snapped forward. All tension, all malice bleached as he slumped to the ground, his eyes hollow. With the exception of his encrusted face and neck, his body was strangely bloodless as if his flesh was now void of fluids.

The demon from Swing Street was dead.

Slammed by the shakes, Athena scrambled out of hiding and hurled herself into Tony's arms. They stood in the middle of the street, crushing each other with tender force.

Over Athena's shoulder, Tony glimpsed a blurred figure at Mr. Rosselli's first-floor window.

"Are you hit?" Tony asked, his hands searching for wounds on Athena's back and arms.

"No," she said with a hitch. "Please tell me it's over."

"Yes. You're safe now." Hoping to quiet her tremors, he held her softly, his hands following the curve of her back. "Well, there is one more thing."

Her eyes saddened. "What? Please, no more bad news."

"On the contrary, I'd like you to meet the man who saved my life. But first this." He knelt alongside Craven, patted him down, and plucked his wallet. "I don't care to explain a century-old ID to the cops," he said as he slipped the billfold into his pocket.

She nodded in agreement.

"Now, get ready to meet one helluva guy," he said as he guided her to a spot under Rosselli's window.

But Tony's favorite baker was not at the window. It was Mrs. Rosselli, a white-haired woman with rosy cheeks, soft eyes, and infectious smile. She was wearing a gray nightgown that tied at her neck and hung loosely over her roundish body.

Tony's face blanched. "Mrs. Rosselli, are you all right?"

"Perfectly fine," she said, her smile nearly angelic.

"But— But Mr. Rosselli. Is he okay?"

The baker's wife angled her head as if trying to understand. "Oh, my dear boy, you haven't heard. Three days ago, my Roberto died peacefully in his sleep."

Tony staggered. "No, that's not possible. He— He just saved my life. Do you understand? He shot the man who was trying to kill us."

Mrs. Rosselli's calmed her face. "No, Tony. Roberto showed me his new pistol. But there was no shooting from this window. I wouldn't know how to hold a gun, let alone fire it."

"But that man"—he glanced over his shoulder and pointed at Craven's body—"lying dead in the street *did shoot* at your window. I saw that with my own eyes."

"Yes, he did," she said. "And I can tell you I didn't appreciate it."

Athena took Tony's arm. "Sweetheart. Don't you see?"

He shook his head and let his arms fall slack.

"How did we get here?" she asked.

Tony wavered. "By a miracle."

"Exactly." She rose on her toes to cradle Tony's face. "It was Isabella. She said she would take care of me, and she has. Craven's death was bloodless because Isabella's ways are more subtle but just as fatal."

"But there were gunshots. And Mr. Rosselli's voice." He scowled. "At least I thought there were."

"I heard all that too. But if Isabella can down a man out of thin air, why couldn't she conjure a pistol blast or Mr. Rosselli's voice?"

Tony covered his mouth and looked down.

The baker's wife broke the silence. "My Roberto was such a tender man. He used to say, 'I love you from here to the moon and back.' It sounds to me your Isabella had the same loving spirit."

Tony lifted his gaze. "Oh, Mrs. Rosselli, please forgive me. I'm so sorry for your loss. I loved your husband so much—always did."

She smiled, which dusted her cheeks even rosier.

Tony was dazzled by the woman. "How can you be so—"

"—perky?" she offered.

"I was going to say 'composed.'"

"What's the alternative? Misery?" Her shrug denoted duty. "I think of Roberto as I've always thought of him. A celebration."

Tony pondered that, turned to Athena, then back to Mrs. Rosselli. "Forgive me again. This is my fiancée, Athena Cruz."

"What a lovely young woman."

Athena took a step closer. "Thank you, Mrs.—" She caught herself. "May I call you by your first name?"

Mrs. Rosselli raised her chin high enough to reveal her pleasure. "It's Juliana, but I'll tell you a little story. I had three older brothers, and they all called me Buddy. It'd make me happy if you called me Buddy too."

Turning to Tony, Athena parted her lips out of wonderment. "Give me a boost."

On a smile, he wrapped his arms under her rump and lifted her to the windowsill.

With soft hands, Athena held the baker's wife by her shoulders, drew her in, and kissed her on both cheeks. "Buddy, you're so sweet. Just like another Buddy I loved. He was a candle in a darkened room, and I see you shed the same light." She paused. "Is it possible your husband helped us too?"

Buddy raised her gaze to the starry sky. "It would be just like him. He always liked being close to the action," she said, her eyes tearing.

As Tony eased Athena down, the still spring night was cleaved by the sound of police cars screaming onto both ends of the street, scattering their red and blue beams across the cityscape. He cupped Athena's neck and gave it a rub. "We have to talk to the police."

"I know," she said, her apprehension evident.

"I'm coming out," Buddy said. "I'll tell them everything."

Although courteous and professional, the police took their time as they questioned all witnesses, including the steward and patrons from Minetta Tavern. Their stories all matched. Two hours later, they seemed appeased, which clearly consoled Athena.

The police were puzzled by a gunman who lay dead without a single bullet wound, but a sergeant dismissed the mystery. "New York City," he said, removing his cap and raking his full head of hair. "Just when you think you've seen it all, something like this lands in your lap."

After the police loaded Craven's body into an ambulance, after the detectives doused their flashing lights and rolled away, after the last neighbors retreated to the safety of their homes, the couple stood alone and stared in a meditative haze around the chalk outline of Cal Craven.

"I guess it's really over," Tony said.

Athena tamped down her emotions. "No. It's just beginning." Squeezing his hand, she gazed into his eyes. "Let's go home."

# 62

Three months after the death of Cal Craven, the couple awaited an engagement at the Village Vanguard. They would be backed by a savvy trio of New York jazz artists on drums, bass, and guitar. Plus, an old-time tenor sax player would sit in to add even more soul.

In preparation, the couple reviewed some of the old tunes from the 1920s along with a favorite or two from every subsequent decade. Athena embraced all the sophisticated rhythms and harmonies of the jazz artists who arrived after Fletcher Henderson. She often asked Echo to play her favorites, including the timeless Louie Armstrong.

For the Vanguard concert, she wore a shimmery full-length purple gown with an understated lattice print. Although she shone with angelic beauty, Tony could tell she was nervous. In sotto voce, she sang all the new songs again and again.

"How are you doing?" he asked.

Her gaze was nearly mournful. "My tummy's a barrel of butterflies, but I be ready."

"I be ready too."

***

Long and narrow, the Village Vanguard reminded Athena of The Nest. Entering the club, they discovered the house already teeming with high-spirited jazz enthusiasts. It would be a night to remember.

They opened with a song whose lyrics were particularly meaningful for them, the 1924 Irving Berlin ballad "All Alone."

Backing her vocal on piano, Athena called for an easy swing feel and set the tempo. She was baffled when her music returned to her from the monitors. She'd never heard her vocal so full and resonant, capturing her three-octave range from her smoky alto to her shimmering soprano. She leaned into the song with even greater tenderness, the band following her lead.

"I'm all alone every evening.

All alone feeling blue.

Wondering where you are

And how you are

And if you are all alone too."

Tony played his trumpet the second time through, and the sax player kicked in on the third chorus.

The saxophonist was a minimalist, lyrically composing with precious few notes to set the mood, while Athena swooned under his spell. He was an older gentleman, probably in his seventies, but he was lean, and his back was straight. He seemed uncomplicated, playing with his eyes closed, rocking at the hip to the tempo.

Tony and Athena closed the song with a vocal duet, embracing each other's emotional nuances to the last musical heartbeat. When they'd finished, the Vanguard customers, well-schooled in jazz history, warmly applauded the band's mastery of the classic.

The evening passed quickly, the audience enthralled by the band's fresh and textured approaches to the blues, swing, and Latin melodies. When the last note had sailed away to join the music of the spheres, the patrons lingered as though recuperating from an emotional high.

Although pleased with their performances, the duo especially enjoyed the smooth and dreamy artistry of the saxophonist. They invited him to join them at a side table near the stage.

"I wasn't going to leave without introducing myself," the gentleman said.

On a warm smile, Athena studied the man's face and was charmed by his features—engaging eyes, strong cheekbones, a handsome straight nose, and a warm complexion, a shade darker than hers.

They shook hands and sat.

"My name is Athena Cruz."

"I know who you are," he said, revealing a handsome arc of teeth.

She was strangely drawn to the man, whose manner—mellow, soothing, with a hint of humor—echoed his saxophone solos on a slow ballad.

"Oh, have we met?"

His eyes were smiling. "Not directly but more directly than you might ever imagine."

"All right, now I'm really curious. What's your name?"

"My name"—his smile appeared tentative, unsure—"my name is Zalo Mangum Cruz."

Athena's eyes transformed from intrigued to astounded to euphoric. "Mangum as in Johnny Mangum?" she asked breathlessly.

"She was my grandmother," he said, his eyes watering. "I'm your grandnephew."

## 63

Athena placed both hands over her mouth, but her eyes told the story. She scrambled to her feet. "You stand up right now."

When Zalo rose, they embraced with all the love three generations could hold.

She looked at Tony. "Get in here."

They formed a three-person hug while Athena murmured and cooed. Her joy was so replete, so effusive she could sail away. As her body heaved, she could hear Tony sniffle.

Once grounded again, they returned to their seats, still shaken by the reunion.

With her hand over his, she examined every pore of Zalo's face. "How did you ever find us?"

"When you left, Tony told my grandfather you'd play at the Village Vanguard in twenty-nineteen. That was easy for me. I love the Vanguard. I've played here for years. I kept an eye on the bill. When your performance was announced, I felt like shouting the news to every patron in the club." He popped a chuckle. "But who'd believe me?"

Athena shook her head and cupped Zalo's face with her hands. "I can't believe you're here. My sweet little grandnephew."

Into the morning hours, they talked, laughed, and cried. Athena wanted to know everything about everyone from 1924 to the present day.

A gifted storyteller, Zalo recounted all his personal experiences and family legends, including the tales of the beautiful and gifted great-aunt. Enraptured, they wandered through the cityscape of Harlem, tracing the lives of her family from the crushing depression of the thirties to the explosive rent strikes and school boycotts of the fifties and sixties. Through it all, Zalo stressed his grandparents' resilience, regardless of the challenges.

Listening in rapt attention, Athena's eyes flooded while her heart drummed, grateful for her family heritage.

The hours passed without notice.

At one point, Zalo gazed at Athena with such intensity her belly quivered.

"I have something for you. I have kept it safe for over fifty years." His eyes glistening, he caught a breath and began afresh. "When I was a teenager, I made a sacred pledge to my grandfather I'd deliver it to you. That day has come."

Zalo reached into his inside jacket pocket and drew out a black leather folder the size of a business letter. He opened the folder, slipped out an envelope, and passed it to Athena.

As one tranced, she regarded the envelope. Immediately recognizing her brother's handwriting, she read the inscription. FOR MY BEAUTIFUL SISTER, ATHENA CRUZ.

She opened the flap. There was a tri-folded letter but something more. Peering into the envelope, she smiled wistfully, then poured her brother's gift into her hand. "Oh, Z." Palm open, lips sealed to stop from bawling, she showed Tony her beloved gold chain and heart. She reread the two-sided engraving. "FOR ATHENA FROM ZALO FOR ALL TIME." Kissing her grandnephew on both cheeks, she asked if he would attach the necklace for her.

"It would be a long-awaited honor."

"Your grandfather was such a wonderful man. So loving."

"I know that right down to my bones," he said, his voice splintering. "I miss him every day."

She withered a sigh and unfolded the letter. As she read, her eyes burned and, without words, she passed the letter to Tony.

As if holding a sacred papyrus fragment from the Dead Sea Scrolls, Tony supported the letter with open palms. His face radiated tenderness and joy as he scanned the handwritten letter. He read aloud.

*My Dearest Thena:*
  *It's 1955. I'm now sixty years old.*

*Johnny and I have two children: Anthony and Athena. Anthony and his wife, Lynda, have two children: Joanna and Zalo. Athena and her husband, James, named their little girl Esther.*

*All our children and grandchildren are loving and in good health, but I especially want to introduce our youngest grandchild, Zalo.*

*Little Zalo was born in 1946. He's now nine years old and loves music. Right now, he's learning to play the saxophone. He'll be seventy-three years old in 2019. I hope he lives long enough to meet you. That would be magical.*

*Johnny and I have been very happy these thirty-one years. She's a wonderful woman. Strong and independent, as you know. The best mom. Though she always profoundly loved our little ones, she never let them get away with any foolishness.*

*It paid off. Our Anthony is a college professor of history. Our daughter, Athena, followed the passion of her namesake. She learned to play your piano, which always gave me a thrill. Now, she directs the Harlem Morning Star Choir. I think of you every time I hear them rattle the rafters.*

*I decided to join the police force. I was sponsored by Samuel Battle. By the way, Samuel made us all proud. He became a sergeant, a lieutenant, and finally a parole commissioner. He's retired now but still active in the Harlem community.*

*In 1938, I became a sergeant. It hasn't always been easy, but I think people know me as a fair and honest police officer.*

*Isabella, bless her heart, died in 1939. I was so happy she saw me make sergeant. She remained our spiritual leader to the end. I often think of her when on patrol, especially when considering the right thing to do in a tough situation.*

*We think about you every day. We love you both so much. Thena, I like to think of you singing and playing the piano. Tony, I see you saving lives as a surgeon. Plus, one day, the angel Gabriel will welcome a great trumpet player.*

*If you receive this letter, remember you have always stayed in our hearts and always will.*

*Love, peace, and joy.*
*Your brother for all time,*
*Zalo*

*PS: Thena, I found your necklace in your apartment. I know you would never leave it on purpose. Imagine. When you get it, it will have been in the family for nearly one hundred years. That's a lot of love.*

As Tony finished reading the postscript, Athena placed her hands over Zalo's necklace, her chest heaving, tears flowing again. When Tony stroked her arm, she took his hand and pressed it against her cheek. "I miss him so much." She turned to Zalo. "Forgive me."

"Believe me, I understand completely."

"When did my brother die?"

"In the summer of nineteen seventy-six, the nation's two-hundredth anniversary. I was"—his emotions seized control—"at his side. He was watching the tall ships sail on the Hudson River when his heart gave out. He was eighty-one years old."

The image of her brother's face came to mind—vibrant, spirited, and loving. "He had a good, long life."

"I was lucky to know him for so long. He taught me what it meant to be a man."

They quieted, all seemingly lost to their memories.

Tony's gaze darted. "You know, this has me thinking about a mystery. How did Craven find us?"

"I was afraid to think about it," Athena said.

Tony bit his lower lip, then spoke as if to a failing patient. "Me too, but reading Zalo's letter reminded me of something. Before we left 1924, Isabella said, 'Leave now.' That was all. Although her tone was curious, I didn't think much about it until now."

She straightened her back. "What are you saying?"

"I can't be sure," he said, "but I think Isabella knew Craven was hiding in the apartment. I think he saw us disappear. It's the only way he could have followed us."

The idea of the monster being so close to her family slashed like an arctic wind. "My god. If I had known, I would've returned home," she said, her back contracting against a cold shudder.

"I'm not sure about that...being with family with Craven on our heels."

Uncoiling from the demonic ghost, she said, "That's true. I'm relieved he never hurt them. Losing Buddy was hard enough. Losing Zalo, Johnny, or Isabella would have been—"

"Unbearable. I feel the same way." He smiled at Athena's grandnephew. "But thanks to young Zalo, we know they were safe."

Seeing the bartender was eager to close for the night, the family of three embraced one last time.

"You're coming for Sunday dinner," Athena said emphatically.

"I wouldn't miss it," Zalo said.

***

On their slow walk home, Athena shared her feelings with Tony, her thoughts awestruck by mystery and discovery. "I'm just one of so many before and after me."

"Yet beautifully connected." Tony's lips curved as he took in the night sky. "You're like a star hanging in space. But you're not alone. You're surrounded by a galaxy of stars. It's beyond my comprehension, but gravity keeps them all hooked in space. Otherwise, they would drop like diamonds."

He stopped, turned to face her, and skimmed his hands up and down her arms. "Just like gravity, the pull of your family keeps you suspended high and mighty. That's not going away. And neither am I."

With a mix of emotions colliding within her, Athena rose to her toes and found his mouth. "Let's go home. I want to feel the tug of your gravity all through me."

Tony chuckled. "Did we just leap from astrophysics to biology?"

She slipped her hand under his belt and tugged him along. "Call it what you like, but get me home. The speed of light ain't fast enough."

After two steps, Tony again dragged to a stop and turned Athena by her shoulders. "Speaking of home, I have a question for you. Now that Craven's gone, do you ever think about going back to nineteen twenty-four?"

Caught off guard, Athena's expression unfolded in stages: perplexed, animated, and finally serenely settled. "Maybe one day, but not just yet. Right now, I want you all to myself."

"But we'll keep your piano?"

"Oh yes. Always."

# Epilogue

*Mooréa, French Polynesia*
*Summer 2022*

The water inside the reef surrounding the island was bathtub warm and brilliantly turquoise. In those shallows, no deeper than three or four feet, exotic sea creatures schooled in perfect harmony. Long, slender needlefish darted past, and reclusive octopi retreated into the crevices of coral or volcanic rocks. Silver-backed stingrays with four-foot wingspans sculled along the sea bottom with the grace of prima ballerinas, and ghosted six-foot blacktip reef sharks, harmless but inquisitive, skimmed by.

Color flourished, including the citrus-striped butterfly fish, the azure peacock damselfish, and the black, white, and yellow-striped angelfish with its fluttering top fin and protruding nose.

Equipped with fins, masks, and snorkels, Athena and Tony slipped among the colorful array of sea life, taking in the dreamworld below. With them, straddling Tony's back, rode the most beguiling mermaid: a two-year-old girl with bow-shaped lips, soft curls of black hair, and hazel eyes filled with wonderment.

The couple stood and faced each other, the weight of their bodies imprinting the white sand as the lagoon's current stroked their waists. Tony folded his arms around his back to support the toddler, who hung like a pixie cherub from his neck.

Tony's chest and shoulders held firm, while he watched Athena shimmer in a stunning canary-yellow bikini glazing her skin, accenting her curves, and lustered the yellow flecks of her eyes.

"It's getting late," he said. "What do you say we head back to the bungalow?"

Dropping her mask to her neck, Athena said, "That works for me."

"Are you hungry?"

"I could eat."

"Maybe Harlan and Jessica would like to join us."

"You mean Sweet and Lowe?"

They chuckled.

"Their names still crack me up," Tony said. "Wacky enough to suit them."

"It'd be fun to have dinner with them if they're back from the whale watch." Her eyebrows went up. "Although they do like their alone time," she added with heavy subtext.

"True enough. But what do you expect? A Freudian psychiatrist is committed to long client hours on the couch."

"More likely Jessica *hog-tied* him to the couch."

With matching grins, they eyed each other and said, "Poor Harlan."

After a laugh, they lingered, steeping in the warmth of the evening sun on their shoulders, splendored by the emerald-kissed shoreline, the thatch-roofed huts clustered on stilts. Beyond, the mountainside was serried by a ravel of ferns, palms, and fruit trees rising to a bastion of saw-toothed ramparts.

"I'm thinking the grilled mahi-mahi with asparagus and pineapple," Tony said.

"Now I *am* hungry."

"I'm 'ungry too," the girl said.

"Oh, are you now?" Tony asked the mermaid.

"Yeah. 'Ungry, 'ungry."

"Well, let's get going then."

Rotating the youngster from his back, Tony set her across his chest. He brushed off the sand on his back, Athena following his lead. They flutter kicked side by side, hand in hand, enfolded by the turquoise lagoon and runnels of pink clouds.

"Hi," Tony said to the little girl. "Have we met? What's your name?"

"Daddy, I'm Isabella."

"What a lovely name. So happy to meet you, Miss Isabella."

"You're silly, Daddy," she said with elfin eyes.

"He is silly," Athena agreed.

As they stroked homeward, Tony said, "You know I think I could stay here for the rest of my life."

Her voice in a swoon, Athena added, "So could I."

"No, you couldn't."

"And why not, Mr. Know-It-All?"

"Well, let's see. For one thing, you'd miss your debut at Carnegie Hall."

She imagined her performance on stage with the Duke Ellington Orchestra lifting her higher and higher. Even in the warm Mooréa lagoon, the vision gave her a shiver. "Oh yeah, I forgot about that."

"Right. Like you could forget Carnegie."

They both laughed and continued their glide homeward.

For no discernible reason, Isabella threw her arms to the sky and shouted, "I'm duh boss a-duh world."

The couple looked at each other and raised their eyebrows.

"'Perseverance—'" Athena said.

"'—and strength of character—'" Tony said.

"'—will enable us to bear much worse things.' *David Copperfield*," they echoed.

# ABOUT THE AUTHOR

Allen's history has been diverse. With a doctorate in psychology, he was a popular keynote speaker and leadership development consultant. He's also an avid jazz vocalist and instrumentalist, cyclist, photographer, videographer, and novelist. He and his wife live in Richland, Washington.

CONNECT WITH ALLEN:

Website booksbyallen.com

Instagram @allen.johnson.phd

Facebook /booksbyallen

Twitter @allenjohnsonphd

272

# ATHENA'S SONG

Allen composed "Athena's Song" for *Athena's Piano*. You can watch his performance at www.BooksByAllen.com. Type in the word "Athena" in the search box located at the top left-hand corner of the screen.

**www.BOROUGHSPUBLISHINGGROUP.com**

If you enjoyed this book, please write a review. Our authors appreciate the feedback, and it helps future readers find books they love. We welcome your comments and invite you to send them to info@boroughspublishinggroup.com.

Follow us on Facebook, Twitter and Instagram, and be sure to sign up for our newsletter for surprises and new releases from your favorite authors.

Are you an aspiring writer? Check out www.boroughspublishinggroup.com/submit and see if we can help you make your dreams come true.

Love podcasts? Enjoy ours at www.boroughspublishinggroup.com/podcast